SMALL GRATITUDE

The Bestial's mouth yawned open, small, sharp teeth lowering to Benedict's neck.

Stellato took three quick strides and jumped. The Bestial gave a hoarse growl of rage and released Benedict. Stellato's hands were clasped together behind the Bestial's neck. Biceps and triceps bulged as, ever so slowly, he forced the Bestial's head down to its chest. Its roar of frustration stopped, punctuated by the crack of neck vertebrae. Stellato released his grip and rolled away.

"You killed him," Benedict said in dull reproach.

"I saved your life," Stellato said. "A simple thank-you will suffice."

By Robert R. Chase
Published by Ballantine Books:

THE GAME OF FOX AND LION

SHAPERS

CRUCIBLE

CRUCIBLE

Robert R. Chase

A Del Rey Book
BALLANTINE BOOKS • NEW YORK

A Del Rey Book
Published by Ballantine Books

Library of Congress Catalog Card Number: 91-91834

ISBN 0-345-36656-5

Manufactured in the United States of America

First Edition: July 1991

Cover Art by Darrell K. Sweet

**For Margaret
This time, for sure!**

. . . God's crucible . . . where all the races . . . are melting and re-forming.

—ZANGWILL

I

SHE DRIFTED DOWN THROUGH A DARKNESS DEFINED BY WAN white lights. They seemed to coil into long helical strands, like pearls adorning a Gargantuan throat.

Or they were in straight rows and only seemed to coil because she was twisting as she fell. Or she was motionless, and the throat was moving up and around to engulf her.

The side of the tunnel grew very close and seemed to blur by her. Ranks of color-coded pipes, each thicker than she was, writhed by like the arteries of a giant. Doorways, silent and closed, moved across her range of vision. Transvator entry points. Cross corridors almost as large as the one through which she was falling.

Seemingly of its own volition, her hand reached out and grabbed a passing grate. Her body swept through a half-circle arc and slammed into the plasmetal wall. Almost, her hand let go.

Legs and torso bounced separately and swung back at different rates. She was panting as if from heavy exertion. She stared at the hand that was her pivot point, at the thin blue veins that seemed suddenly unspeakably important, as did the stillness of the grate itself.

The grate is a main air duct, she told herself. It is silent because the air circulatory system is inoperative, as is nearly every other system on this vessel. Your veins are blue from lack of oxygen. And if you do not get your wits about you quickly and remember what you were doing, you will asphyxiate right here in a cloud of your own carbon dioxide.

Knees and hips reached the end of their respective arcs and impacted again. She grabbed the grate with her other hand and tensed wrists and forearms while trying to make the lower part

1

of her body completely limp to damp her momentum. The maneuver worked pretty well. This time the rebound was in slow motion. She pulled her legs in and hooked her feet through the grate. Her motion slowed and stopped.

There was a prickling through her legs and forearms that couldn't be accounted for by their recent battering. It was like the feeling she got in a standard-gee environment when she had been sitting with her feet tucked underneath for too long or when she had slept with her hands pillowing her head, and they had gone numb with lack of circulation, and she would grimace at the discomfort even as she smiled at the ridiculousness of it all as she said, "Oh, my foot has gone to sleep . . ."

Only this was different. This was the feeling one got from the aftereffects of cold sleep when one had been brought back to consciousness but one's metabolism was not yet up to speed. On large vessels there were always med-techs present to jolt one with bioelectrical stimulation, even a quick shot if it was needed.

There had been no one near her when the lid of her cubicle had gull-winged open and she had floated up through the catacomb of similar containers. Unblinking green telltales were the only light, witnessing that the other cubicles still held their charges in closely monitored hypothermia.

You haven't seen a human being since being revived, she thought. You may be the only conscious human being on the *Crucible*. But that had to be wrong. There had been a voice— hadn't there?—over the intercom, ordering her to report to the bridge.

Get a grip on yourself, Shoshone Mantei. You've been sleepwalking ever since you got out of your cubicle. Use those brains you always boast about. You have only a few minutes left!

The emergency lights at either end of the tunnel seemed fuzzy, as if the atmosphere were thickening with fog. Or the problem might have been in her own eyes, a product of oxygen starvation. She needed to think clearly! There was only one stimulant close at hand. Anchoring herself carefully, she ground her knuckles as hard as she could into the sharp metal of the grating. Indentation welts appeared between her fingers, along the back of her hand. Even those long lines had a sickly blue cast.

But the pain forced itself into her mind, cutting like a blunted knife into the haze that had made her semicomatose. Clarity returned, allowing her to assess her situation.

Engineering Section Two cold-sleep cubicles were two-thirds of the way between the center of the vessel and the outer skin, she reminded herself. Directions on the converted battle-star were a topologist's joke. Either from deference to the ancient usages of the large orbital colonies or, more likely, due to the inherent solipsism of command, "up" was along any radius in the direction of the bridge at the battlestar's center. "Down" was out toward the skin.

Bouncing back and forth on the grate had destroyed what little sense of direction she had. How do I know which way is up? she wondered.

Normally it would not matter. If she wanted to go anywhere shipboard, she could step into the nearest transvator, speak her destination clearly, and let the computer route her capsule through the electromagnetic rail grid that girded the entire vessel. But the transvators would not be working now.

Fortunately, the one emergency drill Captain Nickerson had run before they had left the Centauri system had covered an alternative mode of travel. Four brachirails ran along each of the major corridors within the *Crucible*. In case a power failure rendered the transvators inoperative, one could move to one's destination along the alternating handholds. The possibility that the autolocator might fail had been considered and countered: the corridor was lined with nursery-bright lines of primary color that could be followed to any major part of the battlestar—if the color code was known. The manual chip explaining it all was in her bunk, awaiting its allotment of her carefully rationed spare time.

She did, however, remember the most basic thing. In the wan emergency lights she spotted the nearest brachirail and kicked herself over to it. Even that minor effort made her chest heave. She grabbed on to the rail and pulled her face close to study it. She found what she was looking for almost immediately: a double-headed arrow stenciled onto the rail along its long axis. The crimson red of one arrow shifted to the navy blue of its complement. Doppler code. Red for outgoing, blue for incoming.

She aligned herself with the overprecision of a drunk so that the blue arrow pointed up. Her perspective shifted. No longer was she Alice floating down an artificial rabbit hole. Instead

she was at the bottom of a deep well, trying to pull herself up
to an almost invisible light far above.

Panting as if near the end of a race, she pulled herself hand
over hand into the heart of the dead spacecraft.

At the end there was a wall. A huge cargo lock. Following
standards established when the race had first left old Earth, the
lock had responded to power loss by sealing itself shut. Shoshone could not even imagine manually opening anything so
massive.

Up in the far corner, however, was a shadowed indentation
that ought to be a personnel lock. She pushed off the brachirail,
caught the outer edge of the entryway, and flipped herself
inside. There were bracing stirrups both on the deck below her
and above her. A wheel set into the outer hatch practically
begged for counterclockwise rotation. Shoshone set her feet
into the stirrups and obliged. There was a muffled clank as the
bolts slid free and the hatch swung inward.

The space inside was not quite a meter deep by two meters
high. It was barren save for two weak emergency lights and a
hatch on the far side identical to the one she had just opened.

For the first time since recovering consciousness, she hesitated. Some as yet unknown disaster had befallen the *Crucible*.
As far as Shoshone knew, no battlestar had ever been damaged
by natural agencies. Until the end of the war they had been
considered invulnerable to enemy action.

Yet there was always a chance—"statistically insignificant"
was the term used for it by all her instructors—that a ship might
fall from quantum to "normal" space directly in the path of
some orbiting rock left over from the formation of the planetary
system. The result, depending on the size and relative velocity
of the object, could be anything from a microscopic pit on the
skin of the vessel to, theoretically, instant annihilation.

As minuscule as it was, there were standard procedures to
further reduce the danger. Fully settled systems such as Sol
and Centaurus specified sectors of space for emergence from
quantum drive and regularly swept those volumes for any
dangerous debris. In any system, prudent captains would
minimize the risks of collision by falling to normal space at
a vector matching the orbital velocity proper to the radius
from the primary.

But in an unexplored system such as the one the *Crucible*

was intended to explore, the term ''statistically insignificant'' might be meaningless. A severe meteor strike would explain the loss of main power, the shutdown of the ventilation system. Depending on where the ship had lost integrity, it might mean that she was trying to open her way into hard vacuum.

Shoshone's eyes blurred. Out in the main corridor she had barely managed to subsist on ambient oxygen. In this enclosed space her exhaled carbon dioxide was forming an invisible mask around her face. Were it to come right down to it, a quick death might be preferable.

Besides, she thought as she began turning the wheel, there was every reason to believe that nothing of the kind had happened. Unless they had been struck exactly dead center, any substantial impact would have imparted a good deal of rotational energy. They were not rotating; ergo, there had been no collision.

Furthermore, every air lock she had ever known had a failsafe to prevent opening on vacuum by mistake. The simplest let the air from the pressurized side force the hatch against the exterior seal, at the same time moving the toothed slide, which controlled the bolts, off the opening gear. Therefore, if the far side of that hatch had been depressurized, the wheel she was turning would have been spinning freely because it would have been disengaged. But since she could feel the gears inside the hatch moving . . .

There was a sound like a sharp cough, followed by a quick rush of air. The hatch behind her slammed shut. The wheel jerked itself from her hand as the hatch in front of her swung open to reveal stars burning against blackness.

Shoshone stifled the shriek welling up in her throat so that only a batlike squeak emerged. Fool! she raged at herself. The hatch swung in. And smell that air.

The air from the bridge was cool and wine-sweet. It took all Shoshone's self-control to keep from hyperventilating. Still, the combination of weightlessness and the clear view of deep space provoked subconscious alarms that no amount of rationalizing could still.

The bridge of a battlestar had the most sophisticated holographic display system technology could produce, she reminded herself. A 360-degree display was necessary to control the fleets employed in the just-finished war. All she was seeing was a relatively simple visible light display of the immediate neighborhood.

"Who goes there?"

That's an odd way to greet a crewmate, Shoshone thought fleetingly. "Engineer First Class Shoshone Mantei."

A figure loomed out of the darkness. Even by starlight Shoshone could see the elongated ears, the suggestion of a muzzle, the half hair, half fur. She could smell the . . . *scent.*

"Mantei! Thank God. Is anyone with you?"

There was something of such importance she had to say that she ignored the question. "Look, I don't know who else you ordered to report, but air ventilation is out in the main corridor from Engineering Two—"

Muttered curses sounded from behind the figure who had spoken to her.

"—and I nearly passed out on the way here. Anyone else you revived may be floating unconscious."

There was a series of questions and answers too low to hear.

"Mantei, this is important." The Bestial—no, Shoshone reminded herself, that term was no longer acceptable. The former enemy, depicted by the Defenders of Humanity as a cross between rabid dogs and werewolves, were to be referred to as Gens, for "genetically enhanced." And it was nearly as bad form to refer to oneself as human. *We are* all *human,* was the official line. *Those of us who are not Gens are Norms.*

Both terms had irritated Shoshone at first, smacking of politicians' euphemisms used to paper over a refractory reality. Yet now she realized that the semantic exercise might have some value. Both races had proved their ability to devastate each other in the recently concluded war. The *Crucible*'s crew had been chosen to demonstrate that they could work together in exploiting the star systems beyond the Periphery. Learning new nomenclature might not be too high a price if it aided that mission.

The Gen raised his hand as if to place it on her shoulder. Shoshone stiffened. The hand fell.

"Engineer Mantei." The voice was crisp and formal. Shoshone found that a relief for reasons she did not understand. "Report. When you came out of cold sleep, had any other members of Engineering Two been revived?"

It was like trying to remember a dream of the night before. "No, sir. All the sleeping pallets were sealed."

"Were any of the pallets undergoing revival?"

That was more difficult. Realizing what might hinge on her answer, Shoshone tried to remember the scene exactly. "No. All of the telltales were a bright blue-green. I'm sure I would remember if there had been any yellow lights. Or red."

The Gen made an almost invisible gesture, and she followed him into the inner command sphere. Its only demarcation from the rest of the bridge was a solid ring of instrument consoles and displays. There were about twenty other crew members on the bridge. Few, if any, appeared to be standard bridge crew.

"Given the current state of electronics on this vessel, it is a wonder all the cubicles did not relax into cataclysmic defrost." The speaker was the one who had first challenged Shoshone when she came through the lock—another Gen, bigger than the one with whom she had just been speaking.

"All cold-sleep cubicles have their own battery backups with five weeks power, Dr. D'Argent; more than they could ever use." That was the first officer's voice; Harriman was his name. Shoshone had met him at one of the preembarkation parties on Chiron. At the time she had formed contradictory impressions of him: moody yet overly hearty when talking to her. He had an intensity she found vaguely disturbing.

Now his voice had an understandable edge. "There are power matrices surging all over what is left of our electrical network. It's a miracle that Mantei's cubicle even received the command."

"We do not have any time to wait any longer." That was Nickerson, the captain, easily identifiable by the nasal twang that marked her birthplace. "Mantei, are you fit for duty?"

Shoshone nodded, momentarily forgetting that the captain could barely see her. "Yes, ma'am. A few pins and needles in the extremities from cold sleep, but I'm fully operational. The oxygen in here is the best stimulant imaginable."

"Good," Nickerson said. Command voice, so long a habit, almost managed to disguise an intense weariness. "I'm sending you and Stellato outside."

She raised her voice so that she was addressing them all. "For the benefit of those of you who have not yet heard it from your crewmates, I want you to know that the *Crucible* was disabled at 1530 Standard Hours by an explosion in the main engine room of the number two fusor.

"I am aware that that is supposed to be impossible." An

added irony in the voice instantly quelled a series of protests. "With luck you will be able to maintain lucrative lawsuits against Starpower Ltd. when we reenter the Periphery. For the moment we have more pressing concerns. The number two is beyond repair. Numbers one and three sustained serious damage which is repairable in time. Time, however, is currently in short supply. The reason is above us."

Shoshone's vision had been restricted when she had first entered the bridge. Since then, her attention had been kept to the horizontal. Now, for the first time, she looked up.

It was huge. Belts of mauve and pink mottling—cloud layers at different levels, hot bright clouds rising, cold, dark clouds sinking, Shoshone told herself—writhing through a tumultuous atmosphere. Hurricanes bigger than most planets spun into being as gargantuan opposing jet streams rippled alongside each other. From the outer edge of the atmosphere a ring system spread out like ripples of frozen space.

"Are . . . we going to collide with that?" Shoshone heard herself ask. It seemed unfair as well as implausible. Admittedly, this Jovian had been one of the main objects of their survey—she recognized it from the processed telescopic images. But to be so dead on target after a jump of a dozen light-years was almost unbelievable bad luck.

"No," Nickerson replied. "And that is a large part of our immediate problem. Our course will be deflected by the Jovian's gravitational well, but we will not be captured. We will continue on into deep space. In two weeks at most, our batteries will be too depleted to run the air scrubbers. We can live in suits for a bit longer as the ship cools around us. What we cannot do with the energy and resources available to us is repair the fusors. And if we cannot do that, all we have to look forward to is a tediously prolonged death."

Shoshone grimaced but still found that she appreciated the choice of words. "Tediously." Because you're so tough that to you death is just the ultimate boredom, right? she asked silently. On one level it might be macho bull. On another it was a nearly perfect combination of letting the crew know just how bad things were and taking for granted that the worst would be ennui. It had a bracing effect. In such company, even death would not be so bad. More importantly, a feeling had just flashed across the entire bridge that with this sort of leadership, they might not need to die at all.

"We are going to alter our vector to bring us into the outer layers of the atmosphere. That will both slow us and bring us out into the orbital plane of the rings and the satellite system. We will be attempting rendezvous with this particular satellite."

The focus point of the holoscreen moved sideways and forward. Shoshone gripped a rail hard, fighting a momentary feeling of vertigo. A half disk rose to the apex, swirling white on blue in color.

"This is a real-time image of our destination. Eta Cassiopeiae A.4.4. It is the largest satellite of this planetary system at .75 Terrestrial masses."

Chauvinist, Shoshone thought reflexively, automatically translating the figure to 4.5×10^{27} grams.

"Its importance is that it appears to abound in both oxygen and water. When we make it, we will at least have the resources to survive. We will have the time we need to repair the fusors."

"Does this mean the main computers are back on line?" a member of the science team asked.

"No," Nickerson replied.

"Then, I mean, how can you possibly control the trajectory sufficiently for the proposed rendezvous? Even without the air-braking aspect, you need the computers to calculate the steepness of the gravity wells. And *with* the air braking," he continued, his voice rising, "when we don't even have density profiles of A.4's atmosphere—"

"I will control the *Crucible*'s flight manually." It was a voice Shoshone had not heard before. Squinting at a shadowed area of the bridge, she saw what at first appeared to be a shapeless mass of robes. A head lifted itself above them. For an instant she thought that the eyes were those of a hideously mutated insect. Almost immediately she realized that the eyes were covered by regenepaks. Whoever this was must have been uncomfortably close to the fusor explosion.

"Meaning no disrespect, Father, but even you—"

"I am merely the best and the only chance you have, a fact at least as distressing to me as it is to you."

Shoshone waited for hoots of derisive laughter, for Nickerson to authoritatively dismiss both the speaker and his ideas. Instead, there was only a strained silence, as if the rest of the crew were taking this pitifully arrogant nonsense at face value.

"As leader of our planetological contingent," Nickerson said slowly, "Father Benedict can make the most educated assumptions of any of us concerning our speed to heat conversion in the upper atmosphere of A.4. And as some of you may be aware, he brings other unique talents to this task.

"However, all of this depends on beginning repairs immediately. Three-quarters of our electrical net is out. Energy matrices are rampaging through the lines which are still superconductors. Until both situations are remedied, the *Crucible* is nothing more than a high-tech rock.

"Mr. Harriman will be dividing you into work crews. Mantei and Stellato will report to Lock One."

II

EVEN WEIGHTLESS, THE DEGAUSSER WAS MASSIVE AND BULKY enough to require the efforts of both Stellato and Shoshone to maneuver it into the large exterior lock. Working in pressure suits did not make the job any easier.

The outer lock opened. On Shoshone's command they pushed. The degausser grudgingly drifted beyond the exterior door. A curved silver sea, the skin of the battlestar, stretched away placidly in every direction.

The peacefulness was deceptive, Shoshone knew. When fusor two had blown, it had released a power surge exponentially greater than anything the superconductor lines had been designed to handle. Large extents of line would have become insulators. In between segments of insulation, electrical charges acted as if they were alive, looking for weak points through which they might spill free. Where the patches of insulation were thin enough, the charges might "tunnel" through to new stretches of superconductor.

The plan was for Shoshone to go ahead with the energy bleeder coils and drain the pools of charge down to manageable levels. Stellato would come behind her with the main degaussing unit and nudge the truant atoms of the lines back into their proper positions to make the lines superconducting once more.

The faceplate could display a countdown of time available for completion of the task. Shoshone had suppressed that function on her helmet. She had no need for electronics to tell her that there was simply not enough time.

Stellato finished sliding a guideline through the appropriate notches of the degausser and the energy bleeder and snapped the end to a wall anchor. Quickly orienting herself, Shoshone took the free end of the guideline, attached it to her belt, and tapped a button on her wrist. A short kick, its force spread evenly between shoulders and hips, rewarded her. She was flying forward, the skin of the battlestar falling away beneath her feet.

Of all stargoing vessels, a battlestar was the most difficult on which to perform exterior maintenance. Most starships, not being primarily designed for atmospheric flight, had copious knobs and anchors for attaching wires or overhauling machinery. Battlestars were designed to withstand nova lasers. Their skin was absolutely smooth and almost completely reflective of all visible wavelengths of light as well as most infrared and ultraviolet wavelengths. Coming out of the air lock, Shoshone had for an instant resembled a bizarre playing card, her torso simultaneously extending into space and into the reflection beneath her.

At the far rim of the battlestar hung a glowing crescent, larger and less brilliant in the liquid darkness than the reflected stars. Shoshone angled herself and touched the wrist button again. There was a second burst of thrust. Then she was approaching the battlestar again, an animated geometry lesson from her youth, a point projecting itself into a line that would be tangent to a sphere.

Beneath her, she could just barely make out her own image skimming beneath the surface. She thought of a drowned man floating feet up from the depths.

She forced that image from her mind and emptied herself of everything but Lock Five, which was approaching with ever-increasing speed. Three seconds from impact she pressed another button. She grunted as her forward motion abruptly ceased, and she floated down through the open hatch of the lock.

As soon as it was within reach, she grabbed the wall anchor with her left hand, while with her right she detached the guide-line from her belt and snapped it onto the anchor. Quickly, she kicked herself out of the lock. A short boost from the rocket pack sent her flying back in the direction of Lock One.

A.4 was rising above its own reflection in the silver hull. It was larger than it had appeared on the bridge. Darkness had taken a bite out of the rings. For a moment it seemed to be swelling visibly, but that had to be panicked imagination.

Stellato landed next to Lock One a few seconds after Shoshone. He had run guidelines to two other air locks at right angles to the line between Locks One and Five. With that makeshift system, they could move their machines anywhere on twenty percent of the battlestar's surface.

The strangeness of working with a Gen was slowly ebbing. Pressure suits effectively concealed all physical differences. Stellato had originally displayed a cockiness that Shoshone equated with a lack of professionalism. Nonetheless, he knew how to operate the degausser, and he kept his comments short and to the point. The two of them quickly fell into a rhythm. Shoshone would run the energy bleeder over the hull until the metal proboscis of the instrument, grazing just a millimeter over the surface, sensed an energy matrix. Then she set up a channeling field, allowing the rogue energies into the bleeder, which stepped down voltage and amperage before letting the rest of the current flow through a trailing wire to a receptacle in Lock One and thence to the ship's storage batteries.

As soon as she signaled that the trapped current had fallen to safe levels, Stellato would slowly move the degausser over to where she had been, repairing the superconductor on the way. In the meantime Shoshone would have moved to the next energy well.

Their efficiency increased as they learned to anticipate each other's movements. Patch by patch, the maneuvering impellers came back on line. The recaptured energy flowed through their lines to the engine room, where it was used to effect interior repairs. All they needed was time.

A warning chime sounded in Shoshone's helmet, and she noted with shock that they had been outside three hours. Above her, the ring system of A.4 had expanded across the sky. Clusters of rings and interspersed gaps were clearly visible.

"Five minutes to thrust," Nickerson said. "Mantei and Stellato inside and secure your machinery."

Stellato disengaged the cross lines from both degausser and bleeder, then helped Shoshone guide them into Lock Five. They barely had time to close the inner hatch and clamp the machines to the wall when the warning chime sounded a second time.

"Thrust in ten seconds." A tenor voice this time. During the countdown Shoshone and Stellato wrapped themselves around brachirails. There was no sound at zero, just a feeling of being dragged up the rails. The force pivoted around them, making the outside skin of the battlestar "down." A few seconds later it pivoted again, pressing at their heels.

Then, weightlessness. Shoshone clasped the rail to prevent launching herself across the corridor.

Okay, she thought. We just rotated about ninety degrees so that we could bring to bear the impellers Stellato and I just made functional. That means we should have—

"Thrust in ten seconds," the tenor voice repeated. "Thrust will be one gee on ship's vertical for four minutes."

Shoshone arranged herself as comfortably as she could on the deck. She had grown up on a world with less than one-half standard—Terrestrial—gravity. Despite rigorous adherence to the mandatory exercise schedule, she would never be comfortable with that much drag pulling her down.

". . . two, one, zero. Commencing thrust . . ."

Shoshone's buttocks spread themselves uncomfortably across the deck. The wall was hard against the back of her head.

". . . 238, 237, 236 . . ." The countdown was suddenly muted. "Mantei, stand by for info dump," Nickerson said. Glowing yellow-green lines spread themselves across the inside of her helmet, resolved into an image of the *Crucible*. A blinking red dot marked her position. Red overlay lines indicated the next section of hull they would work.

"This makes no sense!" Shoshone complained. "We'll waste fifteen to twenty minutes setting ourselves up on the other side of the hull. All that time could be saved if we just did the next section from here at Lock Five."

Belatedly, she realized that she was broadcasting. She was about to add an apologetic "sir" when a new voice broke in.

"*Crucible* will hit the outer edges of A.4's atmosphere in approximately eight hours. Were you and Engineer Stellato to work the most efficient pattern for covering area, this much of the impeller drive would be operational at that time."

The image rotated slowly. Less than one-third of the surface area glowed red.

"This would give us considerable unidirectional thrust. However, without fusors, we would be able to maintain full power for less than fifteen minutes. Our strategy is for the planetary atmosphere to provide nearly all deceleration while impellers are used only for course corrections and attitude control. The latter is particularly important. This, therefore, is the optimal achievable configuration.''

The red patch fragmented and flowed. In an instant, evenly spaced red hexagons had spread to all sectors of the image. Her helmet cleared. The cool, precise voice was gone. Shoshone thought of insect eyes and shivered.

''. . . three, two one. Endthrust.''

Shoshone floated off the deck, looking like a levitating yogi. She unfolded her legs and massaged cramped muscles to restore circulation. Stellato was looking at her, his face unreadable through his helmet.

''Back to work,'' she muttered.

Shoshone's time horizon shortened to sixty seconds. Set out the guidelines, position the bleeder and degausser, control wild surges of current that might melt all internal workings. Her breathing was a constant rasp in her ears. Every muscle seemed to ache with fatigue poisons. Sweat collected and stung her armpits and the corners of her eyes. The air in her suit had an increasingly sour smell. And even the best of internal sanitary systems could not eliminate the moist indignities that came with working with no time for breaks.

''Mantei.'' Captain Nickerson's voice. ''Finish up what you are doing. I want you and Stellato inside in fifteen minutes.''

''Yes, ma'am.'' Shoshone hardly heard her. The bleeder snout moved slowly just above the mirrorlike surface. It should have been picking up the strong magnetic fields accompanying the energy matrix. Instead the needles jerked but did not move. Numbers flickered across the digital readouts too quickly to be read and became a row of zeros.

''If there's no matrix, can I ravel the next part of the line?'' Stellato asked.

Shoshone stared at the readings, weighing implausibilities. Every other remaining stretch of superconductor was a reservoir of electricity trapped between segments that overload had turned to insulation. At one point, at least, during the initial surge from the fusor, the entire section had crackled with lightning. Where had it gone?

''Bridge, this is Mantei. If there are any inside repair crews in my immediate vicinity, please have them check the skinward surface of exterior corridors for any signs of intense heat, such as buckling or discoloration. I'm wondering if this stretch may have changed to ordinary conductor and radiated the energy as heat.''

"No time or people to make that inspection, Mantei.'' The new voice on channel was that of Chief Engineer Lumbongo. "Finish up and get inside.''

She made her decision. "Stellato, bring up the degausser. Forget the intervening insulation. Focus about a centimeter in on the insulation and ravel the wire in millimeter segments. When only a millimeter is left, move in .1-millimeter segments. Call out to me before you start each operation.''

Stellato positioned the degausser right next to the bleeder and began the first of his incremental repairs. Shoshone kept her eyes glued to her readouts, watching the ghost flickers. At the slightest real surge she had to be ready to halt Stellato to—

The kick knocked her off her feet and made the stars sweep around her like a flight of panicked birds. For an instant she thought her suit rockets had somehow fired on their own.

Writhing dendrites, searingly bright, burned their images onto her retina. Was this what Benedict— A thunderclap exploding through both earphones had left her partially deafened. She was aware of a long, high-pitched rasping sound. Only when she inhaled and the sound stopped did she realize that she had been screaming.

Her flailing hands grasped the bleeder. Ignoring the blue sparks that crawled along her gloves like phosphorescent inchworms, Shoshone punched in a quick command. The readouts were meaningless: needles swung all the way to the right, digitals alternating between rows of nines and zeros. But slowly excess charge was being drawn off the energy reservoir and channeled through the cable to the ship's batteries.

A strong hand grasped her forearm and levered her around until her boots touched the skin of the battlestar. Stellato's mouth was working comically inside his helmet. Frowning, he pulled her toward him until their helmets touched.

"—happened? Are you okay?"

"I'm—'' She gulped, forcing her voice out of falsetto range. "—just fine. Let's stow these machines. I think we've used up the fifteen minutes Captain Nickerson gave us.''

III

A.4 LIFTED OVER THE HULL OF THE BATTLESTAR AS THEY MA-
neuvered the bleeder and degausser back to Lock One. Circular
bands in the atmosphere made the planet resemble a celestial
bull's-eye. Shoshone could see individual storm systems roiling
their way through the upper layers. It was dreadfully fascinating. Only by a distinct effort of will could she drag her eyes away
and concentrate on getting the machines inside.

The air in her helmet was stifling despite the fact that this far
from Eta Cassiopeiae A she was receiving less sunlight than
Mars did. The suit's insulation had kept the electrical charge
from frying her, but it had not been able to prevent a substantial
portion from being converted to heat.

Her eyes began to tear. In zero gravity her tears did not fall.
Instead they spread across her eyes like liquid lenses. Shoshone
blinked and shook her head, trying to clear her vision. Stellato's image rippled but did not clear. Gingerly, she made it the
rest of the way to the lock, feeling as if she were swimming
underwater.

The air vents were working in the corridor inside. After
clamping the bleeder and degausser inside their lockers, Shoshone swung open her helmet to wipe her eyes. Paradoxically,
the acrid smell of her sweat intensified.

"God, you stink," she muttered.

"Not at all," Stellato said. "Those are pheromones you
smell. They're why you find me irresistible."

He had unsnapped his own helmet, and Shoshone started at
the sight of the matted facial fur. Although she had consciously
remembered that he was a Gen, during their work outside her
subconscious had given the pressure-suited figure the face of
. . . Royce Kingsbury, the daytime serial star.

17

"Christ." Part of her mouth quirked. She was too tired to laugh. Laboriously she stripped off the pressure suit and, because it was required by emergency procedures for air braking, climbed into a fully functioning suit.

It took less than five minutes to pull herself along the brachirail to her own quarters. After a quick check to make sure everything loose had been stowed safely in her lockers, she strapped herself into her acceleration netting. It would have been less awkward without the pressure suit, but safety procedures required that she keep it on.

A stupid rule, Shoshone thought. If the hull lost integrity, their suits might keep them alive for all of a minute more.

The viewplate above her glowed into life. A.4 overfilled it. Only along the top of the screen could an edge of the planet be seen. As she watched, details defined themselves. She could see the planet closing on them.

It was then that a horrible thought occurred to her. It had been trying to force its way to her consciousness ever since she had been on the bridge.

She tried to dismiss it. Surely someone, Captain Nickerson if no one else, would have realized that it was impossible for a blind man to pilot the *Crucible*.

Perspective shifted. A.4 was suddenly *below*, and the cloud tops were rising to meet them.

Shoshone felt the shudder growing inward from the skin. For all its smoothness, the *Crucible* was not aerodynamically contoured. So far Nickerson or Benedict had oriented the battlestar so that ship's "down" was along the direction of their trajectory. That made sense, but what would happen if—

There was a lurch. Her body pressed upward against the acceleration netting. Blood rushed to her head, making her lips swell and her eyes ache. Desperately, she tried to make sense of what she was experiencing.

Attitude control most important, she thought. Benedict said that. Spinning out of control, faster and faster. If he doesn't get control quickly, I'll be pressed into a smear of jelly.

There was a sudden stomach-wrenching stop. Only the acceleration netting kept her knees from buckling and prevented her from being thrown against the wall. The whirling images on the viewplate seemed to fade as her blood was forced into her lower limbs.

Upward pressure ceased. Shoshone sank back into the padding. As her vision cleared, she could see in the viewplate clouds reaching toward a blue sky, cloud banks, row upon row of them, stretching like mountain ranges into unimaginable distance.

The *Crucible* rang like a bell as it hit the first line of clouds. There was an instant of pink-tinged dimness and then sudden sunlight. Shoshone tried to get a sense of scale. How many dozen, hundred—thousand—kilometers was it to the next cloud mass? It loomed up before them like a gaseous Himalayan range. Bright sunlight reflected off wispy peaks, spilled down precipitous flanks, and finally lost itself in the shadowed depths far below.

She counted heartbeats as the cloud bank enlarged, filled the viewplate, then resolved itself into a main mass with groups of smaller clouds as outriders. She blinked as the ship penetrated the mass. It shuddered with the impact. This time the period of darkness was longer. When the *Crucible* emerged, the sky above was a bright slit as if seen from the bottom of an immense abyss. Black clouds billowed and churned, their dark musculature outlined by shifting, interlinked chains of lightning.

And then the sky disappeared. There was only chaotic dimness shattered by concatenations of brilliance. Shoshone felt pressure build on the hull kilogram by kilogram, tightening a grasp that would crush it like an eggshell.

He's gone too deep, she thought, fighting panic. Unbidden memories of Aquaflamme flashed through her mind, of mariminers too eager to sieve the richer suspension plumes, too desperate to heed the pressure ratings of their divers. Sometimes they just left the sub docks and disappeared. Other times, though, there were frantic calls for help, cut off forever in midsyllable.

Light burst from the viewplate. Blinking away afterimages, Shoshone suddenly realized that her room had become entirely dark. She held her breath, waiting for the implosion.

Her room lights blinked and then came on full strength. Blue streaks appeared on her viewplate. They expanded and grew brighter. Sky. It vanished but reappeared a few seconds later, covering twice as much of the viewplate as before. Clouds were falling away to all sides. They were hurtling out from A.4.

Shoshone let herself relax into semiconsciousness. She was distantly aware of thrust from the impellers. There was a series of bursts, each shorter than the preceding one. All, so far as she could tell, along the same basic vector.

"Engineer Mantei."

She jerked awake at the sound of Nickerson's voice. Glowing numbers along the base of her helmet disclosed that she had been resting for nearly half an hour.

"Yes'm."

"I need you and Stellato back outside in twenty minutes. Keep hold of the brachirails. We may need a few more course corrections. I will make sure you get fifteen seconds warning."

Shoshone unsealed herself from her acceleration netting and kicked herself out into the corridor. Stellato was already at Lock One when she arrived. There was one course correction before they unlatched the bleeder and degausser. They wrapped themselves along brachirails, letting their legs trail out like marine plants in a strong current. Vector change acceleration ceased, and they moved their machines through the air lock.

An abstract Euclidian plane divided all space into two halves. At its far edge a sickle of blue-white light slashed its way through the star fields. As Shoshone's gaze moved inward, the plane dissolved into beaded rings. Directly beneath the *Crucible* the rings became irregularly shaped points of light at some indefinite distance closer than the background stars. They moved in stately procession beneath the starship. Shoshone did some quick mental calculations. Precious little velocity seemed to have been shed in A.4's atmosphere. Or they were skimming much too close to the orbital plane of the rings for safety.

She tore her attention away from the hypnotic vista and concentrated on maneuvering the bleeder into position. Some of the lines they had cleared had flipped back to insulating states under the combination of frictional heating and lightning. Sighing, she began reclaiming what she and Stellato had already repaired.

Despite her fatigue, the job went faster the second time. Knowing exactly what to do and how to do it cut waste motion to an absolute minimum. She was actually surprised when Nickerson called them in. Looking up from the bleeder, she saw that they had passed beyond the edge of the ring system. A.4.4 had become much larger. Clouds on the nightside were ghostly in light reflected from A.4.

They unsnapped the line, pulled the machines inside, and sealed all the locks. Only when she was back in her cabin did Shoshone realize how weak she felt. Since being awakened from cold sleep, she had had nothing to eat and nothing to drink save the recycled water of her space suit. Her limbs were shaking as she strapped herself back into her acceleration netting.

A.4.4 grew perceptibly in the viewplate. I ought to be frightened, she thought dully. Or at least excited. But now that she had surrendered herself to exhaustion, she could feel nothing more than a faint nausea. One way or another she would finally be able to rest. That was all that mattered.

The *Crucible* trembled as it hit the outer edges of the atmosphere. An indistinct glow lit up the darkness. Shoshone frowned until she realized that the glow was not coming from the planet. It came from the air the *Crucible* was searing with its passage. They had become a blazing sphere trailing a tail of light.

In an instant the starship crossed the terminator into day. It punched its way through two cloud layers in rapid succession. Below was ocean, close enough that Shoshone could discern individual wave tops.

Acceleration pressed down heavily, driving air from her lungs and pushing her lips away from her teeth. Nickerson's trying to keep us from crashing, she thought. She realized her mistake almost immediately. The *Crucible* had already made its closest approach. Nickerson was using all the power at her disposal to keep the starship from flying off into space.

Then there must have been a short period of unconsciousness. They were back in the satellite's shadow. Every muscle in her body ached. She gulped down air as quickly as she could. The *Crucible* was maintaining a steady deceleration, less than two gees—

Darkness swallowed the room. The acceleration netting held her so tightly that it was more than a second before she realized she was in free-fall. More seconds ticked by interminably. Words rose unbidden to her mind, words she must have learned from some early schoolmate, for surely her parents had never taught her to say:

> Now I lay me down to sleep,
> I pray the Lord my soul to keep.

Over and over she said it, each time with greater dread. The impact, when it came, was almost a relief. Acceleration netting parted like a ripping womb. She never felt her own impact against the wall.

IV

A FORMLESS FIELD OF LIGHT, DARK BLUE. DIM WHITE PIXELS like distant galaxies, courtesy of retinal feedback.

"Now, today we are going to strip the packs off and take a look at our handiwork."

Dr. Spartacus's voice was warm, but with a professional detachment that made it all the more reassuring. A cold spray soaked through the synthetic fibers, chilling Shoshone's face. She felt fabric sag away from her skin. Deft fingers undid the bindings at the back of her head and stripped away the regenepaks. Red light flooded out the deep blue. The "distant galaxies" switched from white to yellow-green.

"Open your eyes and tell me if you see anyone you recognize," the doctor said.

Shoshone forced apart gummy eyelids. The mirror Spartacus was holding showed eyes, nose, and chin in approximately the correct places. Thick black fuzz covered her skull. Irregular jagged white lines webbed her cheeks and forehead.

"It looks like me," she admitted. "An anorexic me with a dyke cut."

"The regeneratives we have been forcing into you have been burning through your body fat to mend bone," Spartacus said complacently. "After all, when you were brought in here, you were less a jigsaw puzzle than a shattered mosaic. It took a lot of work to glue you back together.

"Don't worry about your hair, either. One of the hormone compounds the regenepaks are soaked in is the prime ingredient in most hair treatments. It will come back fuller and glossier than ever."

Spartacus was standing behind Shoshone, looking pleased with her handiwork. Shoshone had spent hours trying to visualize

22

her doctor since a hand covered with soft fur had brushed her cheek during an early examination. It was no shock now to see the large angular ears, the mahogany pelt, the slight protrusion of the muzzle. She wondered how she could ever have considered the features ape- or wolflike. Spartacus reminded her of nothing so much as a well-groomed and undeniably feminine cat.

"How do you feel?" Spartacus asked.

"My teeth hurt," Shoshone replied. "My jaws hurt. My back, ribs, shoulder blades, hips, knees, and ankles hurt. *I* hurt! Whatever happened to painless medicine? I thought you were supposed to fix us up good as new."

"You would have benefited from an extended stay in the regenebox," Spartacus admitted calmly. "However, between power rationing and the fact that the power lines to that equipment have not been repaired, that has been impossible. Your body will have to do the rest the old-fashioned way.

"Be thankful you had no nerve damage. Our lead planetary ecologist suffered severe damage to his optic nerves which will require several sessions of delicate bioelectric stimulation whenever that becomes possible."

Stellato had visited the day before and, as part of a strained, awkward conversation, had explained the situation. With only one partially repaired fusor providing power to the ship, only the bare minimum of services could be run. Because of the degausser's high power consumption, repair of most electrical lines was deemed nonessential.

"A pity you went to sleep just when things were getting interesting." O'Leary was the other patient currently in sick bay. He had fallen and sprained his wrist while inspecting the exterior of the *Crucible*. Now that she had her eyesight back, Shoshone found him more bizarre than Spartacus. Pale, freckled skin covered flattened features. His hair was a carroty red, something Shoshone had never seen before. During the Expulsions from Earth four generations earlier, those displaced had invariably been from the poorest levels of society—because they needed the opportunities of the colonies or because they had the least clout to resist, depending on whose history book one read. In any event, darker skins predominated.

"There we were," O'Leary continued, "just having fallen two kilometers out of the air, when the electrical charge you had so neatly recovered for our batteries finally ran out. Slam into the water, down and down, and then back up again like a beach ball. The sea boiled around for an entire watch, so hot was our skin, and steam flew upward like a comet's tail.''

Fascinating though that might be to Shoshone, Spartacus had lived through it and so gave O'Leary little more than a nod. "Let me help you up," she offered.

Shoshone swung her feet to the floor, half stood, and froze. "I'm afraid something must be wrong," she said tightly. "Everything seems tilted. And the floor is *moving*."

O'Leary stifled his laugh even before Spartacus glared at him. "The floor is tilted *and* moving," he explained. "I told you we hit like a beach ball. That's the way we floated, as well. We spun, floor to ceiling, wall to wall. Friction slowed it down after a while, but wave motion kept us from ever stopping. Only when the captain ballasted us by flooding the lower decks did we regain any sort of equilibrium."

"And by that time nearly everyone shipboard had passed through sick bay, for seasickness if nothing else," Spartacus grumbled. "It was exhausting trying to reach for medicines and dressings in cabinets on the ceiling."

Shoshone stood and made her way tentatively across the room. She stumbled once, but Spartacus was right at her elbow.

"You have been treating a Norm, Dr. Spartacus?" Shoshone recognized the voice immediately. It had challenged her on the bridge. She felt the hand on her forearm tense.

"Very successfully, as you can see, Dr. D'Argent." Spartacus's voice was light. Shoshone wondered if anyone else could sense how tightly it was controlled.

"Your compassion does you credit," D'Argent said, "but it is dangerous. Your training is with Gens. The genetic differences with Norms—"

"Is significant only at cosmetic levels," Spartacus cut in. "Ninety-nine point ninety-nine percent of the genes are the same. My training is in medicine. Yours is in microbiotic biochemistry."

D'Argent loomed massively in the doorway. There were taller men on board, but none so broad across the chest. He seemed to radiate a barely contained energy. The silver that fringed his black fur might have been natural—many of the cosmetic measures available to even the lower classes had not made their way beyond the Periphery—but Shoshone doubted it: the streaks of silver were too bright and arranged too dashingly.

D'Argent's eyes slowly took the measure of the smaller

doctor. Spartacus held her ground, her posture neither threatening nor submissive. After a few moments D'Argent moved his head slightly in an ironic bow.

"No one values your expertise more highly than I do," he said. His bass voice was smooth and incredibly rich. "I merely warn you that there are boundaries which must be treated with the highest respect. Even if you haven't given offense to your patient, there are others who would take offense for her."

Again that half nod; then he turned and disappeared down the corridor. Spartacus unclenched her left fist. Four sharp indentations remained in her palm. With a visible effort she sheathed her claws.

"That man has a way of bringing out the worst in me."

"He's not Mr. Conviviality," O'Leary agreed. His voice had lost the slight accent Shoshone had noticed earlier.

Spartacus looked at him sharply. "You are discharged, Mr. O'Leary. Keep the brace on for the rest of the day. Take it off when you sleep. Work the cream I gave you into the surface skin every eight hours. If you do the exercises I gave you, you should be fully healed in three days."

O'Leary muttered his thanks and left. Spartacus turned her attention back to Shoshone. "Do you feel good enough to report back to duty?"

"I think so," Shoshone replied, ignoring the aches that came with each movement. "At least if I have something to do, it will take my mind off how miserable I feel."

Spartacus smiled. "Good enough. You are to report to Captain Nickerson for reassignment. Let me find out where she is and get you a map."

The transvators were still not in operation except for emergency use. Although the main corridors would provide the most direct route to anywhere on the *Crucible,* it was generally not recommended to climb the brachirails of the main vertical corridor as it pitched and whipped in the swell. A simple program had been developed to work out the most direct route or the easiest route between any two points. In a few seconds Spartacus handed a plastisheet to Shoshone, showing her the jagged path she would have to take, behind laboratories and sleeping areas, to get to the captain's quarters. Fortunately, her destination was only five levels up.

After such a long confinement, it felt good to stretch. Still, by the time she reached the captain's doorway, Shoshone had to pause for more than a minute to catch her breath. The world on which they were stranded had a higher surface gravity than Aquaflamme. That, combined with the strength she had lost while recovering, meant that for all practical purposes she was completely out of shape. When her pulse stopped hammering in her temples, she placed her palm on the visitor's oval to the right side of the door.

"Yes?" Nickerson's voice seemed to be all around her.

"Engineer Mantei, reporting as ordered, ma'am."

"Enter, please."

The door slid noiselessly aside. Shoshone entered a sunken living room. The far wall showed smooth, endless ocean blending at the horizon with an impossibly blue sky. The room rocked gently in time with a long swell that moved through the image.

Nickerson was making entries on a complate mounted on the right arm of her chair. She stood when Shoshone entered. "Dr. Spartacus seems to have done a good job putting you back together," she said.

"Good enough to put me back on duty, ma'am."

"Well, perhaps not quite that good, I'm sorry to say. Have a seat, please."

Shoshone let herself down gingerly. The chair immediately molded itself to her. Instead of relaxing her, however, the configuration subtly improved her posture and made her feel more alert. Nickerson murmured three short words into her complate microphone.

"It says on your charts that you are still very much weakened from the healing process. I could have told as much just looking at you and hearing the way you were panting when you came in. It will take another four weeks before your bones are fully knitted. You are certainly in no shape for the sort of underwater repair work needed now, and which can be done better by Gens in any event."

"I'm certain I can pull—"

"Your own weight and more. Yes, I agree. That is why you have been chosen for a very special assignment. I'm detailing you to act as aide to Father Benedict."

Memories of an insectoid face and a light, mocking voice.

"You already know that he is our lead planetologist, but he is much more important than that. Without him, we would be drifting in interplanetary space now. That, or crushed in the depths of A.4's atmosphere. If there is one person on this vessel who can get us back within the Periphery, it is Benedict.

"But he needs help. He was blinded by the initial explosion of the fusors. This puts him under a tremendous handicap. We must do everything we can to make up for that. We are too shorthanded to spare our fully able-bodied. In any event, many of them would be entirely . . . unsuitable. You can aid me, and all your crewmates, far more in this way than anyone ever could in engineering."

"I—I will do my best, of course," Shoshone said.

"Excellent." Nickerson's smile seemed to flood the room with its sudden brilliance. Yet it was more than successful manipulation, Shoshone felt. On some basic level Nickerson was tremendously *relieved*.

"Give me the map Spartacus called up for you to get here." Shoshone handed over the plastisheet. Nickerson fed it into the recycling slot. "Route map to Father Benedict." A sheet curled out of the adjoining slot. "Here you are. You have my authority in anything you need to carry out this assignment. If anyone acts as a roadblock, contact me at once."

"Yes, ma'am." Realizing that she was dismissed, Shoshone stood and left the quarters.

She paused in the corridor, studying the map and trying to collect her thoughts.

"Is anything the matter, Engineer?" Harriman loomed over her shoulder. Shoshone repressed a start. She could have sworn there had been no one near her when she had stepped out of Nickerson's quarters.

"Nothing. I have just been given a new assignment."

Harriman stared at the map she was holding. "One having to do with Father Benedict, I see. Are you to be his aide?"

"Yes, sir." Even though it was a breach of protocol, she began edging away from the first officer. "Excuse me, sir, but I have been ordered to report to Father Benedict immediately."

His long stride kept pace with her effortlessly. "Do you think you will enjoy this assignment, Engineer?"

Shoshone debated quickly over a safe response. "I am an engineer, sir. I am sure there are others who would be far more suited to this assignment than I am."

"Let me ask you an important question, Engineer. Do you like this Benedict? Do you trust him?"

"I don't know him well enough to like or dislike him," Shoshone said. "But—no, I don't trust him."

Harriman smiled. His arm crossed in front of Shoshone, hitting a transvator button. The door slid open.

"We're not supposed to—" she began.

"Use these without the proper justification? I most assuredly have it. Step in, Engineer."

Shoshone entered the transvator and automatically gripped the handhold. Harriman keyed in the destination code. As soon as the transvator began moving, he pressed two other buttons simultaneously. The light dimmed as the transvator jerked to a stop.

"Now we can be reasonably sure no one will overhear us. You were saying about your detail?"

"I don't like it," Shoshone said, more perturbed than she wanted to admit by Harriman's method of questioning. "I know engineering. I don't know nursemaiding."

"Your feelings do you credit," Harriman said smoothly. "What do you know about this Benedict?"

Shoshone shrugged. "Just that he's some big shot in the Order of Stewards, which entitles him to be our lead planetologist."

"Is that all?" Harriman asked skeptically. "You don't remember the Centauran Sky Marshal at the Battle of Chiron?"

"His name was Rénard . . ." Shoshone said hesitantly.

"Paul Niccolo Rénard," Harriman said. "Within the Order of Stewards, however, he was Brother Benedict. It was an identity he assumed when he fled the Periphery from an assassination attempt. For ten years he pretended to be a humble monk helping the Stewards terraform a planet in the Altair system.

"A Centauran Councillor named Chiang deduced his hiding place and dragged him out of it at gunpoint to be his personal adviser. You're probably too young to remember, but twenty years ago, before Graeme Williams and the Defenders of Humanity started waking people up to the dangers of genetic engineering, the greatest danger facing humans didn't come from Bestials. It came from Multi-Neural Capacitants, self-programming human biocomputers who could manipulate populations the way you could move chess pieces on a board. Except for some timely assassinations, we'd all be their slaves today.

"Chiang needed that sort of power because the other Centauran Councillors had him squeezed in a power play. The Rénard not only got him out of that, he eventually got himself appointed Sky Marshal of the entire Centauran fleet.''

"He prevented the destruction of the Allied fleets orbiting Chiron," Shoshone said slowly as memories of the news clips came back to her. "Not only that, he hurt the Bes—the Gens so badly, they asked for peace terms less than a week later.''

"That is the official story,'' Harriman said with a wry smile. "There are some facts you should have in order to evaluate that properly. Chiron wasn't his first battle with the Bestials. That was around a planetoid named Pearl in the L 726-8 system. Before that battle he had been a guest of a Bestial commander at one of their secret bases. To this day nobody knows what went on during that meeting.

"However, it is on record that after the Battle of Pearl, it was the Rénard who prevented Chiang's forces from moving in for the kill. His main concern then was to get medical supplies to the Bestials, even to the point of threatening to turn his weaponry on one of his own ships that raised an objection. In the end he let most of the Bestials escape.''

"That doesn't make sense,'' Shoshone objected. Harriman was leading her forcefully in a direction she was not sure she wanted to go. Out of general contrariness she found herself resisting. "All the newsnets reported after the battle that the Rénard had been warning for months of how vulnerable the battlestars were. Chiron proved him right. Except for him, all the Allied fleets would have been destroyed.''

Harriman shook his head impatiently. "He did not *warn* of the vulnerabilities of battlestars. He invented the tactics which *made* them vulnerable. He tried out those tactics at Pearl and made sure that the Bestials carried the lesson back to their high command. Hell, that's even on the tapes! That's how he negated the Allies' most decisive advantage.

"Nobody really caught on to what he was doing until after the Battle of Chiron. There was an interesting analysis made of that battle. After Ishige put the Terrestrial forces at the Rénard's disposal, the Rénard bled those forces to the point where Ishige had to both reassert command and disengage. Do you understand what that means? The Rénard destroyed the Alliance. With our forces divided, we were forced to accept a stalemate.''

"Why should he do that?'' Shoshone asked doggedly. "And

if he's as bad as you say, why does the captain say he may be the only person who can get this ship back within the Periphery?"

"She said that because it just may be true. I don't say anything against his ability. All I am saying is that you can't trust him. Our captain is in a delicate situation. The politicians decreed that the *Crucible* should have a mixed crew, representative of every major bloc within the Periphery and among the Clans. They say we are to work together in harmony to erase the bitterness of the war. They don't say that the war so devastated the interstellar economies, always excepting Earth's, that they needed every bloc's support to provide the financial backing for this expedition. That is the main reason we are in a converted battlestar instead of the sort of specially constructed exploration vessel which opened up most of the Periphery.

"The result, however, is that our captain can trust only half her crew. Furthermore, not to say anything against our captain, but you have to recognize that she herself was chosen for political reasons: she never had command of a vessel during the war and so evokes no animosity among the Gens. She is personable, a quick learner, and an excellent administrator, but she has been handicapped by a situation in which her lack of command experience has been her primary qualification."

"If Benedict is as powerful a figure as you say," Shoshone said thoughtfully, "why is he wasting his time here as a planetary ecologist?"

Harriman looked at her appraisingly. "That is a question, isn't it?" he agreed. "It was natural to ask the Order of Stewards to make a recommendation for the position, given their role in the ecological reconstruction of Earth and their more recent efforts in terraforming. And when they proposed Benedict, it was almost impossible to choose anyone else. His work in terraforming Ariel demonstrated that he is a genius in planetology.

"Still, that just underlines the validity of your question. Benedict seems to be, shall we say, overqualified for the position."

He touched one of the console buttons. The transvator shuddered into motion. "As to why the Rénard should do the things he has, I can't say. It may be impossible to know the reasons of somebody so much smarter than you are. I am hoping the reason is that he is a traitor to the human race. Because the alternative is that he is simply insane."

V

Shoshone had to pause as she stepped out of the trans-vator onto the shuttle deck. Sunlight, golden and brilliant, streamed in through the open bay doors, nearly blinding her. The rocking there was slow but much more noticeable. The slope of the exterior walls told her why: The shuttle deck was very close to the top of the battlestar.

A group of figures clustered to one side of the bay doors. Perhaps it was because the backlighting turned them into fantastic silhouettes, or perhaps Harriman's story had worked on her emotions more than she realized, but they seemed to have stepped from an illuminated page of a medieval romance. Lions walking upright like men, dressed in loose-fitting garments bright with heraldic colors. Leather torques and belts contributed an almost gaudily barbaric air.

The figure seated in their midst, though in appearance a Norm, did nothing to detract from that impression. Sturdy half boots folded beneath him as he sat on the deck, Benedict was speaking in tones too low for Shoshone to hear to one of the Gens standing next to him. The large regenepaks that had covered a third of his face when she had seen him on the bridge were gone. Instead, small circular regenepaks covered both eyes, held in place by what appeared to be a black kerchief tied behind his head.

Shoshone walked carefully over to them, shifting her balance as the deck tilted beneath her and leaning into the gale that buffeted her face and dragged on the folds of her one-piece.

The Gens parted before her. She recognized Stellato, who opened his mouth to speak to her and then closed it again. Shoshone kept her eyes straight ahead, trying not to show how intimidated she felt by them.

"Father Benedict." She pitched her voice against the playful roaring of the wind. "Shoshone Mantei, reporting for duty."

Benedict turned his face up at her and smiled. With a few short words and a hand gesture he dismissed the Gens who had been attending him. "I am delighted you are to be my aide. Tiresias had only a young boy to guide him. I have a beautiful young woman. Though if what they say about the old Greeks is true, Tiresias may have been similarly pleased, after all."

"Then you really are blind," she said despite herself. Feeling uneasy about standing over Benedict and still a bit wobbly on her feet, she seated herself across from him. It was an immediate improvement. "After I heard you were going to control the air-braking maneuvers, I wondered how you could possibly read the instruments. I even thought you might be faking blindness." That thought, though, had not arisen before Harriman had talked to her. Normally she would never have spoken so rudely. However, the question had bothered her. Either she would have her curiosity satisfied or Benedict would send her away. Either outcome would be satisfactory.

Benedict was blandly unruffled. "Your modesty does you a disservice. Your hair will grow back—"

How does he know it's cut? She wondered with a stab of apprehension. But of course there were a dozen different ways he might know.

"—your figure will flesh out again, and you will be even more beautiful than you were before.

"My blindness is all too real and more than skin deep. But it was easy to compensate for it while piloting. Even with the main computers out of commission, there were more than a hundred personal units on board. It was a simple matter to jack them into the ship's still-functioning sensors and preset the parameters with which I was concerned. The optimal parabola through the atmosphere generated a pure tone, C above middle C. Anything lower made the tone go flat. Too high and it became sharp. Anyone with perfect pitch could have done as much."

Although sunlight was bright off his shaven skull, the rest of his face was in shadow. Shoshone could not tell if he was teasing.

"We can work out the details of how you will guide me later, whether arm in arm or my hand on your shoulder. Some would suggest a choke collar. A few, in the past, have even attempted it. In the meantime, begin your work as my eyes on this." His hand scuttled across the deck and found a viewplate. Fingers walked along two sides and found the abbreviated keyboard. Thumb and forefinger measured their way to three sets of keys and pressed in a code. An image formed on the plate. An Impressionist's bull's-eye: distorted white ovals on a blue field.

"This world, I think," Shoshone said. "A.4.4."

"Thetis," Benedict corrected. "A Greek sea goddess, mother of Achilles. A.4.4 seemed awkward, and the Centauran contingent won out in the informal name contest."

Clouds and ocean. And, in the gaps between the clouds, occasional darker strands. Land?

"P3 will process the image for you," Benedict offered.

Shoshone pressed the keys. The clouds vanished, leaving only a truncated white oval at the top of the image. It extended halfway to the equator. Jagged rents cut their way northward from the irregular southern boundaries. The dark strands she had seen earlier extended into most of those gaps.

"Stretch marks," she murmured.

"How's that?" Benedict asked.

Shoshone shook her head. "Stupid thought. I see what appears to be an ice cap extending a bit more than forty degrees toward the equator. There are numerous inlets at the margins. Dark discolorations extend from these inlets toward the equator. I think they may be landmasses. If so, they are very long and narrow and show little relief. They are also intermittent, so I would say I am looking at a series of island chains. More than ninety percent of the planet—the satellite, that is—appears to be ocean."

She frowned at the image. Growing up in the floating, submarine colonies of Aquaflamme, she had learned little of above-water geology. Still, something about those archipelagoes seemed wrong.

"Ice can maintain itself more easily on land than on liquid water," Benedict said thoughtfully. "Therefore, I would expect that if the discolorations were landmasses, the ice cap would extend itself south along them. You tell me that the opposite is the case.

"Sonar soundings indicate a seafloor varying from fifteen to twenty kilometers below the surface. A rise from that depth that would break surface is not impossible, but it does seem implausible."

The tone was one of collegial equality, but Shoshone felt the sting of implied criticism in the words themselves. "What do *you* think it is, then?"

There was the faintest suggestion of a shrug. "I don't have enough information for a hypothesis, but if I had to form one, it would be that your first guess was right."

"What—" Shoshone began.

"*Crucible,* this is Scout One." The image of Thetis shrank to the upper left corner of the screen. It was replaced by ocean seen from a height of approximately twenty meters. Lines of waves moved swiftly from the top to the bottom of the image.

"We are ten kilometers northeast of you and have found what appears to be a floating island. Its surface area extends seventy meters by about one hundred twenty. The upper level of the canopy rises fifteen meters from the surface. It is drifting east at four kilometers an hour."

The viewplate image swung up and steadied on a riotous mass of vegetation. Most was brown or green, but here and there Shoshone caught flashes of yellow, red, and even blue. Waves crashed into the sides of the island and disappeared in an explosion of froth. Tall, dendritically branching limbs swept the sky.

As she studied the scene, she realized that she could follow the progress of the waves *through* the island. The whole width of the island lifted up with each wave crest. Treetops scrabbled wildly at the air before settling vertically into the troughs.

She was describing the scene to Benedict when the pilot's voice interrupted again from the viewplate. "Ueda wants to get some samples. I am going to lower him on a line so that he can grab on to one of the trunks."

The viewplate split into two images. The left half retained the picture from Scout One. The right half had to be originating from a stereocam attached to Ueda's helmet. The horizon canted rhythmically from side to side.

There is no excuse for swinging him like that, Shoshone thought. If the pilot isn't good enough to drop him steadily . . .

A trunk top whipped suddenly into view, seemed about to crash into Ueda, slowed—but in the background sky, sea, and other vegetation tossed wildly—and became two overlaid images as one stereocam receptor was ground into the surface of the trunk.

"I'm going down," Ueda said after a few seconds. "It's—snapping about too—too much up here. It—looks steadier—near the base."

For a few minutes the confused images of the descent were

accompanied by heavy breathing and a few muttered curses. Shoshone had to look away and close her eyes to control an onset of motion sickness.

"My line is getting more and more entangled with the top of this trunk," Ueda complained. "I'm going to unhook. There are enough handholds that I should have no problem climbing down far enough to get my samples."

"Shoshone," Benedict said urgently, "is there floating debris of any kind around the island?"

Shoshone fumbled through the help menu and found the PLAYBACK function. Moving back fifteen minutes in memory, she brought up the image of Scout One's stereocams panning up from the sea to the island. She froze the time and zoomed in on the shore.

"There is debris on all sides," Shoshone reported. "I see what appear to be floating trunks, bushes—"

"Ueda! Do not detach your line," Benedict commanded. "The entire island is breaking—"

A high-pitched cry erupted from the speaker. Back on real-time display, Ueda's portion of the viewplate performed a somersault of sky and sea. The surface leapt upward and hit with a palpable slap—

—while the other half of the viewplate showed a third of the island sagging in and collapsing. Trunks fanned out in all directions, pounding the inrushing water to foam. For an instant the surface churned with a writhing carpet of creatures swimming or jumping from their foundering homes to that portion of the island which remained afloat.

Ueda was knifing through water so clear as to be almost transparent. Arms moved through the stereocams' fields of vision in quick, powerful strokes. Shoshone could see, off to one side, the underside of the island. It looked like a faery city floating in air.

"There's a haze drifting away from the base, like a comet's tail, almost as if it were on fire." Shoshone bit her lip to keep herself from sounding even more foolish. Benedict needed precise descriptions, not fanciful impressions!

Ueda's head broke the surface. Like a living sine wave, something silvery rippled from left to right, disappearing before Shoshone could be sure she had seen anything.

"I have Ueda on visual," the pilot said. "I'm dropping down to pick him up."

Scout One dropped down to a heaving sea of half-submerged vegetation. Round, dark tufts, looking like chocolate cotton candy, bounded across the waves and were carried away by the wind. In their midst Shoshone spotted a bobbing torso and two stick-figure arms.

The craft settled into the water. Ueda looked up at a hatch two meters above the water. The line to which he had been attached seemed to have disappeared. Abruptly, the Scout pressed itself down into the swell. A wave washed Ueda into the hatch. Without bothering to drain the water, the pilot sealed the outer hatch and lifted into the air.

"What were you saying about the water?" Benedict asked.

"Ueda is out of it," Shoshone replied, unaware that she had said anything about water.

"No, no, *no*." Benedict brushed his hand impatiently across his face. "You were saying it was clear?"

"Yes," she said, puzzled that he should seize on such an unimportant point. "Almost as clear as drinking water."

Benedict pursed his lips. "This will not do," he said. "This will not do at all."

Scout One settled into the bay less than five minutes later, still trailing the line that had been pinned beneath it by floating limbs. Shoshone's chest and teeth resonated with sympathetic vibrations induced by the craft's repulsor fields. The lock doors slid aside, and the pilot, a Gen named Herald, helped a very cold Ueda down to the deck. Ueda's sodden coverall was unceremoniously stripped from him, and he was enfolded in the waffled depths of a heat robe. A steaming cup was handed to him, but not before its contents had been enhanced by a flask that had mysteriously appeared in Stellato's hand as he passed the cup along. The combination was sufficiently beneficial to slow Ueda's chattering teeth enough for him to talk.

"T-t-that is the g-g-goddamned *coldest* water," he said.

Benedict grabbed Shoshone's arm and gestured in the direction of Ueda's voice. With only moderate awkwardness, due as much to the rolling of the deck as to the novelty of acting as a guide, Shoshone led him to the crowd surrounding Ueda.

"Report," Benedict commanded briskly. "Do I understand that you saw animal life on the island?"

Even smothered within the depths of the heat robe, Ueda stiffened visibly to attention.

"To the extent that any of the life-forms of the planet are

proper analogues to animal and plant categories, there do seem to be mobile forms filling that niche.''

Benedict smiled at what seemed to Shoshone to be an overly precise, almost pedantic distinction.

"There were tubular forms somewhat less than a meter long," Ueda continued. "They wrapped themselves around the upper regions of the trunks, though whether that is their natural habitat or they were just trying to escape the rising waters, I cannot say. I also caught glimpses of arachnoid creatures, maybe half a meter across. I was not able to count or classify limbs before I took my dive.

"Speaking of which, Herald tells me you shouted a warning over the comm-link just as everything gave way. How did you know the island was unstable?"

"You mean, if I was clever enough to discern that it was breaking up, why did I not warn you earlier?" Benedict corrected affably. "I must plead the vicissitudes of age. I was so bemused by the concept of a solitary floating island that I was slow to ask for the data which would have indicated that it was a fragment separated from a larger whole. As long as you were secured by the safety line, it was only an academic concern.

"I was taken by surprise when you unhooked. Then I needed to get the answer quickly, so I had my assistant look for debris around the edges of the island. When she spotted it, it was obvious that there was an ongoing process of decay which might prove dangerous to you."

Herald looked chagrined. "I was right there. I should have noticed that."

"Yes, you should have," Benedict agreed cheerfully. "But with so much kaleidoscopic novelty beneath you, you were unable to pick out the important data.

"Now, Ueda, pray continue your report. Aside from brown, what were the primary colors of the flora you observed? Supposing," he added quickly, "that it is proper to consider them flora."

"Green, yellow, red . . ." Ueda said slowly.

"Chlorophyll green or cupric green? Were the reds orangish, brownish, suggestive of rust?"

Ueda hesitated.

"He was on the island less than five minutes," Shoshone objected, "and most of that clinging to a moving treetop. He had no time for the sort of detailed observations you are asking for.''

"I am not asking for precision," Benedict replied. "I am asking for impressions. They are much more valuable than most people realize in indicating where further attention should be focused.''

"There were possibly cupric greens and rust reds concentrated near the base of the trunks," Ueda said. "I was able to get only a few glimpses through the foliage.''

Benedict cocked his head to one side. "That is suggestive. Now, when you were in the water, how did it taste?''

Ueda grimaced. "Cold. Slightly salty.''

"How salty? As salty as Chiron's New Sea? Or the Pacific Ocean on Earth?''

"Less than either. It was barely noticeable.''

"Was there any sulfur taste?''

"None that I could detect.''

Benedict considered that. "You did not tell me about the icebergs," he said half-querulously.

"What icebergs?" Shoshone asked, confused by the non sequitur.

"The ones Herald, at least, must have seen before he brought the Scout down on the island.''

"They were just on the horizon, Grandfather." Herald's expression was close to awe. "I wasn't even sure I saw them, because of the haze.''

"The northern horizon?" Benedict asked.

"No, Grandfather. The western horizon.''

"The western horizon. We are drifting west to east in a current of unknown extent. At the western limit of our survey we see an advancing line of icebergs, clothed in a suggestive haze. Closer to us we have no icebergs but an undetermined expanse of very cold, almost fresh water. I think—''

"*Father Benedict to the captain's conference room. Executive session begins in five minutes.*''

Benedict sighed. "I lost track of time. Shoshone, please help me to the conference room. Dr. Ueda, continue the water samples but make sure you get a full set of temperature profiles, as well.''

VI

Shoshone guided Benedict across the deck of the shuttle bay to the transvator. She placed her palm on the call plate. The plate glowed briefly, then a prissy mechanical voice informed her that "transvator use is restricted to emergency priorities." Shoshone was about to argue that conveying a blind man to an executive meeting called by the captain met the definition, when she felt Benedict's restraining hand.

"It's not very far from here," he said. "Besides, these old muscles need to stretch."

The map printout showed the conference room to be on the same deck as the captain's quarters. Shoshone led Benedict through a maze of access tunnels. She preceded him down companionway ladders, helped place his boots on the top rungs, and told him when he was near the bottom or needed to duck an obstruction.

It was nearly ten minutes after the summons that she announced their presence at the doors of the conference room. The doors slid apart, disclosing a long table of highly polished Chironese whorlwood. Shoshone guided Benedict to the only vacant chair at the table.

"Stay," he said. "I may need you."

She glanced up uncertainly at Captain Nickerson, who nodded. Shoshone took a seat against the wall, hoping she would be inconspicuous.

"Welcome, Father Benedict," Harriman said. "We are please you could drag yourself away from your work to honor us with your presence."

The tone was so smooth that it took Shoshone a second to

recognize the barb. Automatically, she opened her mouth to protest, but Benedict was already apologizing.

"My infirmity has become quite a nuisance, I fear." Benedict shook his head, a nervous, self-deprecating smile playing quickly across his lips. "I lost track of time until you paged me on the public-address system. Then I was a bit slow in making my way here, despite everything my assistant could do to aid me."

"You should have taken the transvator," Nickerson said.

"My assistant was informed that transvators are for emergency use only when she tried to summon one," Benedict replied.

"I am sure we have enough power to provide you the use of a transvator," Nickerson said irritably. "Especially when you are obeying my summons."

Harriman looked upset. "Begging the captain's pardon, but that is the sort of question this meeting was convened to determine."

"If it turns out that our resources are that slim, I will countermand the order I am about to give," Nickerson said. "Effective immediately, the transvator program will be modified so as to respond without question to the palm prints of either Father Benedict or Engineer Mantei. Furthermore, as a concession to Father Benedict's present handicap, he will be reminded, over private communicator, *not* over the public-address system, of all future executive meetings thirty minutes before they begin. You will be personally responsible for that, Mr. Harriman."

"Yes, ma'am." Hatred and frustration chased themselves across Harriman's face as he looked over at Benedict, as if the Steward had personally contrived the entire series of events just to humiliate him. Although, Shoshone thought suddenly, if half the stories told about Benedict were accurate, that surmise might just be true.

"Very well," Nickerson said. "Dr. Spartacus, we will begin with your report."

Spartacus reported that the sixty percent of the ship's complement still in cold sleep was in stable condition and could be kept that way for another eighteen months. She did not say why so many were unawakened, but from comments and questions from other members of the executive committee, Shoshone inferred that there were two reasons. The first was that there was still damage to the resuscitation programs and even to the hardware itself in some of the cubicles, which made resuscitation medically risky.

"Needless to say," Spartacus commented, "I cannot deal with resuscitation trauma with the few facilities which have been made operative so far."

The other reason was to conserve resources. Even though they were breathing the air of Thetis and water was being made potable through a series of low-energy evaporation stills, it still took a large proportion of the ship's energy budget just to provide basic life-support services. Apparently, some sort of resource management algorithm indicated that the present number of conscious crew members was near the optimum.

"Prospects," Nickerson asked.

"In the near term, moderately good," Spartacus replied. "Those crew members in cold sleep can be maintained there with no danger to their well-being. Injuries have been minor since landing and have not called for anything beyond off-the-shelf organoids and low-level regeneratives.

"Nonetheless," she said, casting a guilty glance at Benedict, "any severe damage to the nervous system is and will remain beyond our capabilities to heal.

"In the long run the major danger is from dietary deficiencies. Although the *Crucible*'s recycling facilities are state of the art, they are not one hundred percent efficient. Without local supplementation, we can expect to suffer deficiency diseases in five to seven years."

"One way or another," Nickerson said grimly, "we will be off this world long before then." The captain was, Shoshone realized, galled by the thought that she might have to be rescued from her first command.

"Thank you, Dr. Spartacus. Engineering, next."

Lumbongo stood up. "Computer: fusor schematics." Fluorescent colors took shape in the air above the table. "The explosion was caused by a rupture in the number two fusor. The resultant explosion vaporized all of that fusor except for the containment shield. The shield was breached, however, and the resultant effects of blast and heat made the entire engine room a shambles. Most of the wreckage was cleared away three watches ago. Last watch, we were able to lay cable to reconnect the remaining fusors to the power supply network."

That is what I should have been doing, Shoshone thought miserably. She felt acutely useless.

"Fusor one was only cracked by the blast. It shut down automatically without further damage. We have been running it in short bursts to recharge our batteries and provide basic power to the ship. It should be fully operational within ten hours. At that time there will be power available for all non-drive uses.

"Fusor three is our main concern. It took the brunt of the blast from fusor two. Its magnetic bottle collapsed without any chance to shunt off the excess heat. Its thermal blast was less severe than that of fusor two, but it nonetheless vaporized four of the six superconducting magnets that formed the bottle.

"The *Crucible* requires the power from two fusors to attain lift and quantum space capability. Our computers contain the specs for the magnets. Our shops have the capability to machine them. What we do not presently have are the raw materials."

A bar graph took the place of the engine room diagram. "As you can see, the magnets are composed of thirty-odd elements—"

"Excuse me," Shoshone interrupted, "but Father Benedict *cannot* see. Please make sure you explain your most important points verbally. And provide a tape of your exhibits to Father Benedict's quarters later."

"Ah, yes." Lumbongo looked flustered and embarrassed. "Your pardon, Father. I forgot—" He bit his lip.

"A full tape of the minutes will be provided," Nickerson said.

"Thank you, Captain," Shoshone said.

Lumbongo cleared his throat. "To summarize, the magnets are constructed from a series of alloys and ceramics which themselves are combinations of more than thirty basic elements. Several of these are in the so-called rare earth series and are crucial in the doping process. Despite the name of their series, these elements are not that rare in either the Sol or Centauran systems, and in younger systems, like the Sirian, they tend to be more plentiful. They are most easily mined in asteroid belts. On Thetis, the nearest mines would be at least ten kilometers below us."

"Can't we cannibalize?" Harriman asked. "The shuttles operate on fusion power. Could you not get enough of the materials you need by stripping them?"

"The shuttles operate on laser implosion fusion, sir," Lumbongo explained, "not by magnetic containment. There are no superconducting magnets to cannibalize."

"Very well, then," Nickerson said. "Could you run lines from the shuttles' power units to our drive systems?"

"Yes, ma'am," Lumbongo said promptly. "The calculations I have run indicate that if we were to take full advantage of all the power produced by our shuttles, we would be able to provide enough power to the impeller pads for *Crucible* to free itself from the gravitational fields of Thetis and A.4. We would still have less than three-fourths of the power needed for quantum drive operation."

"Prepare a contingency plan for doing that," Nickerson directed. "If we cannot find the raw materials we need on Thetis, we will have to go elsewhere in the Eta Cassiopeiae system.

"Father Benedict, if you could give your report, please."

Benedict had been so still that Shoshone had wondered if he was sleeping. His response, however, was quick and clear.

"Thank you, Captain. The fact that we have been breathing the free oxygen of this planet for the last fifteen watches is proof enough that Thetis has an extensive biosphere. Less than an hour ago we had our first extensive encounter with it. Computer: video log of Scout One, this date. Execute. Shoshone, please murmur short descriptions as the scenes change."

The image of the floating forest formed above the table. "This seems to be a fragment of a larger biotic mass. Most of the individual species are buoyant, but as you will see, the upright position of some of the larger species is unstable. We have not yet had time to do an analysis of the data collected, so I cannot present a listing of plant or animal species. However, we can now add nitrogen and carbon to hydrogen, oxygen, potassium, sodium, and chlorine as elements found in quantity. My guess is that we will find at least some of the others Chief Engineer Lumbongo needs at various levels of the food chain as well as floating free in the water itself."

"What is the basis of that prediction?" Harriman asked sharply.

"Construct a model of this ocean in your mind," Benedict said. "No rivers discharge into it, no landmasses divert its currents. With so little mixing, rainfall creates a layer of nearly fresh water. Icebergs melt, adding to this layer.

"We have been making use of this without thinking about it, grateful that our stills function so easily. However, even though we know nothing about the biochemistry of the floating islands, we do know that this layer of fresh water is a desert to them. They cannot survive in it, and that is undoubtedly one reason why the one Scout One encountered was breaking up.

"Dr. Timakata has made a discovery which should be mentioned here."

The chief of the astronomy section cut against the Gens stereotype. He was of slighter build than the average Gen, his eyes darted quickly from side to side, and when he spoke, it was almost always in a low voice with an air of apology.

"It's only a first-order approximation," he said. Shoshone leaned toward the table to hear him. "However, on the basis of the preliminary measurements, it appears that we are not receiving enough radiation from Eta Cassiopeiae A to prevent Thetis from icing over."

"Greenhouse effect?" Harriman asked.

"There is one," Timakata agreed, "but it is not great enough to prevent icing. Of course, if that happened just once, the increased amount of radiation reflected would lower the temperature so much that there would never be a thaw."

"That is not what we see about us," Benedict said. "There must be another heat source. My present hypothesis is that it is the planet itself. Geothermal vents on the ocean floor must be releasing heat into the water. Convection currents carry it to the surface, where it warms the atmosphere. The same upwellings doubtless bring up the nutrients on which the floating islands subsist. Once we find the seas in which the floating islands grow, we will find mines which have come to the surface."

"But you do not say that all the elements required by the chief engineer will be at hand," Harriman said, "or that they will be present in usable quantities."

"Quite correct," Benedict admitted cheerfully. "Until we can take samples from the growing seas, I can tell you neither the full range of elements present nor their quantities."

"Why not go directly to the source?" Harriman asked. "The Scouts are airtight and have more than enough thrust to counteract their natural buoyancy."

Lumbongo rubbed his chin dubiously. "Scouts are specced out for an entirely different environment. Computer: visual model of a Scout-class BAS1E1. Simulate effects of water pressure with increasing depth in a water medium of .857 standard gee. Display depth readout; increase depth ten meters per second. Execute.''

A translucent depiction of a Scout appeared at eye level. Numbers next to it blinked their way through the tens table. Nothing happened for more than a minute. At a depth of one kilometer, rainbow lines shimmered around the entry hatch.

"The colors represent degrees of distortion from specification," Lumbongo explained. "Since these hulls are unicast, the natural lines of weakness are around the hatch and the sensor receptors.''

The simulation ended just beyond one and a half kilometers. Coruscating colors flashed through the spectrum.

"Something just happened," Shoshone told Benedict. "It was too quick for me to catch everything, but the model is broken into three pieces drifting away from each other.''

Benedict nodded calmly but said nothing.

"I don't believe that!" Harriman said. "Oceanographers were going deeper than that before the twenty-first century. Yet with technologies they couldn't dream of, we can't even go down two kilometers?''

Lumbongo shook his head. "It's what I said earlier. Scouts are designed for a different mission. They are supposed to perform in vacuum most of the time, but they're rated up to 1.3 standard atmospheres. The hatch fail-safes use the interior pressure of the cabin to press the hatches flush against the seals.''

Shoshone nodded, remembering her own experience with the *Crucible*'s interior air locks.

"The fact of the matter," Lumbongo continued, "is that battlestar shuttles were never designed to be used for deep-ocean mining.''

"Could you refit the hatches of the Scouts to eliminate the design problem?" Harriman asked.

"That would take a more detailed study—" Lumbongo began.

"My assistant is our on-board expert on submarine mining," Benedict interrupted. "She can answer any questions you have in this regard.''

It took Shoshone a moment to realize that he meant her. He's playing with you, testing you, she told herself. Everyone around the table looked at her expectantly.

She gulped. "I grew up in the Dogfish colony on Aquaflamme. Aquaflamme is the largest satellite of Wolfhound, a gas giant in the Sirius A system. It masses 1.1×10^{27} grams.'' Let them convert that to Earth mass equivalents if they have to, she thought. ''It's younger than either the Sol or Centaurus systems, which is important for two reasons. Like Thetis, Aquaflamme is a world too far from its sun for solar radiation to keep it from freezing. However, its oceans stay liquid because it has not had time to lose much of its heat of formation. Also, because it formed later, its dust cloud had been enriched by nearby supernovas with a greater proportion of heavy elements. Wolfhound sucked up most of them, but it isn't practical to mine the lower reaches of gas giants.''

That brought forth a few dry chuckles from around the table.

''That leaves Aquaflamme as the largest accessible repository of heavy elements, and that is why marine mining is the basis of our economy.'' Harriman was beginning to look impatient. Hurry up! Shoshone admonished herself. They don't need a lecture on astronomy or interstellar economics.

''The solid surface is eight to fourteen kilometers below the surface. Mr. Harriman is right in saying that there is relatively little trouble in getting the mining ships to descend to those depths. The problems derive from the fact that the most lucrative concentrations of the minerals most in demand are found erupting from hot water vents. The heat often exceeds two hundred degrees centigrade. Besides being bad enough in itself, it creates enough turbulence to smash a score of mariminers every year. Some of the vents spout hot acid. If you're lucky, these just corrode the seals around your waldoes and bankrupt you. If you're not lucky . . .'' She thought about her parents talking in low voices over the kitchen table about friends who had been a little too desperate for a big strike and then been reported overdue and then, eventually, been forgotten.

''The point is,'' Harriman said, ''that the technology exists for a mining operation under the conditions we have on Thetis. If it exists, it is almost certainly accessible through an auxiliary data base.''

''The point is,'' Benedict corrected gently, ''that even with the specialized skills and equipment necessary for deep-sea mining, it is still a dangerous and uncertain business. It should be low on our list of options.''

''It isn't on the list at all until we locate minable deposits on the ocean floor,'' Nickerson said. ''Father Benedict, your team will give first priority to identifying sources of all the elements identified by the chief of engineering. Until that is done, all other parts of your mission are secondary.''

Benedict nodded his acquiescence.

''Mr. Lumbongo, you will make sure Father Benedict receives a complete list of those elements. You will continue your repair work. You have carte blanche to cannibalize any part of the *Crucible* in order to make us flightworthy. This includes commandeering, if necessary, personal property from any of the survey teams. You will also check out the Scouts for extended flight within the A.4 system.''

''Yes, ma'am.''

''Dr. Timakata, I realize that your resources are limited at present. Nonetheless, I remember being tremendously impressed during my education at how much was discovered during the golden age of astronomy, when humans were confined to one planet. I need you to do a spectral analysis of all orbiting bodies in the A.4 system. If Thetis does not have the resources we need, we will need to mount an expedition to some place that does.

''Mr. Harriman, make sure the transvators are recoded for Father Benedict. Report any problems to me immediately.''

Nickerson stood. The rest of them scrambled to their feet. Shoshone reached out to guide Benedict, but he had already interpreted the rustling sounds and was slowly rising.

''I'll want summary reports on my desk by 0800 every morning,'' the captain went on. ''For anything *important,* you may contact me immediately whether I am on or off watch.'' Her glance fell on each of them in turn. ''We have five months to make our repairs, complete our mission, and return to Centaurus. Considering that only a short time ago we faced imminent suffocation and an eternity of drifting in deep space, we have done well so far. If we continue to work together''—she put odd stress on that word, Shoshone thought—''we will all be back within the Periphery before anyone knows we were missing.''

They were dismissed. Nickerson said something to Harriman about a Captain's Mast. Shoshone reached out to guide Benedict and stumbled. The room seemed to pivot slowly about her.

''Shoshone?'' Benedict's anxious hand patted up and down her arm.

Shoshone's ribs and cheeks ached. "Just dizzy," she said. She took two deep breaths and forced herself upright. The floor steadied.

"This is your first day out of sick bay," Benedict said. "I should not have let you overexert yourself."

He insisted on accompanying her back to her room. "This is crazy," she muttered. "I'm supposed to be taking care of you." Still, she did feel light-headed, and the deck seemed to move between steps in a way that had nothing to do with the ocean swell.

When they stopped, it took her a moment to realize that she was standing before her own quarters.

"The door was privacy-sealed when you were taken to sick bay," Benedict said. "You are the only one who can open it."

She placed her hand on the palmplate, and the door slid aside.

"Has anything been changed?" Benedict's tone was carefully neutral.

Shoshone grimaced in distaste. "Somebody stripped the bed," she said, "but he didn't take the time to wash the wall." It was smeared with dark brown splotches. She thought of how she must have hit to make that pattern and felt nausea rise within her.

"What about your acceleration netting?" Benedict asked.

"Just lying in a heap," Shoshone replied. She could think of very little except throwing new sheets on the bed and collapsing onto it.

"Please examine the tear," Benedict said. "Is it jagged or straight? Do you see any unraveling of the parted strands?"

The implication of the questions cut through Shoshone's haze. She blinked, forcing her eyes to focus.

"It is completely straight," she said. She ran her fingers along the edge. "I neither see nor feel any unraveling. It is as clean and as straight as—"

"As if it had been intentionally cut," Benedict finished.

VII

Dᴜʀɪɴɢ ʜᴇʀ sʟᴇᴇᴘ ᴀ ᴄʀᴜɴᴄʜɪɴɢ ɪᴍᴘᴀᴄᴛ sʜᴜᴅᴅᴇʀᴇᴅ through the hull of the *Crucible*. The deck canted, rolling Shoshone against the wall. She whimpered without waking. Slowly the deck slid back to something approaching the horizontal.

She woke to the blue-green integers of the chronometer hovering in the darkness above her. She frowned at it for a moment before she realized that it was more than an hour into her watch.

"Command: lights." The room flared into full daylight. Squinting, Shoshone staggered over to the shower. Today the sonic enhancements not only vibrated off dead epidermis, they seemed to finger with special delight each healing crack in her bones.

Nonetheless, she was both refreshed and fully awake as she dressed afterward. She looked over at the acceleration netting and thought about Benedict's last words.

Engineers were recognizable at a distance by two things they always carried. The first was their all-purpose tool. Half again as long and thick as an ordinary stylus, an APT contained within its barrels miniature electromagnets and magnetometers, probes to measure electrical resistance, temperature, ionization, and a dozen other obscure attributes. The other was their severe black pockomp, sheathed in impact-resistant plastic.

Shoshone took the former and plugged it into the latter. She adjusted one of the four rings on the fat end of the barrel to choose function. Flipping open the pockomp, she keyed the display screen. Slowly she moved the narrow end of the APT

49

along the cut acceleration netting. On the screen, the magnified threads showed irregularly shaped bulbous heads. So the fabric had not been sliced by a knife; it had been melted.

Nor had all the threads been cut as she had told Benedict. Closer examination disclosed that two centimeters at the head of the netting had torn, as had three other evenly spaced edges. She pulled her mattress away from the wall. There was the remaining fringe of netting, fastened to the metal frame. Just above it a heat-darkened line on the wall extended most of the length of the bed.

So someone really had tried to kill her. He had taken a laser, perhaps one similar to the one she had in her APT, and cut through enough of the netting that it would be sure to part when put under stress, at the same time leaving enough intact that it would feel secure when she sealed herself in.

It made no sense. Shoshone had never had illusions about her own importance. No one could have any reason to kill her. Conversely, if someone did, why should he choose such an indirect and, as it turned out, ineffective method?

She folded the netting and sealed it in a thigh pocket. As she was about to leave, she saw that she had a recorded message. She hit the play button. Dr. Spartacus, trying to look severe, stated that she had heard of Shoshone's weakness and was placing her on the regimen that would appear in printout. Shoshone smiled as the plastisheet unscrolled from its slot. The doctor's concern seemed excessive, but after nearly having had to be carried back to her room, Shoshone resolved to follow the regimen precisely.

She was already late for her duty with Benedict, but Spartacus had emphasized the necessity of starting with a good breakfast. Furthermore, she rationalized, if Benedict found her performance unsatisfactory, he could always dismiss her. Then she could go back to her real job as an engineer.

Because there was no line in the mess hall, she went straight to the menu board and punched in a breakfast conforming to Spartacus's guidelines. Her covered tray, identified with her name, was already extruding itself as she walked over to the tray slot. She picked it up and looked for a place to sit. That early in a watch there was only a scattering of crew members at the tables. Even so, it was noticeable that all the Gens had congregated on one side, and all the Norms on the other. Since Shoshone wanted to be alone to ponder the implications of her attempted murder, the nearly empty center section was perfect.

The smells that came from the tray as she unsnapped the cover drove all other thoughts from her mind. Even before war rationing had come to Aquaflamme, breakfast had been a matter of differently flavored gruels. On the *Crucible,* however, everyone ate like Exploiters. On her tray was hot, steaming tea; a large glass, glowing with condensation beads, of orange citrall; panfries; and chunks of ham mixed in with scrambled eggs. And that was considered a moderately small, simple breakfast by some members of the crew!

There was even a rumor that much of the food was not high-grade synthetics but was natural—that, for example, the ham might be the actual seared flesh of a mammal and the eggs might have come from the ovaries of a bird. The thought had made her queasy her first day on board, but the queasiness had evaporated with her first smell of the food.

Still, her father's voice asked in her mind, *How many workers had to starve to produce this meal?*

A presence loomed on the other side of the table. She looked up to see Stellato holding a cup of syncaf. Golden torques gleamed in the ceiling lights.

"May I join you?" he asked. When she hesitated, he added, "I have been asked to be a spy."

"On whom?"

"You."

She gestured to the chair opposite. If this was a line, it was at least new to her. "Who asked you to spy on me?"

"Dr. D'Argent—don't look around! He is at the far end of the room behind me. He is very interested in anything you may let drop concerning Gran—Father Benedict. He thought that since we had worked together, you might trust me enough to talk."

"To a spy?"

"You aren't supposed to know that."

Shoshone shook her head. "And now I am supposed to be disarmed by your honesty and tell you everything you want to know?"

Stellato stared into his mug. "You could lean over, slap me, and tell me to take my attentions elsewhere. That would certainly win you the respect of the half roomful of Norms staring at us now. Most would probably rush to your aid."

"The hell with them," Shoshone said, disturbed by the

undertone of bitterness. "Tell you what. Let's exchange information, question for question."

Stellato smiled. The quick glimpse of gleaming white teeth was disconcerting. "Fair enough."

"First, tell me how Dr. D'Argent tells you to do anything. He's not in your chain of command. He's not even a member of the executive council."

"There are at least two hierarchies on board," Stellato said, sounding surprised that he had to explain this. "There is the one you just referred to, based on position and rank on the *Crucible*. The other one, which may be more important, is based on position and honors accrued before we were chosen to be part of this expedition.

"Jean D'Argent is near or at the top of that second hierarchy, at least among the Gens. You know that his specialty is microbiotic biochemistry?" Shoshone nodded. "It was his techniques, disseminated among all the Clans at the beginning of the war, that allowed all of us to survive the blockade of supplies from within the Periphery. It is no exaggeration to say that without D'Argent, starvation would have compelled us to surrender in the first six weeks. For that matter, your own air regenerator/waste processor units on, uh . . ."

"Aquaflamme," Shoshone said tartly.

"On Aquaflamme probably had components produced by Industrial Microbiotics. They are pretty much standard within the Periphery. D'Argent developed all of them for IM before the war. He has an action for royalties in the courts right now." Stellato's mouth quirked. "IM is defending on the basis that Gens were not legally recognized as human beings at the time, so no patent rights could vest.

"He also lost all his children to a raid by some of Chiang's privateers *after* the Treaty of Chiron was signed. Perverse as it may sound, that adds to his stature. He is a well-respected scientist, a war hero, and he has paid more than his share of dues.

"My turn. What is your impression of Father Benedict so far?"

"He is tremendously overrated," Shoshone said flatly. "He is a scholarly old man, very good in his area, but nothing like the gray eminence in all those stories that circulate about him."

"What is the basis for that opinion?" Stellato asked skeptically.

That sounded like a second question to Shoshone, but she felt strongly enough the need to justify herself that in a few minutes she was telling Stellato everything Benedict had done in her presence—everything except his discovery of the cut acceleration netting. After a brief struggle she had decided to reserve that for Harriman or the captain.

When she finished, Stellato regarded her with something like amazement. "Let me see if I understand this. He alone realized that this floating island thing was about to break up. He knew about the icebergs without the pilot mentioning them. At the executive committee meeting he outlined the basic heat flow of this entire world. All this while blind, with his access to information terribly restricted. And from this you conclude he is overrated."

"I didn't say he was stupid," Shoshone snapped. "Although I'd say the robes he wears are some evidence of softheadedness."

"I've heard a lot of things about the Order of Stewards," Stellato said, his voice rising just a bit. "Not all of them have been complimentary. But nobody I know has ever said they were stupid. Or are you just equating religion generally with ignorance?"

"Don't you?" Shoshone asked. "Who suffered more than your people from the Savior of Humanity Churches and its political arm, the Defenders of Humanity? I saw tapes of Graeme Williams preaching on his crusades. He was preaching your extinction. All Bestials were unnatural demonspawn, he said. The Lord delighted in the man who killed such abominations. The man who washed his hands in the blood from the bowels of a Bestial washed away sin. Was that a rational assessment of who you are, of who your people are? I would like to call it ignorance, because the alternatives are worse."

Stellato stared down at his hands gripping the edge of the table. For an instant Shoshone feared that she had offended him, that he would stand and walk away. And why should it bother me if he does? she asked herself angrily.

"Everything important, everything powerful," he said hesitantly, "is two-edged." His hands moved in abrupt half-formed gestures. It was as if words were clumsy boxes, unable to catch the full concept he wanted.

"Look!" He unsnapped his APT from its belt and held it across to her. "Think of this as science, as technology. It has all sorts of tools fitted into it. It has a minilaser that we can use for measurement, for illumination, in dozens of ways to repair and build things as great as this starship. But most of the research in lasers for the past three hundred years has been to make them more effective weapons. I have seen friends *explode* when a battlelaser caught them in the chest. So you hear people say science is evil.

"Religion . . . I'm not qualified to tell you what religion is. But part of what it is, is what people believe most intensely about themselves and what their purpose is in the universe. It gives them a course to steer by, an integrity to their lives. At its best, it provides a framework for lives of honor, love, and forgiveness. At its worst, it allows fears and hatreds to metastasize to monstrous dimensions.

"I know what you mean about preaching hatred and genocide. We had our own counterparts to that during the war. But I also know a man who was killed for preaching reconciliation and love and blessed his killers with the last breath which bubbled through his slashed throat."

Shoshone bit back an angry retort. These were the words she had tried to find nearly two decades before with her own parents. There had been a girl in one of her classes named Sarah. Although she used no makeup, she was the prettiest girl Shoshone knew. Her disposition was sweet and modest. Everything I was not, Shoshone thought. Shoshone liked to spend time studying with her. There was a peacefulness that part of her hoped would rub off.

Her parents forbade the friendship as soon as they learned of it. Her father tried to appear reasonable. "Her parents are Savior of Humanity bigots," he said. "Everything they do, from when they can work to what they can eat, is dictated by some Dark Ages superstition. Right now they're so incensed at genetic manipulation that if they have their way, we will be back to the bad old days of hemophilia and Mongoloid idiots. Just because our so-called leaders lack the courage to eradicate such stupidity is no reason for us to expose ourselves to it, much less to encourage it."

Her schooling modules were changed, and as easily as that she had no more common time with Sarah. An elaborate, fantasized rebellion was aborted less than a week later, when Sarah's parents failed to return from a marimining exploration expedition. A few days later they were officially listed dead.

The day after that Sarah was shipped off-world to live with an aunt.

How odd to find in Stellato something like the same brightness of spirit. Her eyes smarted for no apparent reason.

Shoshone took a deep breath. "We are getting off track. The point I was trying to make is that Father Benedict is nothing like the legends that have gathered around him. Now. My turn." Any number of questions clamored in her mind for answers, but most of them threatened to reheat the emotional atmosphere. "I don't know anything about Catholic religious orders, but I was under the impression that priests were addressed as 'Father.' Yet I have heard a number of Gens address him as 'Grandfather.' You nearly did just now. Does one indicate greater rank than the other?"

Stellato grinned. "That goes back a *long* way. Before the war, even before the Defenders of Humanity became such an important political power. Back to when Snowden's Multi-Neural Capacitants were proving so effective in their indentures to the various power factions within the Periphery that they had become powers in their own right."

"You don't look old enough to remember all this," Shoshone said.

"You'd be surprised," Stellato said. "But you are right. I learned about Benedict in a child's game. He wasn't Father, or even Brother, Benedict then. He was known by the name he had taken during his first indenture, Paul Niccolo Rénard. In the game I was taught, however, he was Grandfather Fox, avatar of trickery, incarnation of cleverness. The purpose of his character in the game was to teach young Bestials—don't look startled. We all used the term then. It was the only one we had—overimpressed with their own strength the value of intelligence.

"When I learned two years ago that he was still alive, it was as if—as if Merlin had suddenly stepped out of the storybooks. By then, of course, I'd realized his purpose in the Game of Fox and Lion. I had learned that there are limits to brute force, that subtlety and cleverness are necessities.

"Even now, most of us can't think of him without thinking of the game we learned as children. That's why we slip up and use the old title by mistake.

"My turn again: Did you notice anything odd about the way Father Benedict behaved?"

"Odd how?"

"I have no idea," Stellato replied, exasperated. "It's not my question." His head jerked almost imperceptibly in the direction of D'Argent.

"Then, no, I did not—not that I have any baseline from which to judge his behavior. If anything, he was like some old university professor, polite to all his colleagues but unable to resist showing off every so often."

Stellato nodded to himself. "That will just have to do, then." He moved his chair back.

Shoshone put her hand out. "One more question," she said.

"We are even," Stellato said with wide eyes.

"I will owe you one. I just don't want to lose track of everything I should be doing. How are the repairs going? And what caused the explosion in the first place? Everything I learned in tech school said catastrophic failure was impossible for one of those units."

Stellato's voice lowered, and he leaned forward. "Repairs are going as well as can be expected. In fact, we have done almost everything we can until someone locates some raw materials for us.

"As to what caused it . . . the chief has been discouraging speculation. However, I saw the containment shield before it was removed. There was a smooth hole about five centimeters across. If I didn't know better, I would say it was caused by an assault laser."

VIII

SHOSHONE SENSED THE DIFFERENCE AS SOON AS THE DOOR
opened on the landing bay. A warmer wind than the time
before, though still chilly enough to frost her breath. Nor was
it a steady gale now. Instead, gusts chased each other across
the bay area, swept in curves along the walls, and jumped out
in ambush from between the berthed shuttles. And there were
odors. With each breath, a complex skein of a dozen odors
invaded her nostrils.

She forgot about them, though, when she turned and looked
through the open bay doors. The sea, except through gaps at a
far distance, had disappeared. In its place was a moving forest.
A childhood image echoed in her mind: Trees marching on
Isengard. Only, even at this distance, she could see that these
tall growths were like no trees known within the Periphery.
Nor did they march, although they did rise and fall in place.

When she could tear her eyes away, she noticed Benedict at
the table that had been set up for him near the bay doors. Ueda,
almost unrecognizable to Shoshone now that he was dry, stood
across from him expectantly.

Shoshone tried to focus on what Benedict was holding. Approximately half a meter across, it seemed like an abstract
sculpture designed to subdivide air. Its framework was thinnest
near the center, with the—hairs? wires? stems?—thickening as
they neared the exterior. Small nodules randomly dotted the
surface. It was light and springy, almost bouncing out of Benedict's hands.

"It followed me into the Scout's lock," Ueda was explaining to Benedict. "I thought you might find it interesting."

Benedict's hands were moving with birdlike quickness and
precision over the entire structure. Watching his fingers trace

the length of the stems and measure the angles of the branch-
ings, Shoshone felt for an instant that she was within his mind
as it constructed a model of what was before him. She also
realized that she had seen it before, bouncing across the waves
in the dozens while the island disintegrated.

"Marine tumbleweed," Benedict murmured. A smile of delight illuminated his whole face. "Do you have any idea
what—" He stopped talking as his fingers found the nodules.

"They are apparently filled with air," Ueda explained.
"They serve to keep the whole structure floating."

"What do you think it is?" Benedict asked.

"My hypothesis," Ueda began carefully, "is that it may be
a seed of some kind. I intend to float it in some water gathered
from outside and kept at the outside temperature. Then we will
see what happens." He lifted the tumbleweed gently from
Benedict's hands.

Shoshone judged it was time she made her presence known.
"Engineer Mantei reporting," she said, stressing the title
slightly.

If Benedict noticed, he gave no indication. "You are sounding better this watch, Engineer. I trust you were not disturbed
when we made 'landfall' in this weed reef."

The lost dream of her tilting bed came back to her. "No,
sir."

"Good, because I am going to keep you busy."

In the next several hours there were pauses that might have
stretched to thirty seconds when she wondered if wry under-
statement was one of Benedict's sources of amusement. She
also wondered how he had managed for any interval of time
without her. Information was streaming into his desk from
Scouts and exploration teams. The Scouts sent back a continuous stream of pictures as they swept north and south along the
weed reef. The desk computer sewed them into a mosaic that
to Shoshone resembled nothing so much as a Julia set from one
of her early math classes. She described the growing composite
as precisely as she could; a few times, at Benedict's suggestion, she guided his fingers along the outlines to help him form
the image in his mind.

Rebekka Shahal was reporting to Benedict on the latest sea-
water analyses when the storm struck. Shoshone happened to
lift her eyes from her data plate in time to see the line of rain
rushing across the weed reef like a rustling curtain. She

watched as if hypnotized, fascinated with the abrupt shift of weather from abstraction to actuality, until the storm hit.

Wind slammed into the hull with a force that shivered through the deck and up through Shoshone's heels. It roared in through the open bay doors, knocking data plates off the tables and skittering pockomps along the deck. Hail pellets blasted her face with pinpoint coldness. As she stood, her chair was blown on its side. She grabbed Benedict and guided him to the shelter of the deep end of the bay. As soon as his free hand brushed the wall, he shook off her arm.

"—et the data plates," he ordered, "—the desk computer."

She leaned into the wind and forced her way back toward the doors, pausing only to pick pockomps out of a stream that had formed in the middle of the flight deck. The desk had cartwheeled into the wall. Lightning split the sky as she pressed the button telescoping the legs. Branching brilliances burned themselves into her retinas. As she blinked, waiting for sight to return, the thunderclap hit her, knocking her to her knees.

Using the desk top as a crutch, she pushed herself up to her feet. Three meters above her, shielded by reinforced plasteel, the flight ops sergeant was watching her progress with an expression of bored unconcern. Monitors behind his shoulders relayed transmissions from the Scouts surveying the weed reef.

"Close the doors," Shoshone shouted.

Flight Ops stared at her. Then, in a slow and elaborate pantomime, he put his hand to his ear and leaned in her direction.

"The doors! Close them! We're being flooded out," Shoshone yelled. Because of the inward curve of the hull, part of the deck by the doors was open to the sky. A miniature waterfall was cascading from the top edge of the open doorway.

Flight Ops regarded the waterfall with a look of aesthetic appreciation. *"Nothing our drains can't handle,"* boomed from the side speakers.

"What about us?" Shoshone demanded. "How are we supposed to continue our work?"

"In your assigned offices and workrooms. While flights lift off and return at twenty-minute intervals, those doors will remain open for safety reasons." Flight Ops turned to his monitors, dismissing Shoshone.

Muttering to herself, Shoshone lugged the desk computer to

the back of the bay. Hailstones floated happily in the little stream that bisected the bay, keeping pace with her until they whirled around and dived into a drain grating.

Benedict stood with Rebekka near the far end of the bay. She had retrieved three chairs and guided Benedict into one. Shoshone set up the table next to them, pressing the button to pop out the legs.

"God*damn* Flight Ops," Shoshone said.

"I hope not," Benedict replied, "at least not over anything this trivial. His main points, after all, are inarguable. This is a flight deck, and we are here at all at his sufferance. Furthermore, we do have perfectly satisfactory working quarters elsewhere. My desire for immediate impressions of this world—its smells, its sounds—is my only excuse for setting up shop here."

Shoshone looked at him sharply. It was the first time she had heard, even by implication, the pain of loss caused by his blindness.

"But Dr. Shahal was about to provide us with something more precise than impressions," Benedict said.

Rebekka Shahal was approximately Shoshone's age but, to Shoshone's eye, better built. Under the strong ceiling lights her jet-black fur glistened with rainbow droplets. It seemed suddenly not at all absurd for Shoshone to feel a stab of envy at the other's good looks.

"I have good news," Rebekka reported. "Most of your hypotheses are proving out. Water temperatures are ten to fifteen degrees higher around the weed reefs than in the surrounding ocean. That heat, I think, is the main reason we have this thunderstorm.

"The hot plume also contains a bouillabaisse of solutes, salts, silicate particulates—we don't have anything like a full catalog yet. However, we do have a preliminary analysis of the elements contained in the plume."

She slipped a chip in the desk computer's data slot. Three-dimensional graphs leapt to fluorescent life. Shoshone shook her head, wondering how she was going to translate the mass of information for Benedict.

"But," Benedict said. "I hear a strong 'but' in your voice."

"Well, bearing in mind that our data are incomplete, I have done a set of calculations which have a definitely odd result. First, I did a rough estimate of the biomass of the square kilometer of weed reef all around us.'' Screen wipe, followed by a single green bar, scale along the left side.

"Next, analysis of the elements composing representative, we hope, members of the weed reef community.'' The green bar shattered into a sloping spectrum: hydrogen, oxygen, then a long dive to carbon and nitrogen and a further dive to a series of elements that looked like stepping-stones. There were too many of them to fit onto the screen without a side scroll.

"Then I matched that with the elements in the hot water plume.'' Highlights rippled across the screen.

"They are the same,'' Shoshone said. "Well, of course.''

"So far, so good,'' Rebekka agreed. "Then Ueda and I looked at the aerial composite of the weed reef the Scouts have been sending in. We paid special attention to the floating islands drifting away on the lee side of the reef. We estimated the total tons of biomass, excluding water weight, being shed over a hundred-day period and compared that to the total mass being lifted to the surface by the plume during the same period.'' She hit the key calling for the next graph.

"The reef is taking in less than a tenth of what it's shedding?'' Shoshone asked, not sure that she was reading the graph correctly.

"Less than one-tenth of what is available to be taken from the water,'' Rebekka corrected. "It is unrealistic to suppose one hundred percent efficiency.''

Shoshone frowned. "I heard at least half a dozen assumptions in the presentation. If any one of them is wrong, the problem goes away.''

"Dr. Shahal is aware of that,'' Benedict said. "The measurements may have been in error, or the time during which they were taken may not have been representative. Or the reef itself may be a transitory structure. But pointing out a seeming contradiction is a valuable indication of where to do future research, since, by definition, contradictions do not exist.''

They were deciding on the next set of measurements to be taken when lunch came. There was a pastry, apparently designed to be hand-held, filled with a scaldingly hot mixture of meat and vegetables, none of which she had ever seen before. It was accompanied by a covered thermomug of tea. Shoshone sipped and bit carefully, savoring the heat almost more than the mélange of tastes.

"Don't you think,'' she suggested between bites, "that it is about time we started concentrating on the main assignment?''

"What main assignment?'' Rebekka asked quizzically.

Shoshone panted, trying to cool a burn on the roof of her mouth. "Captain Nickerson specifically made discovering sources of the elements needed to repair the fusors Father Benedict's number-one priority. Nobody has mentioned that all morning.''

Rebekka squinted at her as if Shoshone were speaking an unknown language.

"At the moment, the best way to carry out Captain Nickerson's wishes is to follow the basic survey outline,'' Benedict said. "There is a program in the desk computer called REPAIR. Call it up.''

The image looked identical to the earlier graph that had shown the composition of the reef element by element. "Now go to the help menu and run DISTILL.''

A figure appeared by the graph. Shoshone blinked and looked again.

"One hundred cubic kilometers? We would have to vaporize one hundred cubic kilometers of reef to get the elements we need?'' she asked incredulously.

"Some of the trace elements are exceedingly rare,'' Benedict observed dryly. "Nearly all of what we need could be obtained from a little more than a tenth of a cubic kilometer. However, there are considerations apart from the aesthetic and ecological which militate against destroying a sizable proportion of the biosphere in order to make our escape. Splitting the chemical bonds requires power of a magnitude usually associated with a fusor. We have only one operational fusor, and if we utilize its power continuously for the next year to vaporize the appropriate amount of reef, we shall have none left over for things like life support.''

Scouts lifted off and landed throughout the second half of the watch. After a while it occurred to Shoshone that Flight Ops had not been entirely unreasonable in refusing to close the bay doors. By then the storm had blown itself out, leaving only dark cloud streamers of fantastical shapes to chase themselves over the horizon.

As the clouds thinned, Shoshone caught her first sight of A.4. It was a multihued arch, spanning the horizon. From this angle the rings were edge-on, invisible. Yet the sight made her catch her breath.

"What?" Benedict asked.

"It's A.4. It's—I have never seen anything like it before."

"Describe it, please."

Shoshone took a deep breath, trying to force herself to think clearly. "It is lying on the horizon, with an angular size of—"

"I do not need you to tell me its position or angular magnitude," Benedict interrupted. "Both are constants from this longitude and have been measured with excruciating exactitude by Dr. Timakata."

"Then what do you want from me?" Shoshone asked, stung.

"I want what *you* see. I want to hear what made you catch your breath when you saw it for the first time."

"I am an engineer," Shoshone said angrily. "I am trained to be analytical and precise."

"Admirable traits. You are also a human being with the capability of comprehending a sensory gestalt in an instant. You don't see a nose, then a mouth, then eyes, then measure the distances and angles between them. You see a face, recognize an individual, judge his or her emotional and physical state. You demonstrated your ability during our last watch together, when I showed you that image of Thetis."

"All I remember is that I gave you the most precise description of which I was capable."

"You remember, but you are ashamed to admit it," Benedict countered. "You said 'stretch marks.' A characterization not likely to have occurred to a male. Timakata had just mentioned to me that Thetis seemed to be receiving too little radiation to prevent ice-over. Either his calculations were wrong or Thetis itself was making up the difference. I was wondering how it might do that when you made your comment. 'Stretch marks.' Exactly! A world giving birth to itself, ocean vents ten to a hundred times more extensive than any on Earth extruding new seafloor, subducting old seafloor.

"I needed a mechanism to power the planetary engine. It could have been that Thetis was just a young world, like Aquaflamme, still churning with the heat of creation. The apparent age of Epsilon Eridani A seemed to argue against that, though.

"I asked Timakata to work out the tidal effects of A.4.3 and A.4.5 on Thetis. He came back with twenty pages of printout. It reduces to a few simple ideas. Both A.4.3 and A.4.5 are trying to lock Thetis in the same sort of gravitational resonance

by which Earth controls the rotation of Venus. They cannot
succeed: A.4's overwhelmingly strong gravitation keeps Thetis
tidally locked with one face constantly regarding A.4. But the
struggle between the opposing tidal forces rubs core against
mantle, mantle against crust; plastic rocks strike across each
other and heat, set up convention currents which over centuries
bring incandescence to the bottom of the seas.

"So we had our answer. All as a result of 'stretch marks.' "

"You would have figured it out eventually," Shoshone said
uncomfortably. "I just made a lucky guess."

"True and true," Benedict agreed. "But your insight provided a shortcut. You should not be embarrassed at having
been correct. Now tell me about A.4."

"It's—it's beautiful," Shoshone said in a small voice. She
cringed, awaiting derisive laughter or a short, razor-sharp re-
mark, dismissive and patronizing at once.

"Speak of its beauty," Benedict said softly.

"It is an arch of color, uniting this world with the heavens,
like an old legend I once read about, a rainbow bridge uniting
the worlds of men to the world of the gods."

"Bifrost," Benedict murmured.

The name sounded familiar. "Or, I was thinking, it looked
like stylized angel wings seen from behind. Only there is a gap
between the wings which makes the angel seem overdeveloped
on its left side. Which I know," she continued quickly, defensively, "is caused by the shadow thrown on the planet by
the rings."

Benedict was silent, as if meditating on what she had said.
Shoshone suddenly wondered if all his sharpness, all his talk of
gestalt perception, might be no more than intentional distraction.

He dominates us so completely, compensates so well for his
blindness, that most of us, most of the time, forget he is crip-
pled, she thought. He does not forget. Could it be that what he
misses most is beauty?

"I am not very good with words," she apologized. "It just
struck me suddenly as one of the most beautiful things I had
ever seen. I wish I could tell you all of it, but instead I can give
only what strains through me."

Later she would remember his answer as the most gracious
thing anyone had ever said to her. "The same may be said of
stained glass."

IX

"IT'S ONLY A COLD," SHOSHONE SAID, SNUFFLING. "JUST give me something—"

"Dr. Spartacus and I will make the diagnoses, thank you," Practitioner Kryuchov said. He pulled the sampler away from her neck, flipped the head around, and sprayed the antiseptic-anesthetic combination on her pinprick wound. The itching vanished in a rush of coldness. Kryuchov slipped the sampler into its holder on the side of his medic's pockomp.

"Your white cell count is absolutely normal," he announced, looking up from the screen, "as are your T cells. Your histamine level, on the other hand, is setting off alarm bells."

Shoshone waited mutely for him to lapse into standard English.

"It means you are having an allergic reaction," Kryuchov explained.

"A what?"

Kryuchov sighed. "You have an allergy. They are not at all uncommon in uncontrolled environments. Dust, dead skin cells, plant matter taken in through the airways—since they are all recognized by your body as foreign, they stimulate its defenses. Thus your congestion, increased mucus flow, and sneezing.

"If we were even attempting to follow proper survey procedure, no human would have been exposed to the biosphere of this world until the forty-day Rhys-Davidson tests proved negative. Even then, only selected individuals would be allowed direct contact; *they* would be tested daily and kept in quarantine for six months."

"I'm sure," Shoshone agreed. "But could you just—"

"But just because engineering has a problem with our power

supply which makes it impossible for us to follow all the rules, people have got it into their heads that they don't have to follow any.'' This was clearly something that had been building in Kryuchov for some time, and he was not about to forgo any part of the full exposition of his grievances. ''The ecological teams which have been examining the weed reefs are the worst. Benedict and your group, insisting on working the flight bay, are hardly better. You know those idiot colleagues of yours were going to pump unfiltered air all through the *Crucible*, all in the name of energy conservation, until Spartacus raised holy hell.''

A pause for breath gave Shoshone her opportunity. ''Is there anything you can give me for the allergy?'' she asked.

''There is, but I won't,'' Kryuchov replied. ''Now, don't make that sort of face. I am doing you a favor. As I just told you, your body is mobilizing its natural defenses against an invader. That is a healthy reaction and one you may have reason to be grateful for soon.''

Shoshone wiped her nose with a tissue. ''Our evolutionary pathways must be way too divergent for the germs of this planet to have any effect on me.''

''God help us when engineers become experts in xenobiology,'' Kryuchov muttered. ''Do the terms 'convergent' or 'parallel evolution' mean anything to you? Has it occurred to you that our experience with alien biospheres is so limited that to trust in divergency for safety is simply whistling in the dark? Or that if evolution is divergent, it will always be less so at the simpler levels, the levels of viruses, or prions?''

Shoshone just stared at him—or she tried to until a sneeze made her grab for another tissue.

Kryuchov regarded her with a mixture of pity and irritation. ''Oh, all right,'' he relented. ''I will give you an antihistamine to help you through the next ten hours. But from now on, when you are in an open shuttle bay or outside the ship, wear this face mask.''

He handed her a square of black cloth with tie strings on all four corners. ''A low-tech solution but one which has worked so far,'' Kryuchov said with ill-concealed pride. ''Notice that the outer surface is both fuzzy and sticky? That is to catch any particles in the air while letting the air itself through.

''Now, drink this and *don't* call me in the morning.''

*   *   *

Her sinuses were already opening by the time she reached the mess hall. Savory smells stimulated her appetite. Yet after she picked up her tray, she found herself hesitating, searching the tables—searching for Stellato, who appeared not to be in the room. Feeling vaguely disappointed, she removed the covers and began picking at her food.

"Hello. Mind if I join you?"

Shoshone looked up. "Of course you may. Do I know you? My name is Shoshone Mantei."

"I don't suppose you do know me yet," the young woman said. She had lightly browned skin and golden hair pulled back from her face. "I'm Sonya Nordstrom. Rich—our first officer would like you to make your report of the day's events to me. He would be sitting here himself, but it would not be to your advantage to be seen with him."

Shoshone wondered why not as Nordstrom continued. "I want you to know that you have all our support. The way you have to endure constant contact with Bestials, put up with obscene comments about pheromones from the likes of Stellato—"

"How do you know about that?" Shoshone asked. "We had just come inside an air lock. I would have sworn nobody was within five hundred meters of us."

"You didn't think we would just abandon you to them, did you?" Nordstrom asked indignantly. "When the *Crucible* was built as a battlestar, a security surveillance system was installed. Every time you are in contact with a Bestial, the system monitors everything."

"Well . . . thanks," Shoshone said, trying to choose her words carefully. "But if this system sees all, why do you need a report from me?"

Nordstrom looked uncomfortable. "The fact of the matter is that with less than a third of the ship's complement out of cold sleep, we don't have enough people for continuous monitoring. Except for the initial check to confirm your loyalties —and your tone of voice as you complained about Stellato's stink settled that for all of us—we have had to rely on the computer program to recognize threat situations from voice tones and body language. Only when it assesses a situation as dangerous does it alert a human. It's the best we can do right now."

"That's fine," Shoshone said sincerely. So she still had

some privacy, after all. But, she wondered, was I really all that sharp with Stellato?

"There is not that much to tell," Shoshone said. "Survey activities seem to be going as well as can be expected, given the resource constraints. There don't seem to be any signs of friction—except with Flight Ops!" Suddenly remembered passion filled her voice. "Which has been needlessly officious and obstructive.

"However," she went on, "there is one thing First Officer Harriman should see." She snapped open a pouch on her belt and extracted the wad within. "This was my acceleration netting. If you look at the side opposite the thermoseal, you will see why I spent such a long time in sick bay."

Nordstrom ran a finger along the severed edge. "Cut," she said. She looked up at Shoshone with sudden surmise. "By a Bestial's claw."

Shoshone shook her head. "If you examine the edge closely, you will see that each strand was melted. Probably by a low-intensity laser like the one in my APT."

Nordstrom nodded. "Makes sense. There's no point in using a method which would immediately be traced to you."

"I don't like the idea of someone trying to kill me," Shoshone said, "but I am almost more bothered by the fact that I can't think of a motive. What makes me important enough to kill?"

"The fact that you are a Norm would be enough for a lot of them," Nordstrom said bitterly. "Also, you are in a very powerful position as Benedict's assistant. The Bestials seem to regard him as a sort of god. They may want one of their own in your position very badly."

Shoshone bit her lip. The combination of bigotry and obtuseness was getting difficult to take. Still, there was no point alienating a powerful faction into whose good graces she had, however unwittingly, fallen.

"I was assigned my position *because* of my injuries," she corrected as gently as she could. "Except for that, I would be at my station as a midgrade engineer."

Nordstrom frowned. "I'll show the netting to the first officer. If we discover any clues, we will let you know. In the meantime, watch yourself. No one else has been actually attacked yet, but tensions have been rising. Captain's Mast has become a daily occurrence—"

"Captain's what?" Shoshone asked.

Nordstrom blinked, momentarily taken aback "I keep forgetting you're not military. Captain's Mast is an informal proceeding the captain can use for minor infractions of discipline. Penalties range from extra duties to fines. On a vessel this size you might expect a Captain's Mast about once a week. Now it has become more or less the beginning of every prime watch."

"Why?"

"All sorts of things have contributed. Minor scuffles, charges of 'insubordination by tone of voice' . . . Only today there was a confrontation over hair clogging a rest room drain." Her voice trailed off uncertainly. Irritation tried unsuccessfully to mask a gnawing unease. "Look, I have to be going now. I just want you to know that we are all behind you. Any time you need help, just call for it."

Alone, Shoshone realized that her food had grown cold. She raised her eyes. All the other diners, Norm and Gen alike, seemed to be studiedly avoiding looking in her direction. With a sigh, she dropped her gaze and forced herself to eat.

X

COLD DUSK LAY BEYOND THE OPEN BAY DOORS. AT THE HO-
rizon, A.4 was a semicircle of darkness outlined by a dull red
glow. All around it, stars pricked a sky of midnight blue.

The weed reef had become a dark mass. Its motion had faded
to a suggestion of moving shadows, a susurration of waving
fronds and branches rubbing slowly against each other. Odd silhouettes, huge and flame-shaped, marched away to the horizon.

Shoshone's jacket kept her upper body warm, but the wind
sliced through her bloused trousers as if they were cheesecloth.
Except for the sticky edge that sealed it to her skin, the face
mask was unnoticeable. From the corner of her eye she could
see that more than half the deck crew wore such masks. No
need to hide her own face in embarrassment. She turned from
the doors. Yet it was only with difficulty that she drew away
from this world's slow-motion embrace with the night.

Benedict was listening to a recorded report from one of
the exploration teams when Shoshone reported for duty. He
pressed the off button.

"Did you notice the sails while you were looking at the
reef?" he asked.

"How—" she began, then bit back the rest of the question.
He would have heard her footsteps approaching from the bay
doors, not from the companionway near the transvator. There
was nothing magical or even terribly intelligent about being
able to identify a given tread and figure out the direction it was
coming from. It would be even less intelligent to gasp over
such a feat, despite the fact that nearly everyone else on board
seemed inclined to react with awe to anything Benedict did.

"Do you mean those tall trees with the flame-shaped silhouettes?" Shoshone asked, taking a guess. She raised her voice

to cut through the low thrumming of a returning Scout. The engines cut off abruptly. Stairs unfolded from the open hatchway. Ueda stepped out, laughing.

"I suppose you might describe them that way," Benedict admitted. "But do not let any of the other specialists hear you. The fact that these biological structures have a series of limbs engaged in photosynthesis, depending from a central trunk, is understood to be merely the sort of detail which always confuses the layman.

"To be fair, they are quite different from anything which evolved on Earth or was genetically modified for Chiron. Their present, informal name derives from their apparent main purpose within the reef system.

"Undoubtedly you have wondered how the reef keeps stationary over the nutrient plumes. After all, you have surface currents driven by more or less constant winds. It should be impossible for any of the weed to stay in place long enough to go through a complete growth cycle."

Actually, no such thought had occurred to Shoshone, though, she realized it obviously should have.

"The reef does move," Ueda said, coming over to them. He unshouldered a dripping sample bag. "Nearly all growth starts on the windward side. As it grows, any given plant moves through the mass of the weed. The *Crucible* is making such a migration itself, moving nearly ten meters a watch because it catches so much of the wind and it isn't moored to anything. Eventually a tree or weed clump emerges on the windward side of the reef and breaks off as a floating island."

"All of which begs the question of why the reef itself does not move with its constituents," Benedict rejoined. "Now, stop trying to confuse my assistant. From the squish of your bag, I would say you had a successful collecting expedition. Did you get the measurements Dr. Shahal asked for?"

"Right here," Ueda said, holding up a data cartridge. Shoshone turned on the deskcomp as Ueda pressed the cartridge into the data slot. A tracery of lines lit up the screen.

"What am I looking at?" Shoshone asked.

"A cross section of reef," Ueda answered, "with emphasis on submarine structure." He tapped three of the keys. A blue line split the image. "As you can see, about three-fourths of the reef is below the waterline."

"You can; I cannot," Benedict said. "Describe."

Shoshone frowned, trying to make sense of the computer-generated abstraction. "As Dr. Ueda notes, approximately three-fourths of the reef appears to be submerged. The underside is uneven: protrusions extend about—" She fumbled with the keyboard. A help window popped down, containing a scale. Deluxe interactive programs like those in the CenCom could have responded to verbal queries. Field programs, Shoshone was rapidly coming to appreciate, begrudged the use of computational power for such frivolous ends. "—twenty meters below the surface." Another menu allowed her to rotate the image. "They seem to be on the order of fifty meters apart, but the spacing is irregular."

"There should be upward projections as well," Benedict said.

"There are."

"Those should be the sails. Now, are the sails directly over the downward projections or off to the side?"

The image responded more smoothly to her fingers now. Her point of view swept over the abstraction of sonar echoes, allowing her to look down *through* the reef.

"Directly over," she reported.

Ueda muttered a curse. "Analogy is powerful," Benedict said reprovingly, "but only as a first-order indicator."

"Of what?" Shoshone asked.

"Of how the reef maintains itself," Benedict said. "The sails are only part of it. In order to hold reasonably steady against a constant wind, a boat needs a keel. Amid calculations of vectors, component forces, and the Bernoulli effect, one of our most respected experts was heard to predict, twelve hours ago, that the reef would have structures analogous to a ship's keel. And not just any sort of centrally located keel; they would have the configuration of bilge keels, angled off to the side of the central mass, like a shark's fins."

Ueda was staring at the deck, biting his lip. Benedict hasn't been picking on me, after all, Shoshone thought, astonished. He's like that with everyone!

"Were resistance to sideways motion the only function of these structures," Benedict went on, "there would indeed be much to recommend the botanical equivalent of bilge keels."

Ueda leaned intently over Shoshone's shoulder. Fingers punched the keyboard quickly as if doing a quick jazz piano riff. The image expanded.

"There are smaller structures extending down at forty-five-degree angles which look very much like bilge keels," Ueda said stubbornly.

Benedict continued as if he had not heard him. "However, there had to be some buoyant support for the sails. Knowing that nature tends to economize effort, it was reasonable to suppose that whatever extended down for buoyancy would be trimmed, so to speak, to function as a keel, as well."

"What are those dots?" Shoshone asked.

"Did you hear what I said?" Ueda demanded.

"Structures like bilge keels," Benedict said mildly. "Well, no reason the reef can't use both configurations. What dots, Shoshone? Describe them."

"Bright points." Feeling malicious, she added, "Looking like stars being born in a nebula."

Benedict considered that. Shoshone could not have described how his expression changed, but she felt an excitement grow within her. She turned back to the deskcomp and called for maximum magnification.

"Whatever they are," she said, "they are less than a meter across. I still can't see any features . . ."

Ueda punched in his own commands. The viewpoint pivoted around a tapering rootlike structure. Long, twisting hairs curved away from the root and did not so much end as lose screen definition. Nearly a dozen of the dots hung in clusters around the root. Halo wisps surrounded several of those lowest on the root.

"Anything giving that bright a sound reflection must be very hard," Benedict said thoughtfully after the data had been described to him. "It would be very interesting to discover what they are."

"I heartily agree," Ueda said.

It took most of the rest of the watch for the diver to ready his attempt. Robot arms were constructed in the machine shop seven decks below and strapped onto a Scout with metal bands. Adequate cross-bracing took several more hours than Ueda had expected, as did adjusting the control system for the servomotors in the arms. The watch was nearly over by the time everything was ready. Nonetheless, Ueda determined to keep working as far into the next watch as might be necessary to make the first dive. Benedict showed no sign of moving, either. Shoshone sighed and decided to extend her own shift—

which would at least save her from having to make conversation with Nordstrom in the mess hall.

It was completely dark by the time the modified Scout Five floated out of the bay, robot arms folded tight against its underside. Ueda was again being piloted by the Gen named Herald, who had volunteered for the mission as soon as he had heard about it. Rebekka Shahal was acting as mission control from her office on the *Crucible*. To Shoshone, after spending eight hours in the flight bay, it seemed overly hot. A disorienting silence took the place of the wind's constant roaring.

She found a chair for Benedict and situated it next to Rebekka. She made room for herself on a credenza behind them by carefully moving to one side a plastic dome of the most elaborate haircare accessories she had ever seen. Her hands came away with a faint but not unpleasant scent. She made a mental note to ask Rebekka about it later.

Rebekka spoke the commands that put her commconsole in connection with the ship's main computers. Two more words, and one of her screens lighted to show a blinking blue dot moving slowly over a pale green grid.

"Ueda could have tried to submerge right outside the *Crucible*," Rebekka said, "but the mat of vegetation is pretty thick around us. It looked a lot simpler to fly out beyond the edge, submerge, and approach our targets from below. The deepest the Scout will go will be one hundred meters."

"You have changed the sonar frequencies?" Benedict questioned. "I am concerned about those tendrils Shoshone described as just fading out. Increased resolution will more than make up for the decrease in range."

Rebekka checked a series of digital readouts. "Yes, we're set on—"

"*Crucible*, this is Scout Five. We are ready to submerge."

"Sounds good, Scout Five," Rebekka responded. "Drop down and commence sonar illumination."

She brushed another series of buttons. A green light on the panel began to flicker. "The *Crucible* is sending out its own sound pulses," she explained to Shoshone. "You can see the responses from the sound cone on the screen. As soon as Ueda turns on his horns, the computer will process both sets of echoes and give us—ah, beautiful!"

It *was* beautiful, Shoshone thought. The image on the main screen, which had shown from the *Crucible*'s pulses only the grosser outlines of the weed mat and the structures, keels or roots or floats, plunging from the mat into the depths, had rippled suddenly into a fineness of detail that so entranced the eye as almost to prevent the mind from inquiring into meaning. The fuzzy mass of the weed became a swirling, tangled hairlike mass. Over the large scale, the observers could see it responding to rising currents that ascended from the burning depths and to the cold currents driving from west to east.

But there were other knots, nexuses, eddies, and cascades that seemed to follow no pattern Shoshone could discern. She described them to Benedict as best she could but with an increasing sense of frustration, a feeling that she was leading him farther and farther astray because she herself could not discern what was important in that fairyland of electronic details.

Scout Five had come beneath its target and was slowly ascending. Above it, like pearls swinging out from a slow-motion carousel, were the brilliant unwinking objects of the hunt.

"I am going for the blip directly above us," Ueda announced. "A few loose tendrils are in the way, but I should be able to push them aside without any difficulty."

Indeed, as Scout Five rose, the tendrils parted around it, shoved aside by a gentle bow wave. The robot arms extended toward the target, the cutting arm above, the scoop arm below. For a few seconds the scissors end of the cutting arm worried at the weed imprisoning the shining dot in silence.

"This stuff is tougher than it looks," Ueda said after a minute. "The claw doesn't seem to be encountering that much resistance, but it isn't severing the root, either. I may have to tug this free."

Shoshone watched, fascinated, as the tendrils that had been pushed aside swept down and around with hypnotic slowness. They were like long fingers closing to caress a precious jewel. Delicately they wrapped themselves around the Scout and lay motionless against its hull.

She leaned toward the microphone. "Scout Five, several tendrils have just coiled themselves around you. Take care not to become entangled."

"Shouldn't be a problem," Rebekka muttered. "That Scout can pull three gees in bursts."

"Our targets appears to be caught in a net of tendrils and seems to be sticking to them in some way," Ueda announced. "I have cut three, but it still is not free."

"The combination of cutting and tugging seems to be working well,'' Rebekka advised. ''My screen shows two more tendrils. If you can cut them—''

Tufts fell ever so slowly from the top of the screen. The whole reef is shedding, Shoshone thought inanely. ''Scout Five, I see whole masses of tendrils descending on you—''

''Got it!'' Ueda exulted. Then: ''Damn!'' For the object of the quest, finally freed, had perversely bobbed upward out of reach. Weed gave counterfeit muscle to the two arms. More and more tendrils uncurled, reaching out to the Scout's hull.

''Mission abort,'' Benedict commanded, interrupting Shoshone's sotto voce description. ''Get out of there, Herald.''

''Roger that.'' A few seconds of silence ended abruptly in an ear-piercing shriek. The image on the screen lost definition and became merely two-dimensional blots of color. There was still enough resolution to see the mass of weed contort and stretch with the strain put on it by the Scout. But it did not break.

''The arms are caught,'' Ueda reported. ''If Herald applies any more thrust, we'll lose them.''

''Better the arms than the Scout,'' Benedict said shortly. ''Apply whatever thrust is necessary.''

''There was also a spray of water from around the hatch at our previous thrust maximum,'' Ueda added, voice crackling slightly as he tried to maintain a steady tone.

''That should not be!'' Rebekka spit the words out as if offended.

Shoshone unclipped her belt communicator. ''Flight Ops, this is Shoshone Mantei. Scout Five appears to be in distress. How quickly can you provide a rescue craft?''

''Mantei, we have been monitoring this channel—'' Flight Ops announced.

''Then why do we have to beg for help?'' Shoshone muttered.

''—and we have two craft within five minutes. I am—''

''No more craft are to be placed in danger.'' It took Shoshone a second to recognize First Officer Harriman's voice. ''Flight Ops, you are forbidden to send any further Scouts under the reef. Scout Five will have to rescue itself.''

''And if it can't, then what?'' Shoshone expostulated. Images of mother and father floated before her eyes in alarm. *Do not needlessly anger those in power. They will not hesitate to punish. Especially if you are right.* But the hot flare of sudden anger drove her on. ''Are we rich enough in resources that we can afford to write off an entire Scout, not to mention its crew?''

There was no immediate response. Rebekka looked over at her and pursed her lips in a soundless whistle. Benedict said nothing. On the screen, it seemed as if an entire section of reef were establishing itself on a lower level. The Scout still returned a brighter reflection than the rest of the weed, but save for that, it was almost indistinguishable from it.

"Scout Five, push all laser switches to the yellow position," Flight Ops commanded. "I am transmitting your arming codes." There followed a staccato chatter of pure tones, peppering the scale with a variety of pitches.

"Pray that that signal gets through," Benedict murmured. "If the tendrils have clogged the sonar receptors . . ."

The image of the Scout convulsed and burst. Bubbles hemorrhaged upward.

"It's exploded!" Rebekka shouted.

Another detonation erupted across the screen. Severed tendrils curled back on themselves and floated to the surface.

"No," Shoshone said slowly. "Those are the lasers. They are cutting their way free."

One never saw a laser beam in space, where energy leapt invisibly from weapon to target. In a Terrestrial atmosphere dust motes scattered enough of the energy of a high-powered laser to make visible a clearly defined beam. But in the waters of the hot plume, turbid with solutes and particulates, power was going to vaporize small but opaque flecks of matter that dumped their heat in the surrounding waters, which flashed into steam.

Water boiled all around the Scout. Some of the laser's energy was probably being reflected back onto the hull. Shoshone uneasily wondered how much.

"They're free," Rebekka said, sighing with relief. Scout Five sank away from the reef, moving to the side of the screen, trailing tendrils like a wounded Medusa.

"We need to be in the docking bay when it arrives," Benedict said.

Awkward with haste, Shoshone guided him out of Rebekka's cramped quarters and down the corridor to the nearest transvator portal. The door opened to Benedict's priority. Shoshone braced herself on the handrails against alternating surges of vertical and horizontal acceleration. Behind her, Benedict spoke tersely into his communicator.

The transvator stopped abruptly. The doors slid aside, letting in the sound of a pulsating Klaxon.

"—ear the landing area. Clear the landing area. All except emergency personnel must stay behind the red line."

Red flashed along three sides of the deck like the pulsing of a gigantic artery. Shoshone led Benedict carefully along its edge, near the racks of piping that had been erected to wash down the Scouts as part of a crude decontamination procedure.

She heard Scout Five before her eyes could make it out. There was the drone of a repulsor field, but with an irregular, rasping undertone. Then she saw it, a clump of reef drifting unsteadily through the air, severed tendrils blowing out raggedly behind it.

It bobbed up and down outside the bay doors as if trying to decide whether to come in. Then, with a sudden motion, it lurched forward and dropped to the deck. There was a crackling sound. Frayed tendril ends swept into puddles left by the washers. The puddles hissed and spit, spraying droplets. A few fell on Shoshone's left hand, making it itch. She rubbed it absently. Her eyes widened as blood oozed to the surface.

Five bay crew, wearing bulky protective garb, moved quickly over the flashing red line. Lasers flashed briefly in deft surgical strokes. Large patches of weed fell to the deck. For an instant Shoshone thought the lasers had been set too high. Then she saw that the searing was too regular and extensive to have been caused by those quick bursts. Even the unseared area had lost its mirror brightness and gone strangely milky. Flakes blew off newly formed pits, diamond-dusting the air.

The outer hatch screeched halfway open and jammed. Water poured from its lower edge. Shoshone bit her lip, wanting to rush over to help but unable to abandon Benedict.

Bay crew wedged two jacks in the hatchway and activated them. As they extended themselves, there was a screeching followed by two loud snaps. More water streamed from the hatchway, splashing on the deck below.

There was movement in the dark opening. Ueda's face seemed to hover in the dimness, eyes wide and astonished. He turned back and reappeared, half carrying a sodden Herald. At the lip of the outer hatch he stumbled and was caught by one of the bay crew. Carefully, they were lowered to the deck and over to powerchairs provided by an anxious Kryuchov. After a quick examination he activated the chairs, guiding them with a hand controller in the direction of sick bay.

XI

"THANK GOD, THEY'RE ALIVE," SHOSHONE SAID. SHE WAS leading Benedict back to his quarters. They could have taken the transvator, but Benedict had wanted exercise.

"I mean, they could have drowned in there," she continued, a little annoyed at Benedict's lack of reaction. "Who would have dreamed the reef would have such formidable defenses? And what sort of creatures must be swimming in the ocean to warrant such defenses?" Shoshone's imagination gave her involuntary shivers.

"No creatures," Benedict muttered distractedly. "I've had sonar scanning the area constantly ever since we wedged into the reef. The largest submarine animal is a snakelike creature approximately ten meters long. It browses quite contentedly on the underside of the reef, provoking no discernible reaction whatsoever. No, that whole reaction was of only secondary importance. The important thing was what happened to the dot they were hunting. Did you see? It *floated*."

"Yes. Well." In the excitement of rescuing Ueda and Herald, Shoshone had momentarily forgotten the purpose of their quest. "But I can't see that that proves anything except that whatever those things are, they cannot be of much interest to us. I mean, I thought the interest in those clear, sharp echoes was that we might have found a source for the elements that we need for our repairs. If there were any appreciable concentration of them, they would sink."

"But that, you see, is why the halos are so important," Benedict said, his voice becoming animated. "Their presence means—"

Several things happened at once. They had stepped through

an interior lock into one of the main horizontal corridors. Shoshone saw Stellato coming toward them. His eyes widened.

"Shoshone!" he called.

She blinked, then found herself wondering how she had fallen so that her face was pressed hard against the plastic intersection of wall and deck. Her nose was pressed uncomfortably to one side. Teeth ground into her upper lip.

Nice spastic move, she thought, feeling slightly lightheaded. Now I'll have to endure comments from Stellato about falling head over heels . . .

A hand grasped her collar, jerked her to her feet, and held her against the wall.

"Are you okay?" Although obviously shouting, Stellato sounded somehow distant.

"Juth clumthy. Nothing theriouth." Tongue and lips had swollen, making clear speech difficult. "Why—" Then she looked over his shoulder.

Nightmare crouched in the middle of the corridor. Video propagandists had tried to create such a horror during the war, but their best and most bigoted efforts paled to daydreams compared to this monster.

The Bestial's coat puffed out, making it seem half again as large as it actually was. Froth matted the fur around its mouth. Its fists opened and closed convulsively. The claws extended so far from the fingertips that to Shoshone it seemed they were being extracted with invisible pliers.

"*Genocide!*" The voice hit her like a blow. Inhuman anger roared itself out in basso thunder. More frightening to Shoshone than the anger was the underlying pain. Even when her acceleration netting had ripped and she had nearly died, she had never experienced anything like the agony she heard in that voice.

"*Traitor. Murderer of children!*" The Bestial howled its wrath, lurching from side to side, claws snapping out in lightning feints so swift that Shoshone saw them only in afterimage.

Beyond it, Benedict stood with head bent, as if in meditation. Four red furrows scored his cheek. Pulsing redness made a sheen along the bottom half of his face.

The Bestial launched itself. At the last possible moment Benedict pivoted. It hit his outstretched leg and toppled as Benedict brought his folded-together hands down hard on the base of its skull. The head slammed hard into the wall and bounced.

Shoshone winced and waited for the Bestial to slump to the deck. Instead, after the length of time it took for a full breath, the Bestial shook its head and whirled on Benedict, claws extended.

"You have to stop it," Shoshone said to Stellato. "Benedict will be killed."

A Klaxon was blaring loudly just behind her. Running footsteps echoed down the side corridors, but help would arrive too late unless something was done immediately.

"Right," Stellato muttered. He moved forward cautiously, flexing his own claws out of his fingertips.

Benedict's head moved just perceptibly in their direction. "Stay *back*!" Command voice was a whip crack. Shoshone felt herself frozen to the deck.

Again the Bestial charged. Again Benedict turned, arms upraised, his robes billowing like the cape of a grotesque matador.

How did he do that? Shoshone wondered. He must *hear* where the Bestial is. Indeed, even from her vantage, Shoshone could hear the hoarse rasping of the Bestial's breath. But how does he know when to move? By a quickening of breath? By the breeze pushed out in front of the Bestial's hurtling body? Could he sense the body heat of an outstretched hand?

However Benedict was doing it, it was an inadequate substitute for sight. Claws had landed on the last pass. Strips of material hung loose from his robes. Tufts fell to the deck.

"Stand aside, sir." Noncoms had come simultaneously up both sides of the corridor. Those on Shoshone's side held laser pistols, wire stocks pressed against their shoulders for stability.

Harriman was on the far side. "Fall back and give us a clear shot," he ordered.

"Hold your fire," Benedict gasped. "There is no need to harm anyone. I can subdue this man."

"I have a shot, sir," the noncom nearest to Shoshone called out. Harriman opened his mouth to give the command.

Benedict leapt forward and grappled with the Bestial. Its arms closed in an iron embrace, claws shredding the back of Benedict's robes. Benedict's hands snapped out like pistons, the heels of the palms thudding hard into the Bestial's side.

Ribs shattered with a sound like exploding firecrackers. The Bestial did not seem to notice and pulled Benedict closer.

The lasers wavered. The automatic target finders, considering Benedict and the Bestial one object, emitted a steady tone.

The Bestial's mouth yawned open, small, sharp teeth lowering to Benedict's neck.

Stellato took three quick strides and jumped. His legs wrapped around the Bestial's hips. He wedged his forearm between its chin and chest, levering the sharp edge of the radius against its throat.

The Bestial gave a hoarse growl of rage and released Benedict. It reached back, trying to rip Stellato off. Staggering sideways, it found a wall and threw itself back against it. Stellato hung on and pushed off, sending both of them to the deck. The bodies writhed together, claws grasping for grips.

Suddenly, most motion ceased. The combined mass lurched uneasily for balance points. Stellato was still on the Bestial's back, both hands clasped together behind its neck. Biceps and triceps bulged as, ever so slowly, he forced the Bestial's head down to its chest. It bellowed its frustration. The roar became continuous, ascended the scale to an ever more agonizing pitch, until—

It stopped, punctuated by the crack of neck vertebrae. The Bestial seemed to collapse in upon itself. Stellato released his grip and rolled away.

"You killed him," Benedict said in dull reproach.

Stellato looked up from his hands and knees. "I saved your life," he said. "A simple thank you will suffice."

A noncom extended a steadying hand. Benedict shook it off savagely.

"Shoshone."

"Sir." She was at his side.

"Guide me to the body."

She took a hand and led him across three meters of deck. The band around his head had been torn off, exposing the two small regenepaks that hid his eyes.

His boot brushed an outstretched arm. He crouched, hands patting the air until they found the Gen's chest. Fingers wandered through the torn tunic up to the collarbone and throat, where the fur was matted and shiny, testimony to Stellato's claws. Bracing himself with his left hand, he rubbed first the palm and then the back of his right hand in the Bestial's blood.

"Stellato!" He held the hand up. "Smell."

Wonderingly, Stellato raised the hand to his face in a macabre parody of courtliness. His nostrils flared. Pupils constricted. For an instant Shoshone saw the shadow of madness pass across his face.

"Testrarch." Stellato choked out the word. "But he was too old. Unless . . . a relapse?"

"There was no relapse," Benedict said wearily. "He was poisoned and set on me. Both of us were supposed to die. You did part of their work for them by killing one of your own people. Someone is laughing very smugly right now."

Stellato fell back, stricken.

"What was his name?" Benedict asked Shoshone.

She knelt and unclipped the dead man's badge. "Konstantin Alexandrov. Clan Tsiolkovskiy."

"I did not know him," Benedict said softly. He lifted his head. "Listen to me!" he demanded. Looking up, Shoshone saw that not all lasers had been lowered. A few were pointing at Stellato, their holders having seen the same expression that had alarmed Shoshone. But others pointed at various other Gens.

"This young man was not to blame for this carnage," Benedict said, turning as he spoke to address them all. "He was poisoned with a hormone complex that induced insane rage. Given a PCP dosage, any of you—*any of you*—would have behaved in the same way.

"I hoped to be able to restrain Konstantin until the hormone complex was fully metabolized. I failed. I—"

Benedict's voice faltered. His eyes rolled up. As he fell, Shoshone was barely able to catch him and lay him gently on the deck.

XII

"HE WILL BE OKAY. I THINK," SPARTACUS SAID. SHE WAS applying spray and gauze to Shoshone's acid burns. Shoshone had forgotten about them until she had accompanied Benedict in the reclined powerchair to sick bay.

"There was blood loss, of course. I have an IV in replacing fluid volume. And substantial bruising. By a miracle nothing was broken. If MNC biochemistry is no more different than I have so far experienced—and that *is* a good question to which I have no definitive answer—then all he needs is sufficient rest to recover. I'll keep him here overnight. He should be able to get around tomorrow, though it will hurt." She finished wrapping regenerative gauze around Shoshone's hand. The furred fingers inside the translucent stretch gloves were remarkably deft. "There. Keep it on tonight. You can wash it off tomorrow."

Stellato came into the waiting room area, escorted by Kryuchov.

"An exciting watch," Kryuchov said to Spartacus. "Accident victims, fights, attempted homicide: just like an intern experience in Goddardton."

"It is not the sort of practice we need," Spartacus said.

"Nonsense," Kryuchov rejoined. "This is the reason we all went into medicine."

Stellato was a patchwork of minor bandages. He moved to walk past Shoshone.

"I want to talk to you," she said stopping him. "You owe me an explanation."

He looked down at her, his stare opaque.

"You and Benedict were both nearly killed," Shoshone insisted. "One of our crew members is dead—"

"Our?' Stellato asked bitterly.

"—and I don't have the slightest idea why. Benedict knows, but he's unconscious. That leaves you."

Stellato was still for a moment longer. "All right," he said finally. "But we'll talk in the mess hall. It was a long watch even before I ran into you."

They both attracted stares as they entered the mess hall. Stellato seemed not to notice. At the ordering stand he called up a menu unfamiliar to Shoshone.

"What is the drink?" she asked.

Stellato grunted. "It has many names among the Clans. We call it Lefeu. It is not very different from what you would call vodka. It is easy to ferment with the wastes from the hydroponic vats."

"Give me the same. And whatever you are having to eat."

Stellato pressed a 2. Covered bowls and cups slid from the appropriate slots, and he and Shoshone carried them to a vacant table. The bowl was filled with barley and vegetables suspended in a meat broth. Even a tiny sip of the drink burned its way down her throat and forced tears out of Shoshone's eyes.

Stellato watched her closely. "The justification for its production is usually medicinal," he said with grim humor.

"Tell me about *testrarch*," Shoshone said, blinking away the tears. "What does that have to do with the attack on Benedict?"

Stellato was silent for so long that Shoshone almost decided he was not going to answer. "*Testrarch* is something every male of the Clans goes through at puberty. It is a farewell gift from our creator, the late Dr. Snowden. While enhancing our metabolic structure to be more efficient in processing foodstuffs, bearing extremes of temperature, functioning in concentrations of carbon dioxide which would kill unenhanced human beings, he found it necessary to tinker with our hormonal balances in ways which had unforeseen consequences. One of those is a period of extreme emotional instability. When he became aware of it, Snowden used it as a means of culling strains he considered less fit to reproduce.

"I went through *testrarch* when I was eleven years old. My mother had had a daughter six months before. It was a time of great joy, not just for our family but for our whole Clan. By another of those trade-offs in genetic engineering, our women find it more difficult to conceive children and more dangerous to bring them to term.

"I was delighted by Dolci, my baby sister. I learned how to change her, to feed her, to keep her clean. It got to the point where my parents complained that I was spoiling her by holding her all the time. But they were both so busy maintaining the atmospheric system for our asteroid colony that they needed all the help they could get. Maybe that is why they didn't notice the changes in my voice and bearing, a growing abruptness in my manner, or any of the dozens of warning signs that should have alerted them that my time of testing had come.

"I didn't notice anything myself. I had heard about *testrarch*, that it was the dangerous—and, therefore, to my mind, exciting—entry to manhood. I probably would not undergo it for another year, which is forever at that age, so I spent no time thinking about it.

"Only . . . there were headaches, more or less continuous, which spread from the base of my skull, down my neck, and into my shoulders. Most of the time they hovered just at the threshold of awareness. More and more often, though, flashes of pain would erupt inside my skull. When I came to myself again, I would find that my teeth were clamping my lips shut to keep me from screaming."

"Couldn't your parents do anything?" Shoshone asked.

"They did not know. They were working two shifts at the time. Most of the time they were away or asleep. And most of the time the simple remedies in our medicine cabinet seemed sufficient.

"There was something else as well, a feeling that is hard to explain. I thought people were watching me, looking for weaknesses. I did not want to admit, even to myself, that I might need help.

"Then, one day while I was doing my lessons on my terminal, Dolci began to cry. I ignored it as long as I could, then logged off. I changed her and tried to feed her, but she wasn't interested. She only cried louder. I started rocking her in my arms because she always liked that. Not this time.

"My father came out of the sleeping room, awakened by the crying. He yelled at me, said that I was hurting Dolci."

Stellato paused. Shoshone saw him tightening rein on himself, bringing his breathing under strict control, leaching his voice of all expression.

"I don't remember what happened then. I just remember Dolci's screaming. She was lying on the opposite side of the room. My father was on the floor between us. The back of his head was bloody.

"We were able to reconstruct things later. There had been a short argument. I ended it without warning by hurling Dolci at my father. The impact snapped his head back against the corner of the overhead cabinet.

"That is how I learned about *testrarch*. By nearly killing my father and baby sister."

"What did happen after that?" Shoshone asked after a pause.

"Neither of them was seriously hurt. Dolci's screams had brought me to myself. I was belatedly told the facts of life and subjected to the confinements and diets appropriate to my condition.

"There are stories of Clans where *testrarch* is a rite of passage to be mastered, where those who can control themselves are considered fully adult, while those who succumb to the rages are thrown into the reprocessing tanks. There is no truth to any of them. Every young man, without exception, is mastered by the rages. All that can be done is to alternate confinement with self-discipline sessions. Eventually the hormonal imbalances subside, and discipline prevails.

"You can ask members of any Clan to name their greatest fears. Some will say that they fear that the megacorporations will reduce them to bondage again. Jean D'Argent will tell you that fanatics like the Defenders of Humanity will be satisfied with nothing less than our total extermination, so we should fear them most of all.

"The real fear, though, the one they won't admit, is the one they see in the mirror. The fear that the Defenders of Humanity are right, after all. That our devotion to obedience and discipline, our elaborate hierarchies and courtesies, are nothing but bright and brittle veneer. That we really are bestial, and since the beast cannot be tamed, it must be killed."

"You know that is not true," Shoshone said with more firmness than she felt. "As you said, neither your father nor Dolci was seriously injured."

"She grew into a fine young woman," Stellato said thoughtfully. "During the war she was evacuated to a colony far from the Periphery. For three years all we got were occasional messages. She did well, was selected to be a monitor to help with the younger children. But her notes always had at least a touch of homesickness to them. That is why we were so overjoyed when the treaty was signed and we got word she was coming home.

"She was killed in the same privateer's raid that killed D'Argent's children. Now, if you don't mind, it has been a very long watch for me, and I need rest."

He stood abruptly and strode away. Her mouth tried to close on words that might give comfort. She found only emptiness.

XIII

A MESSAGE ON SHOSHONE'S SCREEN THE NEXT MORNING TOLD her to report to the meeting room adjoining Benedict's office. It was not surprising that he would not be in the flight bay, which in the course of Thetis's long night had become too cold to be used as an operations center. What was astonishing to her was that he should be out of the sick bay at all.

Nonetheless, except for moving with a deliberate stiffness, he showed few effects of the battle he had engaged in scarcely twelve hours before. The rents across his cheek pulsed in puffy red lines. He was dressed in a new set of gray Steward's robes, those loose, incredibly sturdy all-weather garments that closed tightly about wrists and ankles and had an extremely practical hood that could be pulled loosely over the head for shade or tightly around it for warmth.

Several rows of folding chairs faced a long table in the front of the room. Near the corridor door, on a smaller table, was a silver dish of what looked like crackers. It was evident to Shoshone that Benedict was going to be hosting a meeting of the planetological contingent, probably a strategy session to assess their next move.

Through a second doorway Shoshone saw Benedict moving around in his office. A bottle of wine held in his hand suggested that the meeting would be at least as much a social gathering as business. Good, Shoshone thought. Everyone had been getting overly tense during the last few watches. Maybe if they could all loosen up a bit, they would be able to make some progress.

He must have recognized her tread. "You should be able to find my pockomp," Benedict said. It was in fact in plain view.

"Please call up the READINGS file and enter today's date. Tell me what it says."

Shoshone entered the appropriate data. A short but incomprehensible group of letters and numbers appeared.

"Ess, aye, arr, two, seven, colon, two, two, dash, two, eight, colon, one, one. Next: em, tee, one, eight, colon, two, one, dash, three, five."

She studied the legend along the top of the screen. "I can call these up if you like."

"Thank you, no. I have them memorized. However, I may need your help with moving things about and some pouring."

Kryuchov entered from the corridor. "I did not know you made house calls," Shoshone said brightly. "Your patient is in his office, looking remarkably well, considering. I don't think you can see him just now, though. He is preparing for a meeting in a few minutes."

"He discharged himself against Dr. Spartacus's advice just two hours ago," Kryuchov said. "That is not why I am here. I came for the meeting you mentioned." He gave Shoshone an odd look and took a seat against the wall.

Three Gens came in next. Two were members of the astronomy team, assistants to Dr. Timakata; the third was Stellato. His eyes widened when he saw Shoshone, but instead of saying anything to her, he sat with his companions on the opposite side of the room from Kryuchov.

A continuous stream of crew members entered, filling the seats back to front. Following the already established pattern, Gens and Norms kept to their own sides. Soon only standing room remained. Only a fifth of those present had anything to do with the planetological survey team.

A horrid suspicion formed in Shoshone's mind and blossomed into certainty when she saw the formal robes Benedict had just put on.

"I'll give you the cues for when to pour the water, and so forth," he told her. "Now, just precede me through the door."

Gens and Norms rose as one. Benedict stopped behind the center of the table and turned to face them, extending an upraised right hand.

"Greetings, in the name of the Father, and the Son, and the Holy Spirit."

For the first few minutes of the service anger at being tricked into serving as an acolyte kept her from paying much attention to what was being said. More than once she decided simply to stalk out of the room. What held her back each time, she could not say.

The congregation sat for a series of readings that Benedict had memorized. Someone named Sirach tiresomely predicted bad ends for the proud and wrathful, contrasting that with some idealized paragon of merciful forgiveness. Sirach, in fact, sounded very much like Shoshone's grandfather in one of his more querulous moods.

The second reading dealt with a master handling the debt owed him by a servant, at first forgiving the debt when the servant could not pay but then throwing him in jail when the servant dealt harshly with the debt of a fellow servant. But that's stupid, Shoshone thought. However will he get the money to pay the master if he's in jail?

With the conclusion of the reading, Benedict was silent, waiting for the room to become still, becoming so completely still himself that Shoshone had a momentary fantasy that he would disappear if she blinked.

" 'How many times must I forgive my brother?' Peter asks. He suggests seven times. It's a 'magic' number, after all, right out of Genesis, and is large enough to suggest forbearance, not to say moral superiority. But most importantly, it is *definite*; it sets a bottom line. Like any lawyer, any bureaucrat, any practical human being, what he wants to know about his brother is *When can I cut him off?* Christ's answer, seventy times seven, is worse than the ratio of 7 to 490. By trumping one magic number with a higher one, he has effectively said that there is no bottom line.

"This is the first of three stories in Matthew which I call the Bad News of the Gospel. He follows this with a prohibition against divorce, prompting his disciples to grumble that under these conditions it would be better never to marry at all, and caps it all with the statement that it is easier for a camel to pass through the needle's eye than for a rich man to enter heaven. At this the disciples throw up their hands in utter exasperation, asking if anyone can be saved under this standard.

"I never got that far. For me, the admonition I just read you was the worst of all. It was not merely hard; it was insanely ludicrous. When Juliet, my mistress, was murdered before my eyes in the Olympus Mons spaceport by a Defenders of Humanity fanatic, forgiveness was the emotion furthest from my mind.''

Mistress? Shoshone thought in surprise. Yet suddenly the thought of this aging cleric having a mistress seemed not at all absurd.

"In my first profession forgiveness was weakness, always dangerous, often fatal. Even after I joined the Stewards, I sympathized most with those early Church Fathers who considered that a truly satisfying heaven must contain a box seat over hell from which one could watch in detail the sufferings of one's enemies in life and, if necessary, adjust the gas jets to raise the screams to the proper pitch.''

The words, so gently spoken, sent a shiver down Shoshone's spine. Irrationally, she found herself believing what Stellato had told her about how dangerous this man had been.

And might still be.

"What, then, can I preach to you about a text so uncongenial to my own temperament? Only that it is crucial to all of us and must be understood and followed even as we must understand and obey the laws of motion to get about in free-fall, or the rules of nutrition in order to keep from starving.

"Set up a computer program if you want proof. Simulate several groups of several members each. Allow each member the freedom to destroy any member of any other group but make a rule that any such action must trigger retaliation in kind. You can call the rule honor or deterrence, justice or vengeance; it does not matter because the cycle of revenge set in motion can end only in genocide or mutual annihilation.''

Benedict turned his head slowly. Despite the patches held on his eyes by the knotted black cloth, he gave the impression of studying each person in the room in turn. Clever effect, Shoshone thought, angry with herself for being impressed.

"Everyone in this room has just cause to be angry, to cry out to heaven for vengeance. Every one of us has suffered the loss of those we loved, has seen our friends maimed, has lost home and possessions to the ravages of war or the simple vagaries of fate. And everyone can claim a right to have the score evened.

"Only, if we take that right, there will be no end to the cycle. Peter wanted a bottom line on forgiveness. Christ gave him something more important instead. He gave him a bottom line on vengeance. He showed how the endless cycle of horror and retribution could be broken.

"We are here on a new world, a world which has never known sin, if only because we are its first sentients. We are granted a chance to start over. Release your wounds, release your hates, that you may be able to grasp this chance firmly."

How anticlimactic, Shoshone thought, still seething. Because his heart really isn't in these warmed-over platitudes or because he really is not that good a speaker?

The rest of the service went quickly, though it seemed forever to her. Following Benedict's cues, she was able to provide him wine and wafers for the consecration. To her intense relief, communion servers came from the congregation.

Then it was over. A few Gens and Norms chatted briefly with Benedict. Stellato gave Shoshone a mysterious and infuriating smile but darted out the door before she could say anything.

Only when she and Benedict were alone did she trust herself to speak. "Is that quite all?"

"You are angry with me?" Benedict asked, wonder in his voice.

"My parents were Rational Ethicists," Shoshone said evenly. "Therefore, my view of Dark Ages superstitions should hardly need expounding."

"Your parents *were* Rational Ethicists," Benedict agreed. "But I was under the impression that you had rebelled against your parents. Was it only a partial rebellion?"

Shoshone suddenly found herself thinking of Sarah. Sarah's beliefs might have seemed incomprehensible, but they had been anything but silly. A second wave of anger swept through her. Shoshone shook, frightened because she was suddenly unsure of the object of her anger.

"Or perhaps your records are misleading in this respect," Benedict continued meditatively. "For example, all of the reports state that Sirian colonists were particularly fervid in their support of the war. After all, they were on the front lines, suffered the greatest number of raids, and would suffer the most economically if Bestials were suddenly granted human status and freedom. Was that really the case? I wonder."

"Among the elite it may have been," Shoshone said. Why is he trying to distract me this way? she wondered. Does he really think he can make me forget why I'm angry with him? "The people I knew were those who were likely to lose their jobs to—to Gens slaves, so their independence might have worked in our favor.

"The real bitterness was directed against the Terrestrial and Centauran high commands for not providing adequate forces to protect us. It was funny in a way. Few of us were directly hurt by the raids, which were always against military targets. And since there was a war on, after all, we didn't resent the raids. On the other hand, everyone felt the pinch of short supplies and blamed our so-called allies for being more eager to avoid combat losses than to support their own friends."

"Fascinating," Benedict murmured. "Now, that is precisely the sort of detail that tends to get lost. Anyone looking at your official file would think that you had grown up in a hotbed of anti-Bestial sentiment. He might even use the names your parents gave you and your sister Sapi to support that conclusion. How easily he might overlook the disdain in which Rational Ethicists have always held the Defenders of Humanity . . ."

Shoshone heard no more. She turned at the sound of approaching footsteps and found herself looking down the barrel of a laser, close enough to see the unwavering red dot of the arming light. There were two others to either side of it.

None of them were pointed at her. "Paul Niccolo Rénard," Harriman said, stepping forward, "alias Father Benedict. You are under arrest. Follow me."

Benedict did not move. "May I ask the charge?" he asked mildly.

"Sabotage of the *Crucible*," Harriman answered, "and the attempted murder of everyone on board."

XIV

THEY MARCHED BENEDICT TO HIS MAKESHIFT CELL ALONG THE
main axis corridor. Things were moving far too quickly for
Shoshone, but still she had time to wonder why Harriman was
parading Benedict through the main part of the ship rather than
simply bundling him into the nearest transvator.

For the present course was clearly dangerous. Crewmen were
gathering in knots as they spotted the curious procession and
realized its purpose. A disproportionate number of them
seemed to be Gens. A murmuring steadily increased. Beneath
it Shoshone could hear the sound of running footsteps.

Abruptly, there was a traffic jam of bodies and equipment—
a dolly containing huge spools of infrared optical cable had
become diagonally wedged against a cart carrying rice and
vatmeat from the reprocessing tanks to the galley. Both vehicles were primarily designed for zero-gee use; the rollers were
little more than an afterthought. They seemed to have been
frozen with the impact.

Crew members rushed past Shoshone to get at the vehicles.
She was pressed against the wall, unable to move forward.
Harriman was likewise immobilized. He looked around in ir-
ritation and opened his mouth to demand that a way be cleared.

"Good morning, First Officer," Stellato said courteously,
forestalling him. "Where are you taking Father Benedict?"

The air was heavy with the smell of the massed Gens. Harriman's escort, all of whom were Norms, suddenly realized
that they were pressed too closely together to make effective
use of their firepower. From the corner of her eye Shoshone
caught glimpses of portable hydraulic jacks and welding lasers.
They would be nasty weapons in close.

"Father Benedict is being confined until he can be tried for sabotage," Harriman replied, sounding not at all disconcerted. "We have evidence that he caused the explosion of fusor number two, which nearly killed all of us."

"What evidence?" Jean D'Argent asked harshly.

Shoshone waited for Harriman to explode and order D'Argent out of his way. Instead, he answered as calmly as if he were reciting one of the responsorial prayers in the mass just ended.

"While in quantum space, the autolog maintains a record of the movements of all crew members not in cold sleep. Until a few hours ago we thought that part of the computer memory was wiped out by power surges when the fusor blew. We have just been able to construct enough of that memory to show that Father Benedict had just positioned himself next to the fusor when it exploded. It is a simple inference that he had planted an explosive device on the side of the fusor which detonated prematurely."

"Simple but weak," Stellato said reprovingly.

"There is also the matter of the other individuals who were conscious during that period. What my technicians have been able to piece together proves that at least six individuals were conscious and in the drive room at the time. They are now in cold sleep with records indicating that they have never been awakened since the last jump and that their cold-sleep cubicles were damaged during the power surge.

"There has obviously been tampering with the data base. I hope it is not too much to suggest that the person with the greatest motive for such tampering would be the person who sabotaged the fusor."

"But it makes no sense to suppose that anyone sabotaged the fusor," Shoshone objected. "If it would kill or maroon us, it would do the same to him!"

To her surprise, Harriman gave her a small nod of approval. "I agree. It would not be the act of a rational human being. But there is reason to believe that we are dealing with one who is irrational. Although it is not well known, it is a fact that Multi-Neural Capacitants are extremely sensitive to the stresses of quantum space. My informants tell me that repeated jumps during the Battle of Chiron reduced Benedict for several hours to a state of complete idiocy. It appears that there were longer-lasting effects, as well. Or if he was not insane before this expedition, he went over the edge when he revived during our last jump through Space$_4$."

"What say you, Fox?" D'Argent demanded. "Can you explain your presence by the fusor?"

"I can," Benedict said, cocking his head to one side. "But I choose not to at this time."

Stellato shot him a look of astonished exasperation, then faced Harriman. "Your case is so circumstantial that it hardly warrants refutation. There has never been any secret about Father Benedict's proximity to the fusor when it blew. That is why he is blind, after all. You're taking evidence of victimization, turning it on its head, and turning it into evidence of guilt."

"A ship corridor is hardly the place to present an entire case," Harriman said. "There will be time for that at the trial, as well as for any defense Father Benedict may wish to make.

"This is not a move against Gens generally. This man is not necessarily your friend."

"Pardon me if I remain skeptical," D'Argent rumbled.

Harriman raised his voice. "Communications. Tape R-N2."

A voice came over the loudspeakers, clear and, to Shoshone at least, unmistakable. ". . . but some are still very worried," Nordstrom was saying. "Those same qualities you just mentioned make them appear dangerous to a great many people. And the fact that they control the Periphery is a long-term worry. If they keep expanding outward, won't the rest of us be denied the stars forever?"

"Any such long-term fear is baseless." Benedict's tone was light, ironic, self-assured. "Earth has sent an expedition to Betelgeuse which will puncture the Periphery if successful. In any event, the final solution of what you would call the Bestial problem is even now being executed. In the long term there will be no problem because there will be no Bestials."

A roar broke loose from the Gens. Harriman suppressed almost all traces of a smile.

"Sound tapes can be altered," Stellato said, sounding desperate. "Words taken out of context—"

"Or created out of whole cloth on computer," Harriman agreed. "But that was not done here. Ask Benedict himself."

There was a moment of suspended silence as all eyes turned on the figure in the Steward's robes. After a few seconds

Benedict seemed to realize that they were waiting for him to speak.

"The tape is accurate," he said in a low voice.

"And do you *choose* to explain that accurate tape?" D'Argent rasped.

"Could any explanation make any difference, do you think?"

D'Argent shook his head violently. "No!"

"Then there is no need to waste everybody's time with an attempt," Benedict said gently.

The crowd melted away as dolly and cart were unjammed and moved aside. Harriman marched his prisoner down the corridor in restrained triumph.

XV

"WELCOME BACK, MANTEI," LUMBONGO SAID. HE LOOKED her over with that air of critical irritation that Shoshone had come to recognize as being a permanent part of his temperament. "I have you back full time now?"

"Yes, sir."

"Too bad. No, I don't mean that the way it sounds. I had been hoping that Benedict could run a series of materials trade-offs for me. Doesn't look like he'll be doing us any good for a while now."

Lumbongo wanted the computation because, according to the ship's data base, the *Crucible* contained sufficient quantities of all elements necessary to repair the fusors. That suggested that with a bit of intelligent cannibalism, they should be able to make the ship operational.

The catch was that so far every plan anyone had been able to come up with had the result of disabling the ship in some other way. For example, they could cannibalize part of the quantum drive system itself if they did not mind never being able to leave the Eta Cassiopeiae system. Or they might recover elements from all the ship's electrical cable. In that case, the *Crucible* might survive the return trip through quantum space, but without constantly monitored cold-sleep cubicles and suppressor fields, the crew would not.

So far, none of the various mathematical approaches had demonstrated that there was *not* a solution, so the attempts continued.

Most tasks already had their own assigned teams, so Shoshone was used as "utility personnel." That was Lumbongo's term. Her own was "gofer." Despite which it was good to be back doing what she had been trained to do. The team she was

99

assigned to was laying a primitive ceramic semiconductor from each of the Scout berths to the main engine room. When completed, it would carry power from each of the Scouts to the impeller converters, giving the *Crucible* the ability to range at least through the A.4 satellite system.

The work was heartbreakingly slow. Holes had to be cut through bulkheads in the most direct routes possible without severing the ship's plumbing or electrical systems. Then a substrate was laid along the decks and walls to serve as both anchoring and insulation. Only then could the moving kiln Lumbongo had jury-rigged move along the substrate, laying superconductor. That was the most crucial, and the most frustrating, part of the entire operation. Cracks spiderwebbed the ceramic as it extruded onto the insulation and cooled. Three times while Shoshone was stationed there a jar in the movement of the machine caused a crack to run all the way through the ceramic. Then the kiln had to move back, carefully rebaking the cracked portion into wholeness. The third time that happened, the operator's face worked as if fighting back tears.

It was only between assignments or when grabbing a quick bite to eat that Shoshone had time to gnaw on the problem of Benedict. Nothing about his arrest made sense. Harriman had squelched Stellato by making a plausible case that Benedict was insane. It was a necessary case, Shoshone realized, because the more she thought about it, the more cogent seemed Stellato's objection that Benedict would *have* to have been insane to have damaged the fusors. Among the engineering crew, Benedict had both puzzled supporters and vindicated detractors, but no one from either side thought him crazy, unless it was "crazy like a fox."

And they are right, Shoshone thought, sucking hot tea from the nozzle of an insulated cup. As infuriating as Benedict had been, she had seen not the slightest hint that he was either insane or suicidal.

Then why had he raised no objection on being arrested? Both the news files and her own observation documented that he could be extraordinarily persuasive when he wanted to be. The Gens had been willing to overpower Harriman's rather pathetic guard force at a word. Benedict had not spoken that word. Why not? Could it be that he had wanted Harriman to arrest him? That made no sense, either.

She wished she could talk to Stellato, but according to the

locator, he was outside the *Crucible*. His crew chief informed her that he was one of a group of Gens inspecting the outside of the hull. Apparently it had suddenly occurred to Harriman that if the reef could nearly disintegrate a Scout, it would be well to see what it might be doing to the starship itself.

It was getting toward the end of her shift. She reported back to Lumbongo to see if he had one more assignment for her.

"I need a supergofer to get some more of the ingredients for our ceramic superconductor," he said. "Our manifest has located a storeroom containing hydroponics supplies, among other things, which we could put to good use. Our colleagues in ship systems will object, and of course it is the captain's call. However, if we expend the effort to recover it, that should give weight to a claim for at least part of the raw materials."

"No problem," Shoshone said. "Just give me the location and a dolly and I'll bring it up here."

"It *will* be a problem," Lumbongo corrected. His smile, ivory flashing from ebony, made it obvious why he was so attractive to the female half of the ship's crew. "The reason it will be a problem is that it is underwater."

Shoshone climbed carefully down the brachirail. The pressure suit muffled not only all sound but even the feeling of pressure from hands and feet. It was all too possible for her to misjudge a step or grip and plummet down the dark shaft. The fact that water was less than twenty meters below was illusory comfort. With the shaft canted off the vertical, the odds were good that she would hit wall or brachirail itself on the way down. A shattered helmet would at the very best be a considerable embarrassment. At the worst . . .

It was only imagination that made the entire shaft seem to lurch and sway. That far down, the pitch and roll of the ship were minimal. Still, the extra gear that Shoshone was carrying, lights fixed to her helmet, collapsed flotation bags with attendant gas bottles attached to her back, all exacerbated the effect of each motion the ship made in response to the waves outside.

Even through the gloves and boots of the pressure suit, she felt the brachirail tremble. Looking down between her feet, she watched the surface of the water churn itself into foam as it raced up the shaft, stopping less than two meters below her. The shaft acted as a funnel, greatly exaggerating the change in water level as the ship swayed from side to side.

"Communications, this is Mantei in shaft VM 180. I will be dropping underwater with the next upward surge. I expect to be out of contact for as much as an hour."

"Copy that, Mantei." Communications sounded inordinately cheerful. "Bring us back something nice."

Again the shudder raced through the brachirail. Shoshone looked down. In the light from her attached helmet lamps reflected along the walls, the only light in the shaft, she saw black water laced with white froth geysering up. She waited until it slowed and seemed to come to a halt less than two meters below her boots. Black waves smashed white against the shaft walls.

Shoshone opened her hands and pushed off with her feet. Water slapped at boots and backpack, slowing but not stopping her descent. She twisted herself around to bring the brachirail back in view. Its rungs slid upward with increasing speed as the water began its plunge down the shaft. Turbulence tumbled her away from the side. Clumsy in her pressure suit, she tried to right herself and swim back to the brachirail.

She had just grabbed on to a rung as the column of water slowed and reversed its flow. She wrapped both legs around the brachirail and hung on as the current tried to tear her from her perch and hurl her upward.

"Map!" she commanded.

Fluorescent green lines etched the inside of her helmet. Her own route was marked in glowing yellow. Had power been on in that part of the ship, her own position would have been marked by a blinking dot. However, as a conservation measure, all power had been cut off. She would have to rely on her internal systems for guidance.

Again the flow reversed. She put her head down and her hands out, almost flying down the side of the shaft. When her downward motion slowed, she was in sight of the crosscorridor indicated on her map.

Her breath sounded like a windstorm in her helmet. She tried to bring it under control so she would not be completely deaf to outside sounds. The tunnel vision caused by the lamps strapped to the sides of her helmet made her feel vulnerable enough.

What sort of creatures justify defenses like that? she had wondered when the reef tendrils had nearly disintegrated Scout Five. *Crucible* had ballasted itself with water from the ocean. What else had it drawn into itself?

Nothing! Shoshone thought angrily. Nothing large could get through the intake ports.

But something sufficiently small to get in would then be able to grow in these dark shafts and corridors with none of its own predators to molest it.

Enough of that, she told herself. Any monster that has been waiting all this time to make a meal of me must have starved to death by now.

Hand over hand on the rungs, she pulled herself down to the cross corridor. At its mouth she paused to call up the MAP function again and match the corridor's number with the one she was supposed to enter.

A sudden surge sucked her into the darkness. She thrashed about for a handhold, beams of light from her helmet corkscrewing the darkness ahead of her. Her fingers brushed by doorways and pipes unable to grasp a hold. Her momentum leaked away, and slowly she began to slide back the way she had come. At that moment, out of the corner of her eye, she spotted a brachirail. Arms fluttering like some ungainly bird, she managed to grab a rung and hold against the steadily increasing force of the water.

Getting materials out of the storeroom was going to be more difficult than any of them had imagined. The flotation bags would give buoyancy enough, but the increased surface area of the inflated bags would make it nearly impossible to resist the alternating flow of water in the corridor. Perhaps because the corridor was smaller than the shaft, its current was correspondingly stronger and faster. If she did find anything, Shoshone promised herself, she would take back only a small amount. Lumbongo could have a crew rig lines to pull the rest of it into the shaft, where it could float to the surface.

MAP gave her destination as being twelve doors in from the shaft. Shoshone took her time, letting herself hurl forward with the surge of the current, then holding tight against the backwash. Despite her growing proficiency in working with the current, she was exhausted by the time she reached her goal. To her surprise, she saw that the doorway was on her left—she must have been pulling herself along the ceiling brachirail rather than the one embedded in the deck. The underwater environment was more confusing than weightlessness.

The palm pad for the door mechanism was located midway

up the right side of the doorway. It would be inoperative without electricity, of course, but there were ways around that.

After waiting for the next lull in the current, Shoshone kicked herself away from the brachirail, grabbed the edge of the doorway, and twisted so that she could brace herself inside it. The chisel came easily from her belt. She snapped the cord around her right wrist. With two quick, flowing movements she inserted the narrow end of the chisel in the narrow side slot of the palm pad and flipped out the entire box unit. Feeling around with the chisel in the hole that was left, she engaged the manual lock release. It resisted her leverage for three seconds before letting go.

The current was strengthening. Moving very carefully to avoid being whirled away by it, Shoshone shifted herself until she was completely within the doorway. The edge of the chisel found the join where the sliding doors met. She wrenched over the handle. The doors slid easily aside.

The first thing she saw was a blinking red light. But how could that be, with all the power out? Shoshone reflexively raised her head to check the number over the door. 14H135. Being pulled into this corridor had disoriented her even more than she thought. Up was down, and left was right. Her destination, 14H136, must be behind her, across the corridor.

But there was no way she could turn her back on that blinking light. She pushed into the room, feeling its calm waters displace and flow around her. Locked cabinets lined both walls, floor to ceiling. The light was coming from the far side of the room.

Close up, Shoshone saw that what was lit up was a sophisticated arming panel, one that would require both palm print and coded sequence and perhaps an enabling command from the bridge. A display, previously hidden by its angle, showed a hologram: a circle enclosing a minus sign being orbited by a circle with a plus sign.

Shoshone felt the blood drain from her face. That explained the self-contained power source. No one would risk the dispersion of the magnetic containment fields of an antimatter bomb.

"MAP: 14C135: nomenclature."

ARMORY. But this was totally converted into a parts storage bin before I even joined the crew. I saw the plans on my data base.

How can I prove . . . She looked around at the cabinets and unhooked her chisel again. The cabinet proved far more resistant than the palm pad box, but it had been designed with electronic safeguards as the primary line of defense. The metal latch was little more than a redundancy. There was a satisfying snap as it cracked in two.

Hinged at its bottom, the cabinet swung open. Light dazzled off nested silver leaves. The cabinet seemed to be filled with two rows of huge metal flowers. Shoshone reached deep to grasp a dark pistol grip. The leaves folded together, clasping her forearm. Gently, she raised this new extension of herself for examination.

It was a beautifully balanced heavy-duty assault laser. During her brief stint in the Aquaflamme militia she had seen training films of Allied shock troops using such weapons: Dogfish had been too poor to afford any. Power packs shielded by light splashers clustered around the thick central portion below the grip. A humming, barely felt through the knuckles, confirmed that it was fully operational.

There was motion at the far edge of her peripheral vision. A figure, feet braced in the doorway against the current, was gesticulating with his left hand. In his right hand was a wire-stocked laser pistol such as those carried by Harriman's guards. Moving with dreamlike slowness through the water, it came up to bear on her.

No, Shoshone thought, shaking her head incredulously. But the expression inside that other helmet, both frightened and determined, carried its own conviction. She brought up her arm instinctively to shield herself, clenching her fists.

The assault laser was self-targeting. Light pulses swept fifteen degrees to either side of the muzzle, looking for a target. Although the chip could be programmed, the default setting was for a human form. Normally it would aim at the target's center. But when the return was characteristic of human flesh, as it would be through a nearly transparent helmet, it would switch to that.

The water, sucked into the *Crucible* when it was dozens of kilometers from the warm water upwelling that made the reef possible, was nearly transparent. Nonetheless, it would still have heated sufficiently in a long-lasting beam to have started dissipating convection currents. The packet of energy coming from the assault laser came in so short a pulse that the water molecules had no time to move. Energy flared through the attacker's helmet, superheating flesh and bone. The helmet exploded. For an instant the head was replaced by expanding red mist. Then body and blood were swept away in the current surge.

Shoshone clamped down on her throat muscles, trying very hard not to be sick in her helmet. His other hand, she thought. He was gesturing to a companion. *And here I am with a light-house on my head which says, "Here I am, shoot me!"*

Not far from panic, she wrenched off the lamps. Slipping them around the assault laser, she unstrapped the floatation bags from her back. Deprived of their weight, she floated to the ceiling. Fingers stiff and awkward in their pressure gloves clamped the lamps to the uninflated bags. It would have been considerably easier with two hands, but she did not dare let the muzzle of the assault laser stray far from the open doorway.

Next came the air bottles originally meant for the bags. She clipped them onto the lamp bands, trying to get them as close as possible to where the center of mass should be—not that her ruse had much chance of working at all, much less of fooling someone who might be out in the corridor, waiting for her.

She bounced across the ceiling, muffling the light from the lamps. A meter from the doorway she opened the nozzles of both air bottles. They bucked, trying to tear loose. Making sure everything was pointed in approximately the right direction, she let go. It was like letting go of an inflated balloon. Light corkscrewed across the deck and wall of the corridor as lamp and bags and bottles tumbled through the doorway in a froth of bubbles.

Lasers *from the left* shattered both lamps, leaving Shoshone in the dark with searing afterimages. Her left hand found the edge of the doorway. Her right arm, clad in the assault laser, she stuck outside, pressing the trigger. There was a burst of light, as at the end of a long tunnel.

In the blackness she held the trigger down, sweeping the laser in a 180-degree arc in front of and behind her. Nothing. So either there were no further targets or the laser had ceased functioning.

The corridor current was waning. Shoshone stepped out of the armory and let herself float to the ceiling. Her free hand scrabbled around for the brachirail, finding it just as the current began to freshen.

She could go only a few meters with each forward surge of the current. She needed to feel the brachirail, to make sure that she would not lose it and be forever tossed about in currents of darkness. Time stretched out endlessly. Shoshone wondered if she had been going the wrong way. Certainly she should have come to the shaft by now!

"TIMECHECK. From Armory."

Less than five minutes had elapsed according to the display that flashed across the inside of her helmet. She kept going, her arm aching with weariness, her breathing becoming labored.

The surging became stronger. Gurgling noises she had not noticed on the way in increased in volume. Abruptly, the brachirail she had been following right-angled to the vertical.

The rest should be easy, she told herself. Float up to the surface, climb from there to the lock, and I'm home.

She realized almost immediately how wrong she was. The rocketing surge of water was so strong that she dared rise only rung by rung for fear of being torn off. When she was high enough that the water dropped below her, she found that she had to wait for it to return to make any further progress. The surface, as it swept over her, was a roiling chaos, arrhythmic waves chopping at her back and reflecting off the wall at her front.

At last there came a time when she was above the highest surge. Legs and arms trembled uncontrollably, threatening to spasm. She could not make the rest of the climb with only one arm. Regretfully, she let the assault laser fall. In the continuous oscillating roar that filled the shaft, she never heard it splash.

Ten rungs at a time, then a pause for breath. She pressed her helmet against the wall, fighting dizziness. Five rungs and then a rest.

Then she found herself staring at a green pinpoint. Unbelievingly, she put out a hand to cover the light. The buttons were just above her fingers. At their pressure, a crescent of brilliance appeared and widened into an oval.

Hesitantly, Shoshone swung into the blindingly bright safety lock and collapsed.

XVI

I DON'T . . . HAVE TIME FOR THIS, SHOSHONE TOLD HERSELF. Without rising from the deck, she forced trembling fingers to undo her suit seals. Wind whistled through the gap between helmet and pressure suit. A few more snaps and she was able to wriggle out of both halves.

She staggered to her feet and pressed the button to close the lock. Wind rose to a shriek and abruptly cut off.

There was a transvator almost directly across from her. She pressed the palm pad. Doors slid noiselessly apart to admit her. Inside, she braced herself against the side railings.

"Captain's quarters," she said.

The doors opened to the sound of surf. A gentle swell moved across blue waters to crash on a sandy beach spread with seaweed. At the far horizon, between light-strewn waves and fleecy afternoon clouds, was a dark, irregular line of land.

"Hello, Shoshone. How nice of you to . . . to visit me."

Shoshone looked around for the voice. Except for the wall-length holo, the room was in shadow. It took her a few seconds to spot Nickerson, leaning back against the corner of a sofa, a tray of food in front of her. Too-bright eyes regarded the seascape.

"Do you like it?" the captain asked. "It is Chatham, looking north across the Breach to Provincetown Island. My home. For as long as anyone can remember, there have been Nickersons and Chases and Snows on Cape Cod. You see slate markers in all the graveyards with the names of those who fought the sea all their lives. And even after they are dead, the sea keeps gnawing, dissolving, until dune bluffs tumble into the waves and the graveyards crack apart and the sea has its final victory.''

Her glass slipped from her hand and fell gently to the carpet.

"Captain," Shoshone said, alarmed.

Nickerson frowned down at the glass, breathing heavily. Her mouth moved as if trying to form itself around a difficult word in a foreign language.

"Shoshone," she said clearly, "something is wrong. I need—" Her eyes rolled up, and she collapsed into the cushions. Shoshone knelt and reached for her wrist. The pulse was as strong and sure as the sound of the surf. Nickerson's breathing was deep and even.

Faint corridor noises penetrated into the room. "I don't hear anything," an unknown voice said uncertainly. "Are you sure the drug has had time to take effect?"

"I'm sure," Harriman said. But his voice betrayed his own nervousness.

Both voices came from the entryway. There was no time to get back to the transvator. Shoshone stepped quickly around the sofa and through a doorway into what turned out to be a bedroom.

"She is all right," Harriman said, sounding defensive. "Didn't even hurt her head on the way down."

"Lucky for you."

"Lucky for all of us, including her. Make sure you don't touch the glass. I'll call sick bay."

Sick bay attendants took less than two minutes to respond. Then the room was empty again. It would not be long before Harriman learned that the two crewmen he had sent to the armory had been killed. He would hear that Shoshone Mantei had been sent down to that same corridor and had not reported back. Putting two and two together, he would at least revoke her transvator priority. He might even realize that there was only one place on the starship she could go for help.

Taking a deep breath, she strode across the living room to the cry of sea gulls and entered the transvator.

The guards to either side of the door stood at parade rest, looking uncomfortable. One was a Gen, the other a Norm. Body language suggested nearly terminal boredom.

Shoshone identified herself. "Timakata sent me down to get some computer codes from him," she said.

"That has been the story all day," the Norm said. "They don't trust him running around the ship, but they can't run it without him."

"It would be a lot easier for everyone if they reactivated the room terminal," the Gen said.

"But then he might use it to take over the ship."

"If they can't protect themselves from one old, blind man, they ought to give up right now."

The dialogue had a worn, familiar ring to it. Shielding the palm pad from Shoshone's sight, the Norm pressed it with his hand and then tapped in a code on the alphanumeric lock that had been wired in beneath it. The door sighed open. The Norm sketched out a bow, inviting her in.

Only when the door closed behind her did Shoshone realize that the room was pitch black. There was a soft sound she could not identify.

Just suppose that the simple explanation is the correct one, she thought. That he really is insane. Where there was no alternative, there was no problem, her father had taught her. That bit of pragmatic advice brought with it no comfort at all.

"Visitors?" the familiar voice asked. "Ah, you need the lights. On the wall, just to your left. In my present state I tend to forget such things."

Shoshone brushed her hand over the sensor. The room flooded with warm, golden light. Benedict sat cross-legged on the floor, Stewards' gray cloth draped across his knees. At his side were tubes and tapes used in cloth mending.

Shoshone strode quickly across the room and sat down facing him. She would make it an engineering report, she decided. Facts in order, without opinion or hypothesis. Undermanned as the crew was, Harriman was unlikely to have detailed anyone for full-time eavesdropping. If she was concise, she might finish before anyone did a spot check.

"I need your help," she began without preamble. "The armory has been reconverted to its original purpose. There are racks of assault lasers. Two crewmen, I think under Harriman's orders, were down there just—" She looked at her chronometer in disbelief. "—one hour ago. I—I killed both of them. I think they were going to take weapons up to the main part of the ship. They might have wanted to activate the antimatter bomb—"

That got a reaction.

"Antimatter bomb?" Benedict said, letting fabric drop from his fingers. "That I did not know. I wonder which faction was insane enough to think that would be useful."

"I tried to warn Captain Nickerson. When I got to her, I found that she had been drugged. Harriman and some goon came in and called in sick-bay staff, who carried her away."

"What was her state, as far as you could tell?" Benedict's words carried an undertone of urgency.

"Aside from being unconscious, she seemed well. Harriman seemed concerned that no serious injury befall her."

"Good," Benedict said. "He has sense enough to realize that even if he needs her out of the way to effect his own designs, he still needs the legitimacy of commanding in her name. I would guess that he will have her put in cold sleep 'for her own safety.' "

"What can we do to prevent his mutiny from succeeding?" Shoshone demanded.

Benedict picked up the cloth again. Shoshone saw then that it was the Steward's habit that had been shredded by Alexandrov's attack. Hands deftly located a rent, pressed all wrinkles out of the fabric to either side of it, squeezed a line of white paste from a tube directly onto the tear, and followed it with sealing tape, pressed on with both thumbs spreading carefully to allow no wrinkle to remain beneath it. In a matter of minutes the fibers would melt into each other, making a mend that, if it was not as good as new, would at least make the garment serviceable.

"Our first officer," Benedict murmured, "believes that he can rise by placing one foot firmly atop the other and stepping up. He will learn his error in time. Until he does, he is liable to thrash about at those who attempt to point it out to him. Right now there is little that can be done to hasten the process. Certainly there is nothing I can do from here."

Was his response just an expression of petulance? Shoshone wondered. Or was she being invited to participate in a jailbreak?

She felt rather than heard the door open behind her. Footsteps advanced quietly across the deck. Shoshone's back tensed as she waited to feel a laser muzzle on her neck.

"Good day, Grandfather," Stellato said courteously. "Forgive me for interrupting this meeting with your assistant, but I urgently require your advice concerning the Thetan plague which has so endangered all of the ship's company."

"There is no such plague," Benedict said evenly, "as your tone of voice indicates you are very well aware. The biochemistry of life here is such that there can be no plague which could endanger us."

"So I thought," Stellato agreed, "although an engineer has little understanding of such things. That is why I was both concerned and surprised to learn that the *Crucible* had been sealed to prevent any further sources of infection from entering."

"Leaving a great many Gens outside," Benedict surmised.

"Leaving only Gens outside," Stellato said.

"You were out checking the hull," Shoshone said suddenly. "If the *Crucible* is sealed, what are you doing here?"

"I performed a manual override on a below-surface lock. Since there is no power to the lower portions of the ship, I was able to let myself in without even registering on the status boards."

Right! Shoshone thought, remembering the dead darkness from which she had so recently returned. Then a second thought: Only chance had prevented her from killing Stellato as she sightlessly swept the corridor and shaft with her assault laser.

"I went to engineering. Nobody there had heard anything about a plague. Mr. Lumbongo could not reach Captain Nickerson, and I did not want to entrust myself to anyone of lesser rank, since my presence aboard is insubordination at the least."

"Quite wise," Benedict said. "Our captain has been drugged by First Officer Harriman, who has put me in here and most of you outside."

"So," Stellato said quietly. "I thought it might be something like that. That is why I have come to you."

"Did you come with nothing but questions?" Benedict asked.

A sudden brilliant smile flashed across Stellato's face. "While in engineering, I picked these up, thinking you might find them a useful gift."

From a pouch pocket, he took out three translucent disks. Seemingly random pinpoint patterns of shimmering iridescence shattered the light like a spray of water droplets. He handed them to Benedict. Even without sight, Shoshone thought, they were unmistakable.

Benedict's fingers caressed their surfaces. "Optical switch disks. Excellent. What do these come from?"

"The suppressor field generators. I also located and wiped the specs in the engineering data base—after I copied them into a cartridge, which I also have."

"Subtle as a serpent, Stellato. But now that you have these things—" He paused. A muted snapping sounded through the walls. Shoshone heard running feet in the distance. "—how are you going to use them?"

"I don't know," Stellato admitted. "It was all I could grab in the time I had. I was hoping you would find them useful."

"Assuredly. However, your options are rapidly narrowing. With most of the Gens out of the way, Harriman is consolidating his hold on the *Crucible*. You hear some of the resistance. It is futile: Harriman has too much of an edge in arms and numbers.

"If you stay on board, you will be caught, and at best you will have an ad hoc cell like mine. More likely, you will be put in cold sleep. If you are lucky, you may someday be awakened.

"There is no place on the *Crucible* where you can hide the switching disks. You must take them outside. Since there is nothing more you can do here, I would appreciate it if you took me, as well."

"I will come with you," Shoshone said suddenly. "You will need my eyes more than ever out there."

"This is not your fight," Stellato objected.

Shoshone frowned. "I killed two of Harriman's men down in the armory. I heard him confess to drugging the captain. I don't think I have much future here with him running things."

"What about the guards?" Stellato asked Benedict.

"I can help there," Shoshone said. She rapped on the door, afraid her nerve would fail her if she hesitated. "I'm finished here," she called. "You can let me out."

The door slid aside. "Are you okay, Ms. Mantei?" The Norm's laser flicked uneasily between the room and the Gen who had been standing guard duty with him. The Gen's laser lay on the deck between them. Indistinguishable words crackled from both headsets.

Shoshone stepped into the corridor. The laser swung back at her.

"Stay back, Stellato!" the Norm ordered. "There seem to be problems in the rest of the ship. All Gens are confined to quarters. Some jerk in command group is probably overreacting to something, so it would be a shame if I burned somebody before they all sobered up.''

It was almost pitifully easy. Shoshone stepped on the laser on the floor and stumbled into the Norm. Even as he tried to disentangle the laser barrel, he gave an explosive grunt and folded to the floor.

''You didn't have to hit Sven that hard,'' the Gen said to Stellato. His laser, kicked over by Shoshone, lay at his feet. ''He was only following orders.''

''His orders were coming from Harriman,'' Stellato replied, ''who has mutinied against Captain Nickerson and seems inclined to restart the war. In less than an hour every Gen remaining on board will be either dead or captive. We are going outside. If you wish, Gerry, you may join us.''

''That is not much of a choice,'' Gerry grumbled.

''It's all you've got.''

Shoshone went back for Benedict. He thrust the Steward's robe he had been mending into her hands. ''You will need this as protection against the cold.''

Shoshone began to object, then thought better of it. She shrugged into the garment, tightening the wrist and ankle straps and pulling the inner cowl snugly around her face at Benedict's direction. It was surprisingly comfortable despite being four sizes too big.

''One deck down there is an access hatch to the outside,'' Stellato said. ''There is a companionway we can take twenty meters down this corridor.''

''You'd better hurry,'' Gerry suggested, pressing his headset against his right ear. ''Audio traffic is confused, but apparently somebody on the bridge did a monitor check on Father Benedict's quarters and did not like what she saw. It sounds like a squad is on the way to put us all back in the box.''

Benedict's hand on her shoulder, Shoshone with difficulty kept up with Stellato's distance-devouring stride. Gerry, coming behind with his laser rifle, acted as rear guard. As Stellato reached the door to the companionway, they heard the *whoosh* of a transvator coming to rest nearby. They ducked through the door, sealing it silently behind them.

All the way down the steep, narrow stairway, then out into the deserted corridor, Shoshone listened for the sound of pursuing footsteps, expecting to hear a command to halt and then the hiss of burning beams of coherent light. All she heard, however, was the slow, steady pulse of the waste regeneration pumps.

Then they were at the air lock. Stellato regarded the cycling switch thoughtfully. "As soon as I activate the lock, that will show up on the bridge. The computers should already be set to seal off the area if that happens. So let's do something a little bit different."

He pulled out his APT, flicking a side stud. It extended to more than twice its length, terminating in a flat, dull blade. "Shoshone, grab the hatch wheel and be ready to rotate at my command."

He slid the blade end of the APT into the cycling switch. There was a spark, and the switch's ready light winked out.

"Now!"

The wheel rotated easily under Shoshone's hands. She had not quite completed a turn when the lights were extinguished. Bulkheads slammed shut at either end of the corridor. Klaxons filled the air with angry-goose rage.

Shoshone kept turning. The hatch suddenly lifted from the inner hull and slid to the side. She felt Stellato and Gerry step into the lock. Taking Benedict's hand, she moved carefully after them.

A sliver of starlight etched itself on the darkness, followed by a knife-edge blast of thin, cold air. The outer hatch swung the rest of the way aside. Wind moaned around the edges of the opening. Beyond it, a river of pink-tinged mist swirled quickly past, illuminated by the bright red dot of Eta Cassiopeiae B high above.

"Jump out as far as you can," Stellato instructed. "We are just above the *Crucible*'s equator. You don't want to leave any part of your epidermis smeared along its hull on the way down."

Shoshone must have made a noise. Stellato turned to her, his smile brilliant in starlight. "Don't worry. I'm told a ride like this would command quite a price at the Terrestrial thrill parks."

Then he grew serious again. "I'll go first, then Gerry, then Shoshone. Ten seconds between jumps, and swim away from the *Crucible* as soon as you come up to make sure nobody lands on top of you. Grandfather, I want you to go last so the rest of us can already be in the water and ready to guide you onto the reef.

"See you in a few seconds." He perched himself on the edge of the lock and sprang out. Fog swallowed him almost immediately. After what seemed far longer than ten seconds, Gerry followed.

Shoshone turned to Benedict. "Call out for me as soon as you surface. I'll come right over to you."

"I have no doubt of that." For once his voice was devoid of its characteristic irony.

Then, fearing that she would lose all courage and turn herself in to Harriman if she waited any longer, she stepped to the edge of the hatch and hurtled into the middle of the air.

XVII

Icy mist rushed past her face. Shoshone twisted and straightened out into a dive, trying to force herself away from the *Crucible*.

Water slapped hard and closed above her. It was . . . *warm*. Her plunge slowed, stopped . . . *Fairy fingers, mermaid webs, touching, caressing, grasping* . . . Across her mind flashed the image of Scout Five imprisoned by tendrils, acid gouging its hull.

She kicked hard. Slowly at first, then with increasing speed, she ascended. Her chest ached. Abruptly she bobbed to the surface. Voices were calling. Their distance and direction seemed to shift with every second.

There was a loud splash to her right. That had to be Benedict. How can he be that far over from me? she wondered. "Over here," she called, striking out in the direction of the splash. A head popped up in front of her, darkness against darkness. He swept past her. She reached and caught. They pinwheeled slowly.

Her feet brushed a hard surface, then her knees. Whatever it was seemed to surge through the water, trying to scoop them up.

No, that was wrong, Shoshone realized. The thing was still; it was the water that was moving.

"Try to climb," Benedict said. "We must be on a floatation bladder. We should be able to climb up to a drier part of the reef."

It was not easy. The current tried to suck them away. Feet and hands slipped along a surface that felt like taut leather. The bladder itself bobbed unsteadily under their weight as they emerged from the water.

"Shoshone!"

She paused, gasping, and looked around for the voice. An immeasurable distance above and to the right, a pinpoint of light, aureoled by fog, bobbed unevenly.

"Shoshone, where are you?" Stellato sounded worried.

Feeling as if the water had congealed her brain, Shoshone remembered her APT. She fumbled inside the Steward's robes and found it, still clipped to the inside of a coverall pocket. She flipped it on to its narrowest, most intense nonlasing setting.

"Over here," she shouted. "Father Benedict is with me."

She widened the beam and swept it around her to get a better idea of her situation. Rows of black humps peering out of the water bobbed up and down to an unseen swell. Between clusters of humps ran swiftly flowing streams. They were on one such hump. Above them a bewildering complexity of branches and vines twisted together in helices and exploded in starburst patterns. All were in constant motion, up and down, backward and forward, like a fairy-tale forest that had come alive.

"Shoshone, is that you?" It was a woman's voice behind and above her. "There is a trunk over here you can climb up."

Shoshone clipped the APT to the side of her hood for illumination and, guiding Benedict, half walked, half stumbled over to where a thick tangle of rootlike structures plunged down from a trunk to the massed flotation bladders.

"Step carefully," she warned Benedict. "I'm not sure these things will bear our weight. And even if they do, we may twist an ankle."

Sleet slapped coldness on her cheeks. Treacherous as the uneven, constantly moving surface was, they managed to ascend perhaps two meters. Then the roots joined and smoothed into hard, uneven trunk. The slope was too close to the vertical for Shoshone to even think of climbing it.

"Take my hand." An arm extended to her. In the rifts of the driven fog, Shoshone saw Rebekka Shahal's face.

"Hold on tight," she warned Benedict. Rebekka grasped her forearm with surprising strength and pulled both of them into the cold fog.

"Stellato, I have them!" Rebekka shouted. She had to shout because of the constant cacophony of the reef: a blustery wind moaning through the branches, the gurgling rush of the current forcing its way through the undergrowth, a near symphony of creaks as limbs rubbed against each other.

The bouncing APT light that marked Stellato's position was suddenly right next to them. Galaxies of water droplets caught the light on both his and Gerry's fur.

"Follow me," Rebekka said. "I'll lead you to the Scout. Although I was hoping that when you reappeared, it would be to invite the rest of us in rather than to bring more refugees."

Footing was a nightmare for Shoshone. They would go perhaps three meters along a horizontal limb, then either climb or drop to another limb going in a different direction. With uneven slipperiness rocking beneath her, Shoshone seemed to stumble with every third step. That none of the Gens seemed to be having any difficulty just made things worse.

"These are actually quite interesting adaptations," Benedict said, helping her up. "They seem to have been water roots originally. As they have evolved, they have become the structures which hold the entire reef together. They also act to stabilize the individual plants against tossing motions of wind and wave. Rebekka thinks they may have retained some of their rootlike characteristics and that they may take nutrients from the plants they brace against. If so, what started out as a parasitism may have grown into a circulatory system for the entire reef."

"It doesn't make them any easier to walk on," Shoshone muttered. Less than a minute later a branch whipping back from Rebekka caused Shoshone to stagger. Her hand shot out to a trunk to steady herself. A vine writhed to life beneath her hand, twisted over her wrist, and slithered up into the darkness.

"What—was—*that*?" she asked. She described it.

"A tree snake," Rebekka said after listening to her description. "They're harmless. I don't think we taste good to them."

Just when Shoshone felt she could go no farther, she smelled smoke on the wind. Below and ahead of them a light flickered. It was a small fire, illuminating the hull of a Scout that nestled in a web of bracing roots and vines.

"Who goes there?" a voice in the darkness above demanded. Shoshone thought it advisable to stand completely still while they named themselves.

"I am glad you were not captured, Stellato." It took Shoshone a few seconds to identify Jean D'Argent's voice. "Almost glad enough to forgive you for not letting me know that you could open an underwater lock. All of us could have entered and made a stand inside the *Crucible*. By now we would be in control.''

"I had to make sure the story about the plague was false,'' Stellato said defensively.

"By now you would be dead,'' Benedict said. His voice was as quietly confident as if he were seated back in his quarters. "Harriman's men are armed with assault lasers. My assistant killed two of them with one.''

"I am not sure I am pleased to see you, Fox. Too many of my people have died at your hand. As for your assistant . . .'' D'Argent turned and stared down at her. Distantly, Shoshone was aware that she should be terrified. Exhaustion and body aches, however, muted all other feelings. "She is human. She has no place among us. Send her back.''

Shoshone looked up at lips drawn back from sharp, white fangs. *The better to eat you with, my dear,* bubbled up from the depths of her childhood. An urge to laugh hysterically swept over her and died to nothing.

"I hurt,'' she said. "I am chilled and bruised and exhausted. If you intend to get your grins by ripping out my throat and drinking my blood, like all the war propaganda said, be quick about it. Otherwise, get out of my way. I'm going into the Scout to collapse.''

There was a rustle of quickly repressed laughter from several points around her. She moved to go past D'Argent. A hand spanning from her shoulder to the quickly pulsing jugular vein in her throat rested lightly on her, claw points as fine and sharp as needles.

"Not into the Scout,'' D'Argent rumbled. "You cannot be trusted there.''

Shoshone shrugged the hand off. "Then at least over there by the fire,'' she said, teeth chattering. Without looking at him, she moved away.

Multicolored flames danced in the fire, green and orange and blue. For an instant Shoshone had the feeling that should mean something to her, but she was too tired to follow the thought. Warmth from the fire seemed to melt her bones. It occurred to her to wonder how the Gens had set the fire so that it would not spread to the rest of the reef.

On the other side of the fire a Gen glowered at her, flexing his fingers so that his claws flashed through the night like flaming daggers.

Screw you, too, she thought, stretching out to parallel the warmth as much as possible. The Steward's robes were much more practical than she had thought. They had kept her main torso dry during her plunge and protected her from the wind during the walk. Even with her repeated falls, the cloth had not torn. The fact that the garment was overlarge turned out to be an advantage, as well. Lying down in it was like being in a collapsed tent. Wind snapped at folds of cloth. Beneath her, the rush of water rose and grew softer as the entire reef rocked her to sleep. In the distance she heard Stellato telling D'Argent the story of their escape.

Benedict sat in the crotch of a bracing limb and tree trunk. The join was wide enough that D'Argent could pace slowly from one side to the other in a semicircle while considering his guest.

"What shall I do with you, Fox?" he mused. "You are a Gen, if not of the Clans. Harriman thinks you are dangerous to him. I played the Game of Fox and Lion often enough in my childhood to know him right in that. From Pearl to Chiron, I know the damage you have inflicted on my people. Far too well to want to be part of any final solution you may have to the 'problem' of my people's existence."

"I warned Commander Lupus that he might choke on Pearl," Benedict observed. "At the time I was legally bound by Councillor Chiang, whose interests I upheld. At the Battle of Chiron I served the Centaurian Councils as Sky Marshal."

"Who is your patron now?"

"For the term of this mission I owe my loyalty, as do we all, to Captain Nickerson. Beyond that, and above that, is my vow of obedience to the Church Universal."

A low growl seemed to come from D'Argent's chest. "That I can never forgive you. As an archetype in a children's game, as an actual opponent, you taught us craft and subtlety. No matter how painful those lessons may have been, those of us who survived were the stronger for them.

"But now, when we most need strength, you come among us preaching a religion of weakness. We are to suffer blows with a sickly masochistic smile. You would extinguish the cleansing flame of anger against injustice and substitute for it a saccharine, suffocating 'love.' Only a few watches ago you preached that we should 'forgive and forget' and therefore make virtues of moral laxity and amnesia. If I believed you were sincere, I would say you were the most contemptible man alive.''

Other Gens had gathered as close as they might to hear the interrogation. Low growls erupted from several of them at this last statement. D'Argent gave no indication that he heard.

"If?'' Benedict asked lightly.

"I know my history, Fox. The Multi-Neural Capacitants, of whom you are the last, were created by Snowden to be bio-computer servitors for whoever would bid highest. He did not foresee, or did not care if he did, that his creations, dwarfing the mental capacities of their patrons, would inevitably further their own interests, no matter whom they professed to serve.

"You are who you always have been. You are the Fox. You go your own way, alone. Those Steward's robes are merely the latest in your lifelong series of disguises.''

"And if this judgment were correct,'' Benedict said after a pause, "what follows from it?''

"It follows that I can never be sure of your loyalties, nor can I match you mentally to determine where you think your self-interest lies. You are a dangerous wild card. To protect my people, I should probably shred you right now.''

The wind veered and seemed to batter against itself in confusion. A large limb in the fire snapped, loosing a cascade of sparks into the night.

"Grandfather Fox has come to us at considerable danger to himself,'' Stellato said. His voice shook with the effort to control his anger. "Why do you insult an honored guest who wishes to aid us?''

"He has come to us because he prefers freedom to a cell,'' D'Argent replied. "He intends to use that freedom by betraying us, thus buying his way back into Harriman's favor.''

"It is certainly a possibility which must be considered,'' Benedict said, forestalling another outburst from Stellato. "We have a choice of mutually exclusive propositions: Either I work against your interests, or I do not. If I do, it would appear that I achieved all my ends while safely within the *Crucible*. You are out here. There is no way for you to force yourself back in. If nothing else intervenes, your deaths will be an unpleasant race between vitamin and amino acid deficiencies. I would estimate that you have three months.

"On the other hand, if I am not set against you, I am the most powerful tool you have. Far too powerful to simply throw away.

"You have nothing to lose. I can do no worse than leave your situation unaltered."

"We are not without resources," D'Argent said harshly.

"Of course not," Benedict agreed. "If you were, even I could do nothing for you. You have, in fact, three resources Harriman desperately needs, two of which he is intelligent enough to want. Can you name them?"

It was a shift of balance as palpable as that which propelled a judo throw. One second D'Argent was interrogating a prisoner. The next he was a student being quizzed by a patient teacher. Even those who had listened to every word were not sure how it had been done.

"We have Stellato's optical switching disks," D'Argent said. "Without them the *Crucible* will never reenter the Periphery. You will not be told where they are being kept."

"One," Benedict said, nodding. "We will have to make sure Harriman realizes they are missing. Stellato may have accomplished that so smoothly that their absence has not yet been noticed. I have no need to know where they are. Later I will tell you where not to keep them. Number two?"

"The power plant in the Scout behind us has a set of lasers powerful enough to initiate fusion by inertial implosion. Those lasers can be removed from the Scout and directed at the *Crucible*."

Benedict shook his head slowly. "This is the idea of an intelligent microbiotic biochemist. Your engineers would point out that beyond the basic difficulties of mounting your lasers with a clear line of sight in this environment, the fact is that the *Crucible* was originally built as a battlestär. Its hull surface is twenty nearly one hundred percent reflective monolayers designed with no other purpose than to reflect nova-attack lasers."

"I am not so stupid as you believe," D'Argent said, voice trembling with repressed anger. "The beams will not be directed at the hull. They will be directed at the vegetation pressing against the hull. Each will vaporize with the force of a bomb. The *Crucible* cannot stand up to that indefinitely."

"It would not have to," Benedict replied. "It would have to last only long enough for the defensive laser batteries on the

Crucible to locate the source of incoming fire and silence it. We are talking less than three seconds. The only thing that would save you from annihilation is that your laser would not fire that long. Internal batteries start an implosion laser, but after the first second, it needs to draw on the power it is producing to keep going.

"Nevertheless, you get fifty percent on that answer, because your second resource is the Scout power plant, as you said. Not because of what you can do with it but because Harriman can do nothing with it while you have it. Lumbongo has been busy laying makeshift superconductor from each of the Scouts to the impeller converters. The idea is to give the *Crucible* at least normal space capability within the A.4 satellite system.

"I have gone over the output figures. With all Scouts hooked into the system, there is just barely enough power to get the *Crucible* out of Thetis's gravity well. With one Scout missing, the ship will not be able to rise.

"It was clever of Harriman to get all engineering Gens outside to check the hull. Increasing his numerical advantage by stranding one of the survey teams outside was shortsightedness which he may even now be regretting."

"What is our third resource?" Stellato asked after a pause in which it became evident that D'Argent was not going to ask.

"I have been expecting D'Argent to throw it in my face for the last fifteen minutes," Benedict said. "It is something he should know well. I hear instead uncharacteristic silence. No matter for now. We must consider how to keep your first two resources out of Harriman's hands—and mine, as well, if you wish."

Their voices became as rough and indistinct as the wind. Sometime much later, Shoshone turned over and found a strange Gen crouched beside her, the embers of the fire reflected in his eyes.

"You are just as D'Argent has taught us," he said when he saw her eyes open. The voice was almost too low and guttural to be heard. "Too weak to do anything but slow us down, eat our food, betray us to others of your kind. Grandfather Fox may help us, for he is as different from you in his way as we are. But you . . ."

A clawed hand moved toward her face with mesmerizing slowness. Shoshone tried to force sound through a throat gone suddenly dry.

A second hand reached over, enfolded the outstretched claws, and forced them closed.

"I used to believe that myself," Stellato said conversationally. "But in my Clan we were taught that the weak are to be protected, that strength is to be restrained, to be used only when necessary and with precision. We learned that force should be the servant of both reason and honor.

"What did they teach you in your clan, Morgenstern?"

Morgenstern made no answer.

"You seek to frighten a weak female Norm from her sleep," Stellato said softly. "She has been the eyes to Grandfather Fox all the time we have been on Thetis. She has survived at least two attempts on her life. She is also both the toughest and most technically proficient partner with whom I have ever been paired. I feel sure that on reflection you wish to apologize for your discourtesy."

The locked hands jerked convulsively. Patches of wetness spread through the fur caught beneath Stellato's fingers.

"Stellato—let—"

There was a straining, an aborted shift of balance. Morgenstern gasped.

"I am sorry—any breach of honor—unintentional."

Stellato did not immediately let go. "Good. For starters. So that you will mean it, listen when I tell you that if Ms. Mantei is frightened, is harmed in any way, if she simply disappears, I will not try to prove who or how or why. I will simply come for you. Now go!"

Morgenstern stumbled away, turned once to glare at them, and vanished into the darkness. Stellato gave Shoshone a slight bow, a quick smile, and disappeared himself.

Sleep was a long time in returning.

One more time she woke that night. Sobs burst from her chest and tears streamed down her face. Sorrow had overwhelmed her in her sleep. Not since she had been very small had she ever felt so completely desolate.

Like a dream of her mother, a hand stroked her hair, giving mute comfort. "If you wish, you may talk," Benedict said.

"The two men," Shoshone said, trying to keep sobs from exploding her words into incoherence. She grasped the shards of dream that remained in her memory. "I didn't know them. I don't think I ever even saw them before. But the first one, he was at the doorway, and his laser seemed to be coming up, and—'' She took a deep breath, trying to get herself under control. ''And I killed him. Then I killed his friend.''

There was hardly a trace of nausea in her memory, even though the image of superheated blood and tissue erupting through skull and helmet remained vividly precise. Instead, she felt an overwhelming sense of loss.

''I would not have you cease your tears,'' Benedict said surprisingly. ''Not though you acted in self-defense, not though without your action you would probably be dead and we would not know of the arms aboard the *Crucible* or of how Captain Nickerson was drugged.

''Two humans are dead. Someone should mourn them. Who better than their killer? If you can, pray for their souls and for those who loved them. That is the last service you can give them.''

After that, slumber was complete and undisturbed.

XVIII

SHOSHONE OPENED HER EYES ON A MIDNIGHT-BLUE SKY. FOR
an instant overhanging branches framed air like luminous
stained glass. Then wind rushed into the calm, whipping the
branches aside and dissolving the image.

I'm awake, she thought. And nobody slit my throat while I
was sleeping.

She got unsteadily to her feet. She had been sleeping on a
bracing root overlaid with a netting of vines that the Scout had
pulled down in its descent. In the gaps between the vine and the
tangle of broken limbs brought down with them, the gurgle and
wash of the waves drifted up from a darkness not yet penetrated
by predawn light.

If I'd been restless, I could have rolled right into empty air,
she realized.

There were two immediate needs. One called for privacy.
Shoshone picked her way across the clearing to where the tall
floating trees rose and fell with the swell, creaking when they
jostled against each other. Ten meters in, she was sufficiently
shielded from the area around the Scout to relieve herself.

I wonder if this could get me prosecuted for an eco-crime,
she wondered, remembering a briefing on the damage human
waste might do to an alien ecosystem. Of more immediate
concern were the consequences of losing material for recycling. But the only alternative, since she was not allowed access to the Scout, was to surrender herself to Harriman, which
did not seem like a good idea.

She looked up to see an eye regarding her. It stared unblink-
ingly from an irregular ovoid perhaps four centimeters in diameter. Four, no *six*, jointed limbs sprouted at ninety-degree
angles from each other. The creature hung from one of them as

it surveyed her. Then, almost faster than the eye could follow, it hauled itself up and hurled itself in a zigzag blur from branch to vine to branch up the tree until it disappeared from view.

Suddenly curious, Shoshone searched for handholds and began to climb. This was one of the sail trees. It had long since lost its lower limbs, but the remaining knobs provided convenient handholds. As she ascended, she moved around the trunk so that its rocking motion was side to side rather than forward and backward—she did *not* enjoy the sensation of climbing at an angle that was suddenly greater than ninety degrees.

Twice she startled clusters of the six-limbed creatures. They exploded in all directions, scampering up the trunk, hurling themselves across the void to catch adjoining limbs, a few even clutching Shoshone's hair or shoulders as they jumped over her and down.

By the time she reached the horizontal sail limbs, most of the reef was below her. The *Crucible* appeared startlingly close, less than a kilometer away. Behind it lay a path of water stretching almost to open ocean. As she watched, it rose and fell with the swell, burrowing itself deeper into the reef.

Everything else was moving, as well. Not just up and down with the waves or side to side with the wind, but each tree was shifting its relationship to each other tree as if dancing to a slow pavane or as if each plant were one piece in a huge and torpid kaleidoscope.

Cold wind scoured the remainder of sleep from her eyes. A pale yellow line etched the eastern horizon. In less than half a watch Eta Cassiopeiae A would rise lazily above the horizon to begin Thetis's hundred-hour day. The red dwarf companion had just passed zenith, a brilliant ruby embedded in velvet. On the western horizon A.4 flooded the dark ocean with mauve and pink bands of light.

Here I am, she thought, marooned thirty-odd light-years from home, with no particular prospect of ever getting back. Most likely I will undergo a slow, painful starvation unless some of my less friendly companions have their way and rip out my throat. If I am very lucky, I may even get back on board the *Crucible* to be tried for murder and mutiny.

So why do I feel so happy?

For it was as undeniable as it was inexplicable that she felt a joy dancing within her so strongly that she could scarcely contain it. She clung two-thirds of the way up the sail tree against a wind that roared in her ears as it tried to blast her loose. Out beyond the reef it chopped waves into ribbons of white. The reef itself, curving north and south, undulated like a great serpent or a living road as it sailed against the current to stay above the hot plume.

She maintained her perch until the cold numbed her hands. Coming down was more difficult than climbing had been. She had to be careful to keep the Steward's robes from snagging.

Rebekka was waiting for her at the level of the bracing roots. She was chewing on something in the form of a black curlicue.

"Sweetroot," she said when Shoshone asked. She broke off a coil and handed it to the other woman. "Grows below the waterline. It has a high concentration of sugars. For a wonder, their handedness is right, so that our bodies can metabolize it."

In texture it had an outer flakiness surrounding a tough inner stringiness. There was a definite sweetness as well as other, less definable tastes.

"It's safe," Rebekka said, as if reading Shoshone's mind. "D'Argent and his team checked it out pretty thoroughly in their shipboard labs before they were tricked out here. Come along and I'll show you what we're doing to supplement our protein resources."

Shoshone followed her across, through, and occasionally under the debris of the clearing to the fire. For the first time she noticed that all stray vines and branches had been cleared away from the surface of the branching root surrounding the fire. It was flanked by two water-filled plastic containers from the Scout's storage lockers. Here, as on shipboard, as in any enclosed habitat, fire was one of the primary fears.

As they approached, a Gen lifted the slender branch that had been functioning as a makeshift spit to examine the broad ribbon of meat skewered upon it. Judging it to be done, he unclipped a vibroblade from his belt, one designed for taking quick samples of local flora, and sliced it into thin strips, then sliced those strips across their width. The resulting chunks he deposited on several leaves beside him. Rebekka took one, crimping the leaf to keep any of the contents from spilling out, and handed it to Shoshone.

The leaf was salty. Its contents . . . hot but without much taste. And tough. The reason for the fine work with the vibroblade was suddenly obvious.

Rebekka watched Shoshone's struggles sympathetically.

"Tree snakes—obviously not bred for tender succulence. But they slithered next to our cook last night for warmth and paid the price. You can't live on them, but you can live longer with them to stretch out the Scout's emergency supplies."

"Easier for you than me." Shoshone abandoned all pretense of manners and tugged at a strip with her fingers to help her incisors tear gristle.

"Not really," Rebekka said, nonetheless handling her own meal more deftly. "Our dental work is almost exactly the same. It has to be. The same technology produces the same diet. Not only is there no payoff for massively muscled jaws, there is a definite disincentive. All those muscles would need to anchor themselves on a sagittal crest on the back of the head. That would result in a thicker skull, which would result in a smaller brain. Bad trade-off. Much better to use the extra brain cells to invent selective breeding, steak knives, and tenderizer."

And so, Shoshone thought, another "fact" everyone knows turns out to be wartime propaganda.

Benedict appeared from the Scout's entry hatch, accompanied by D'Argent. Guiltily, Shoshone crammed the rest of the meat in her mouth and hurried over to assist him through the moving obstacle course of the clearing.

"This is a Thetis fajita," Shoshone said as she seated him by the fire. "Rotisseried tree snake wrapped in tangy salt leaf. Chew carefully so you don't choke."

Rebekka handed him a common cup filled with distilled water. Benedict gave every indication of hugely enjoying both.

"Excellent! Now, Shoshone, can you find a close-by location with line of sight to the *Crucible*?"

"I was just up in a sail tree on the far side of the clearing," Shoshone said, surprised by the question. "It had a clear view of the *Crucible*."

"You see, D'Argent? We have our outpost, our speaking platform, and our converted radios for early warning. The only question now is whether Harriman will attack or parley first. As soon as we move away from here, we will be prepared for either eventuality."

"And just what are we to do while we wait for Harriman to seize the initiative?" D'Argent asked.

"We are a survey team," Benedict said. "We should, to the extent that we can, continue the survey. Diet supplements should take first priority, I suppose, but I am very interested in further explorations of the reef base.''

At his insistence, they moved camp just out of the clearing. The new site still had a direct view of the Scout. Shoshone at first thought he would explain the change. Instead, he confined his conversation to technicalities: Perelandrian masses, Red Queen progressions, and other terms of art—some, she suspected, only recently invented—that conveyed no meaning at all to her.

The day wore on slowly, brightening by infinitesimal degrees. Exploration parties went out in groups of four and returned with data, which Rebekka fed into a pockomp. A three-dimensional map took shape in the too-narrow screen, flashing numbers marking footnotes to warn of dangers or points of interest for future investigation.

''I don't know why you bother,'' Shoshone said. Midwatch had brought an unsuccessful experiment in living off the land: boiled sixer legs garnished in minced sweetroot that could not disguise their sourness. It kept coming back on her now, accompanied by sharp cramps.

In addition, her sinuses were beginning to throb as her antihistamines wore off.

''I mean, as soon as you map anything, the position changes,'' she continued, trying to justify her ill temper. ''In just the past four hours parts of the clearing have pinched together, other parts have elongated, and the thing as a whole has rotated ten to fifteen degrees. In fifty hours it may not exist at all.''

''True enough,'' Rebekka agreed. ''But it gives us a general orientation, at least. And part of what I'm working on is a program to predict the shifts. The strength and direction of the current is a constant. Wind patterns change in generally predictable ways during the day-night cycle. The variables I really don't have a handle on are the ways the sail trees adjust to wind shifts and the underwater config—''

A buzzer began a loud electronic chirping that sounded across the clearing.

''Oops,'' Rebekka said, hitting the SAVE key and slapping her pockomp shut. ''Time to go. See you around. I hope.''

In a second she was on her feet, loping into the reef's interior. The bracing root of a neighboring tree wedged itself across the path of the one on which she was running. She vaulted the obstacle without breaking stride and disappeared on the other side.

All the other Gens were scattering in apparently random directions. Only Shoshone, Benedict, and D'Argent were staying where they were.

"Anybody care to explain to me what's going on?" Shoshone asked.

"The sound is an alarm we set up while you were sleeping," Benedict said. "It is a radar detector we made out of scavenged radio parts. It just registered a series of pulses sweeping over us. Although our instruments are too crude to confirm it, I am sure that we have been swept by two separate sets of pulses. A computer in the *Crucible* will have already integrated both sets to pinpoint the location of the Scout. We can expect a strike force from Harriman in less than a minute."

"That explains the evacuation. Why are we hanging around?"

"I am remaining because I wish to see how the rest of the plan works," Benedict said. "You are staying because I cannot see without your eyes. Dr. D'Argent favors us with his company because he trusts neither of us and wishes to be able to open our jugular veins quickly should we wish to betray his people to Harriman."

"Oh."

"In the meantime," D'Argent said, "it would be well to conduct our reconnaissance from deeper in the reef. From here, we can be too easily spotted and captured. Or is that your plan?"

"It is neither my plan nor Harriman's," Benedict said evenly. "He did not go to all this effort in getting you outside the *Crucible* in order to round you up again. You eat too much, take too much manpower to guard, and too much electrical power to keep in cold sleep."

"Disadvantages easily dealt with by our deaths," D'Argent replied.

"There is always that," Benedict said surprisingly. "But we cannot run fast enough to get beyond the blast radius of an antimatter bomb. Where is Harriman? They must be more disorganized than I thought."

It was more than two minutes later that the overhead canopy was shattered by a Scout plunging out of the sky. Last-second deceleration brought it to a motionless hover just above the grounded Scout. A wave front of displaced air rushed out to the edges of the clearing and brushed by Shoshone an instant later. She shook her head with admiration for the pilot. Her shoulder muscles were still tensed for the impact.

Broken branches cartwheeled lazily down into the clearing as a bottom hatch opened in the hovering Scout. There was a flash of momentarily captured sunlight as silver figures leapt directly into the open hatch beneath them.

"Full armor," D'Argent said. He muttered a curse.

"Irrelevant," Benedict said.

"What is this plan I am supposed to watch unfolding?" Shoshone asked.

"Harriman's attempt to retake the Scout," Benedict answered. "In which, he hopes, are the missing optical circuit boards."

"Are they?"

"No. That is the one place I have told D'Argent he must not keep them."

"So Harriman gets only half a loaf?"

"If Stellato and Gerard do their jobs, he gets nothing."

It took her a second to realize what he meant. "Stellato is in there?" Her voice went high.

"Why should that concern you?" D'Argent asked.

"Because he's—he's a good friend," she said, unaccountably confused by the question. She felt her face heating. "He has been a good partner to have at my side the times we've worked together. He also went out of his way to protect me from someone named Morgenstern who was questioning my genetic right to exist. He deserves better than to be sent up against assault lasers."

D'Argent was silent.

"Maybe you believe all your own propaganda," Shoshone continued, "but the fact is that not all Norms are bloodthirsty. We can care about your people just as much as about our own."

"I do believe you," D'Argent said. "That is the problem."

"His danger is minimal," Benedict said. "Visualize the interior of a Scout, Cramped space, short, narrow passages leading forward to the cockpit, aft to storage. Those assault lasers may be able to vaporize a human being, but they can also do serious damage to the inside of a Scout. Unless Harriman is a complete fool, he has ordered his team to use the lowest power settings and to fire only if necessary.

"And you should know, Shoshone, how awkward it can be to carry an assault laser in a confined space. They will be pointing the barrels straight in front of them as they enter the unlighted cockpit. Hands will grab the lasers and disable their owners before they know what has happened to them."

"Unless Stellato gets fried first."

Benedict shook his head. "Bestials"—his mouth seemed to caress the word—"have faster reflexes and are much stronger than Norms. One on one there is no contest. That is why, whenever I have been at cross-purposes, shall we say, with the Clans, I always cheat."

D'Argent grunted.

"Nothing seems to be happening," Shoshone said nervously.

"Harriman should be getting quite frantic by now," Benedict said, a beatific smile lighting his face. "His plan hinged on taking us by surprise. That having failed, I imagine he is at quite a loss. He doesn't dare send in another assault team until he is sure what happened to the first one.

"Neuronic shockers, stunners, knockout gas . . . any of a dozen simple crowd-control tools would have more than sufficed to disable any of our defenders and take control of the Scout. However, the plotters who stocked the armory clearly considered nonlethal weapons to be useless concessions to squeamishness."

The minutes stretched out. Abruptly, the attacking Scout lifted and vanished through the canopy.

"Good," Benedict said when Shoshone told him. "Let us go and claim our prizes."

XIX

THE PRIZES WERE NAMED FITZWILLIAM KIM AND MOHAMED Nujoma. Both limped as they walked. Livid bruises on cheeks and collarbones hinted at the reasons. Herald and Gerald stood just behind them, within easy arm reach.

"Please be seated," Benedict invited, himself cross-legged. He indicated the space in front of him. D'Argent towered over him in a patch of shadow only intermittently invaded by dapplings of sunlight with the rocking of the trees. "I wish we could offer you more in the way of hospitality than cold water, but our circumstances are constrained. You have not been ill treated, I trust?"

"Ill treat the two largest available sources of nourishing protein on planet?" Herald muttered. "I should think not."

Kim paled and stumbled. Nujoma nearly succeeded in keeping the quaver out of his voice as he spoke, his eyes shifting nervously between Benedict and D'Argent.

"I argued with those who spread rumors about Gen savagery and blood lust. I told them they were reviving old Defenders of Humanity lies, that our experience working with them should convince us of the truth. I regret that I was wrong."

Benedict's laugh was low and, to Shoshone's ears, unforced. "You were right, and we are quite properly corrected. We have just a few questions—"

"You can't make us talk," Kim interrupted.

"Don't be too sure," D'Argent rumbled.

"There will be no coercion," Benedict said. "I would think, however, that you would want to explain why you have attacked your shipmates with weapons the mere possession of which is illegal to all but members of the armed forces."

"We did not attack anyone," Kim said hotly. "It was all the

135

other way around. We were trying to get back a Scout which is vital to getting the *Crucible* powered up again when your goons jumped us.''

''A mere misunderstanding, then,'' Benedict said. ''We can remedy everything by crowding everyone into the Scout and flying it to its berth in the shuttle bay.''

''You . . . cannot be let on board until a treatment is found for the plague,'' Nujoma said, watching Benedict very carefully.

D'Argent grunted.

''Tell us about this plague,'' Benedict said after a pause. ''What exactly are the symptoms? Who has come down with it?''

''Gens seem to be the main carrier,'' Nujoma said. ''I don't have a list of everyone who has come down with it, but Captain Nickerson is definitely the most important victim.

''As for symptoms, there seems to be a short period of violent irrationality, possibly coupled with hallucinations, followed by coma. We have lost two crewmen, Krenz and Zolotas, to someone who forced his way into the armory and started blazing away with an assault laser.''

Shoshone cleared her throat. ''That was me,'' she said.

Nujoma turned his gaze to her, the whites of his eyes startling against the brown of the pupils and the brown of his face.

''I lost my way while looking for material for Lumbongo,'' she continued. ''I had reason to believe they were going to burn me to keep me quiet about what I found in the armory. I may have been right or wrong about that, but it wasn't caused by any plague.''

Kim cursed under his breath. ''And to think we were supposed to risk our lives to rescue you, if possible.''

''It would take only a few hours for us to show you the entire group of Gens out here,'' Benedict said. ''You may see some traces of hunger, but you will see none of the symptoms you have enumerated.''

''That makes it worse, you know,'' Kim said abruptly, as if surprised at his own daring. ''If there is no plague, then the other rumors must be true. Captain Nickerson was poisoned in an attempted coup, which the first officer nipped by forcing the ringleaders out of the ship.''

''Clever,'' D'Argent commented. ''Harriman has two stories floating around so that whatever he cannot justify under one, he can justify under the other.''

Benedict shook his head. "Not clever at all. He would do much better to choose one lie and stick to it. This shows a basic indecisiveness. Is he trying to put down a mutiny or deal with a health problem? It is only a matter of time until some of his supporters notice that his actions are consistent with neither scenario."

"What happens now?" Nujoma asked.

"You will both give your parole not to take up arms again against any Gens crewmates. Then we will escort you to that part of the reef nearest the *Crucible*. If you are lucky, Harriman lets you in."

"*What!*" D'Argent's voice was scarcely above a whisper. It was as if outrage had taken his voice away. "You would just take their word and let them go?"

"Certainly," Benedict said placidly. "We have no reason to doubt their honor. And we have nothing to lose even if we are wrong. As I think you would hasten to point out, it would take manpower we do not have to guard them and food we do not have to feed them. So we strip them of their armor and send them back. After they have seen that there is no plague, that their crewmates have been exiled without cause."

"I suppose," Nujoma said, attempting a smile, "that the alternative to giving parole is to be converted into protein supplement."

Benedict shrugged, a smile on his face.

"You have my word," Nujoma said. "No more will I bear arms against Gens of the starship *Crucible*."

"Harriman won't stand for this, you know." Kim's voice cracked into shrillness. "You brutalized the two of us in the course of our lawful attempt to prevent your theft of that Scout. Since then you have been attempting to terrorize us. Harriman will make you answer for this treatment."

"Your treatment will speak for itself when you reappear unharmed in the *Crucible*. As for how much the first officer will care about it . . . You do know why you were chosen for this assault, don't you?"

Kim glared at him without speaking.

"You must already suspect that Mr. Nujoma was chosen because of his Gens leanings," Benedict said. "If he succeeded, he would prove himself both loyal and useful. But if he became a casualty, Harriman would count him no great loss."

"My loyalties have never been in doubt," Kim snapped.

"Quite so. On the other hand, your position is in Timakata's astronomy section. Your specialty, as I remember it, is subjovian gas giants."

"That is correct."

"An area of expertise for which the first officer will have no pressing need in the foreseeable future. So, you see, you and Mr. Nujoma have your most crucial quality in common, after all. You are both expendable."

There was a quiver in Kim's jaw, quickly stilled.

"Blindfold them and take them to the *Crucible*," D'Argent ordered. He faced Kim and Nujoma. "Whether Harriman lets you in is his problem. If you starve, you starve. But if you come back into the reef looking for us, we will kill you."

"If you are allowed back on board, ask the first officer to check the suppressor field generators," Benedict suggested. "He may wish to consult with us on what he finds there."

After they were led away, D'Argent stood for a minute, regarding Benedict. "It won't work, you know. Harriman won't let them back in, so those seeds of dissension and doubt you were so artfully sowing will never have a chance to flower."

Benedict shrugged. "He may risk inconsistency with his supposed fear of plague in order to find out what they have learned from us. Or he may not. Did you know that most stratagems fail? The success rate is comparable to that of predator attacks: about one in ten. Military historians tend to be romantics. They concentrate on the brilliant set piece battles of a Napoleon, or a Rommel, or a Wu. They rarely note that most battles, most wars, for that matter, are decided like a boxing match between two punch-drunk fighters, with the victor nothing more than the one who collapsed second."

"Present company excepted, of course." D'Argent's voice was edged steel in velvet.

"Not at all," Benedict said seriously. "During my brief stint as Sky Marshal I had no intention of laying siege to the Clanworlds or destroying their fleet. All I hoped to do was to keep the Allied fleet from being destroyed by your forces. Because I succeeded, there was a treaty."

"How far you have fallen."

"Yes." Benedict's tone was thoughtful. "It had been my intention to study living worlds, to puzzle out their everchanging balances, to learn how to heal damaged ecosystems. Instead, I find myself among ghosts refighting a war that was over years ago.

"But the strategy remains what it was: conserve my forces and give my enemy every opportunity to make a mistake."

"That lack of aggression is why I am the leader and you are the gadfly," D'Argent said. "If we wait for mistakes, we shall be dead of deficiency diseases."

Benedict shook his head. "Harriman has already made his mistakes. The only question is how soon it will take him to realize their extent."

"Stellato!"

Stellato looked up, surprised by her shout. Benedict, beside her, was deep in a discussion with Herald concerning how they might get work crews beneath the surface of the water to examine the underside of the reef. It did not appear he would need her for some time.

She excused herself with a few words and ran along the bracing root to the edge of the clearing. Stellato waited, a curious smile on his face.

Shoshone stopped a meter from him, suddenly self-conscious. "I was afraid you might have been hurt," she said.

"Why?"

"Why what?"

"Why were you afraid?"

"Because—well, I didn't want to lose my protector against goons like Morgenstern. Or the best partner I've ever worked with." The last words came in a rush. She felt her face heating as if she had said something shameful.

Stellato stood still for just an instant more, an infuriating smirk on his face. "Partner, huh? I'll have to think about that proposal." Before she could get angry with him, he had grabbed her and brought her mouth up to his.

"That—" Shoshone gasped. Her hand went to her lips. "*Itches!*"

Stellato gave her a rueful look. "Battle holds no terrors for Gens. Impending starvation we can bear stoically. But if we can't groom, we may as well be dead."

Shoshone frowned, chasing a memory. "All those clippers and curling irons in Rebekka's room . . ."

"Any one of us would kill for them now," Stellato said. "You don't understand why? Let me see. When you had biology, or life science, or whatever it was called in your edu-packets, do you remember seeing pictures of the Terrestrial species called chimpanzees?''

"Yes, because they are humanity's closest relatives in the animal world.''

"Do you remember how they looked?'' Stellato stared at her intently.

"Not particularly. They were small, I remember that. Sort of hunched over, hairy—''

"Ragged, ratty hair, which they have to groom constantly to keep from being overrun with lice. Hair everywhere except the face, the ears, and each side of the butt, as if they had been designed to be props of an off-color joke. Just like us. That is why personal hygiene, grooming, deodorants, and polish are so important. Our natural state can stand a good deal of polish.''

"Oh,'' Shoshone said in a small voice. "I was not criticizing. I was just—noting a sensation which may take some getting used to.''

Stellato's face underwent several changes of expression as he considered the ramifications of her response. "Well. Maybe I was just exercising our inferiority complex again. At least I don't turn it into a religion like our fearless self-appointed leader does.''

"What do you mean?''

"That's the real reason he and Father Benedict don't get along. They're direct competitors. D'Argent is ordained, believe it or not, in the Church of Evolutionary Advancement. There are similar sects throughout the Periphery: The Fellowship of the Next Step, the Spencerians, the *Homo Superior* Society—which we always called the society of superior homos. Sorry, bad joke.''

Shoshone laughed. When next she looked at her watch, she was astonished to find that what seemed a few minutes conversation had consumed an hour. She excused herself and hurried back to Benedict.

As she turned, a shadowed figure in the gently moving depths of the reef stepped behind a trunk, but not before Shoshone saw him. It took her a few seconds to recall the name. Morgenstern.

But he was keeping his distance, at least. Maybe he had learned his lesson from Stellato. She dismissed him from her mind.

XX

SHOSHONE WOKE TO FIND HER HEAD HALF OVER THE ROUNDED top edge of the bracing root. Small gusts from the depths chilled her brow. Level below level of twisting branches and writhing vines, more intricate than any wiring conduit she had ever had to straighten out, bewildered her eyes until they vanished beneath the crest and recession of waves' surfaces. Reflected sunlight strobed the veinlike structure across the inside of her eyeballs.

She pushed herself up to a sitting position. Her head throbbed as if it were being pulled apart. Air rasped through a dry throat; all her nasal passages seemed to be stuffed with rubber. Distantly, she wondered if allergies could be fatal.

Even though the sun was now halfway up in the sky, sending shifting shafts of warmth deep into the reef, Shoshone shivered, huddling within her Steward's robes until the fit passed. Despite the discoveries of the foraging parties and the ingenuity of the cooks, there was still little that was nourishing or, except for the water, even filling. The Scout's emergency rations—as well as those stripped from Kim and Nujoma—were added in almost infinitesimal increments to all meals but, even so, were almost half-gone.

As she approached the new, more sheltered cook fire, she saw Benedict sidle around a trunk and hold a hand stiffly out in front of him, feeling for obstructions. She hurried over to him.

"You are a mess," she said, straightening his robes and pulling his hood up to cover his nearly bald head. "Everyone here is looking to you to save our hides, but if they see you the way you look now, they may just curl up their toes and die. And if you don't know enough to ask to someone to guide you, you'll slip and kill yourself."

Benedict bore her attentions without complaint. "Are you uncertain?" he asked curiously. "Your voice trembles with doubt." He sounded as congested as she was, but it did not appear to bother him.

"What you hear is a combination of phlegm and frustration," Shoshone said. "And cold and hunger, and maybe a little impatience for you to live up to your brilliant reputation."

She realized she was being unfair as soon as she said it. The worst that could be said against Benedict was that for all the right reasons he had chosen the losing side. Given the disparity in resources, there was nothing anyone could do. Except, as Benedict had said, wait for Harriman to make a mistake.

"They have been calling for eight hours," Benedict said, apparently changing the subject.

"Who?"

"Harriman. His communications officers. They have been hailing us over the Scout comm-link for the last eight hours. They seem quite eager for a parley."

"What is our answer?"

"No answer. I don't want them to know for sure that that comm-link is operational, much less who we have inside. It might make another assault just too tempting to pass up."

Shoshone helped him seat himself near the fire. Catch of the day was a revolting gelatinous mass, which Shoshone forced down piecemeal. Benedict ate daintily as a cat, showing no signs of distress. His allergies, she thought, must have completely destroyed his sense of taste.

"Every one of those communications specifically asked for parley with me." Shoshone had not heard D'Argent come up behind her. She hoped no one noticed how she had jumped at his voice. "Why do you suppose that is, Fox? After all, I'm not even senior civilian."

"The reason is that the last thing Harriman wants is to deal with me," Benedict said promptly.

"He won't deal with either of you if you don't respond to his message," Shoshone noted. "Why the coy act? I thought you wanted him to negotiate?"

"When we talk," D'Argent said, "it must be on our terms."

"Do you know why they are calling?"

D'Argent's lips drew back from his teeth in a very disconcerting smile. The incisors seemed extraordinarily sharp. "It started less than an hour after my observers reported Kim and

Nujoma entering a *Crucible* air lock. I would guess that the first officer has discovered he is missing some optical switching boards.''

"D'Argent." The voice of God thundering through the reef. *"Jean D'Argent. Come to the* Crucible. *I can aid you. And your people."*

"That's it!" D'Argent said, ears twitching as he looked up.

Not the voice of God, Shoshone thought; just the highly amplified voice of First Officer Harriman, reproduced with such fidelity that even his hoarseness was perfectly clear. Could he be nervous? she wondered.

"So now you trek over to that canal the *Crucible* is smashing through the reef?" she asked.

"Use your head," Benedict said. "That would in some ways be more unsuitable than the Scout comm-link, and for the same reason. No, we shall use the vantage point you discovered. D'Argent will climb until he has line of sight with the *Crucible*. As soon as they spot him, they can focus exterior microphones on him. Resident programs will have no difficulty deleting wind sounds."

Shoshone gazed upward along the trunk. "The assault laser I had . . ." she began hesitantly.

"Would have no difficulty picking off a target like that," Benedict said, finishing her thoughts. "Quite right. I have offered to conduct negotiations myself in order that our leader not be exposed."

"That would send two messages I would not care for," D'Argent said. "To Harriman you would appear to be our leader. To my own people I would appear to be sending a blind priest into a situation I was too fearful to deal with myself. My authority would be undercut two ways at once."

"Of course," Benedict said thoughtfully, "it could be that I suggested going up only to make sure you would forbid it and go yourself."

Shoshone glared at him. This is a very dangerous and angry man, she thought, hoping that intensity would translate itself into telepathy. Don't play your games with him!

"I considered that," D'Argent replied. "I will trust my safety to the antimatter bomb your assistant saw. If Harriman merely intended to kill us, he would not have to get us in his sights.

"Of course, I would not be so vain as to think I could match wits with Grandfather Fox. So instead of going into an infinite progression of what you would think I would think you would think, I just decided to do what seemed best to me. I will ascend, but you will go with me, staying just out of sight. I am not so insecure in my position that I will deny myself the benefit of the most devious mind in the Periphery. I will just keep my own judgment about how much of your advice to follow.

"Those most loyal to me will stay at this level directly beneath us. Two of them will have the assault lasers we took from Nujoma and Kim. Both will be trained on you. Should anything happen to me, they will fire immediately."

He paused, letting them consider his words. "Now, would you like to revise your advice in any way?"

"No," Benedict said immediately. "Lead on."

At D'Argent's hand signal, Gens converged around them. If it had not been for the assault lasers, the whole procession would have looked ludicrous to Shoshone. Especially once they started climbing. What had been so easy only a little while earlier by herself was definitely laborious now that she had to guide Benedict's hands and feet to every hold. D'Argent leapt from branch to branch, devouring the tree in giant strides.

It took them perhaps three minutes to catch up with him. As soon as she caught her breath, the absurdity of their appearance struck her afresh. In the holovids of her childhood, confrontations invariably occurred on the bridges of starcruisers or in palatial office suites perched atop kilometer-high buildings. Not clinging awkwardly to the side of a tree, hoping to be noticed.

D'Argent stepped out from the trunk, extending his arm until only his fingertips touched. Then the arm dropped to his side.

The wind was nearly constant, a gale occasionally interrupted for no more than two or three seconds, as if the sky were taking a hurried breath. Trunk and limbs, however, moved to an offbeat syncopation imposed by the interaction of the waves below the surface of the reef. This high up, Shoshone clung with both arms, afraid that a moment's inattention would result in being flung into the air.

Yet D'Argent moved along the branch with perfect balance, looking so ridiculously heroic as the wind blew back his mane that Shoshone did not know whether to laugh or cry. This was breathtaking daring carried off with perfect poise. For the first time she could step away from her own feelings of intimidation far enough to understand why D'Argent commanded such respect and loyalty among the Gens.

"Jean D'Argent. Come to the Crucible. There are misapprehensions which must be cleared up . . ."

Each word was almost painfully loud, as if Harriman had decided they must not have heard the previous entreaties and so had turned the volume up. There was a rustle of panicked movement with each word. Tree snakes, sixers, and other half-seen creatures for which Shoshone had no name ran or jumped randomly to escape the painful assaults of compression and rarefaction.

"I think," D'Argent said, "that we can discuss everything needful from this vantage." His voice was loud and forceful but not shouting.

"D'Argent, where . . . is that? Dr. D'Argent, come down closer to the Crucible. We are having trouble hearing you."

"Then turn up the gain on your zoom mikes. You should be able to hear my every word with no difficulty."

"Uh, Dr. D'Argent. We have supplies we wish to transfer to sustain your people while we work on a way to contain the plague."

"He has an audience," Benedict said urgently. He was counting on his location on the side of the trunk opposite D'Argent and his voice projecting up and away from the *Crucible* to allow him to advise D'Argent without being overheard. "We know there is no plague, so he is not playing to us but to some other listeners he feels he must convince."

"Two watches ago you transferred battle armor and assault lasers to us," D'Argent said, referring to the items confiscated from Kim and Nujoma. "The memory makes us wary."

There was static, then a sudden cessation of even the background noise. For an instant Shoshone feared the conversation was at an end.

"We believe Stellato broke into the Crucible and stole components vital to the suppressor fields, probably at the instigation of the Rénard, Father Benedict. Without them, none of us will ever get back within the Periphery."

"You could have asked," D'Argent suggested.

"Perhaps . . . a mistake was made." To Shoshone, it sounded as if the concession had been ripped out of Harriman's chest. *"The plague induces violent hallucinations. Nujoma*

and Kim confirmed this before we put them in isolation. That is why we wished to protect them.''

"As you well know," D'Argent began, "there is no plague. We were tricked out of the *Crucible* so you could carry off your coup unopposed. You have quarantined Kim and Nujoma because you don't want them spreading the story that all they saw among us were the effects of cold and hunger."

"Plague is the most charitable interpretation I can put on acts which would otherwise be mutiny! Returning the optical switches will be considered evidence that the disease has run its course and you can be admitted to the ship for further observation.''

"It is not only becoming your prisoners which makes that unattractive. The Wartime Emergencies Act, making mutiny a capital crime, has never been rescinded, to my knowledge. Submission to your authority might be considered taking part in the mutiny.

"By the way, I trust Captain Nickerson is in good health? That may mitigate your sentence to some extent. Engineer Mantei was speaking with the captain when she fell victim to the drugs you put in her food. She was in the next room when you and your stooge entered the captain's quarters to make sure she had succumbed. She will testify—"

A series of sharp sounds cut him off. Shouts, Shoshone thought; she could not make out any words. Maybe a scuffle. Then silence as the speakers cut out again.

They came on again almost immediately. Heavy breathing was nearly as loud as the gusting wind. Harriman's voice had a definite tremor, though whether from exertion, anger, or some other emotion, Shoshone could not tell.

"No more need for games, D'Argent. I know you were planning to take over the ship, relying on the Rénard to prevent Nickerson from opposing you until it would be too late. I know that you have tampered with the programming of the cold-sleep cubicles to prevent the resuscitation of key crew members. You think that possession of the Scout and the optical switches gives you enough bargaining power that I should set you free to be about your plots again.

"Hear me: I have three antimatter bombs at my disposal. Any one of them can obliterate all of you completely. You could run for an entire watch without getting beyond its range. If I cannot have the resources you have stolen, cannot have you under my

command, I can at least be rid of the danger you represent. You have three hours for consideration. At the end of that time one antimatter bomb will be launched and detonated.''

Shoshone felt a hollowness at the pit of her stomach. "He must be bluffing," she said desperately. "He can't afford to lose both the Scout and the optical switches. And exploding an antimatter bomb this close would have to damage the *Crucible* itself."

"For a man with Harriman's military training, it should be an easy matter to set the impact point sufficiently beyond us so that we are incinerated but the craft is not damaged," Benedict said. "It is a battlestar, after all. In any event, we had better hope he is *not* bluffing.

"D'Argent, tell Harriman he must not put the bomb in the launch tube. A Scout should carry the bomb off to a safe distance and not begin the detonation sequence until it is beyond the destruction radius."

"Who is with you? Is it the Rénard?"

D'Argent stared down at Benedict. "Why should he do a thing like that?"

"Because all the antimatter bombs are set to detonate less than a kilometer beyond the tubes once they are armed. Close enough to ensure everyone inside the *Crucible* is killed. Now tell him!"

D'Argent did so. There was no response from Harriman. The speakers had gone silent again.

"Even if you are correct," D'Argent said after a few minutes, "it will be a simple matter to correct the software codes."

"The change will be hardwired," Benedict said. "Harriman will know that there is no point in sabotage which will be disclosed by a simple safety program."

"How did you arrange that, Fox?" D'Argent asked. "Why did you arrange it?"

"I had no idea the bombs had been smuggled aboard. But when Shoshone told me of them, I realized there could be only one use for an antimatter bomb on this expedition. That would be to destroy the *Crucible* itself."

After a few more minutes Shoshone began to wonder how long they would wait. Superhuman endurance was all very well for D'Argent, but her thighs and calves were beginning to ache. She looked up at D'Argent, intending to ask him if he had seen a Scout leave the *Crucible*.

White brilliance flooded the sky, turning trunks and limbs and flesh to insubstantial matchstick silhouettes. Above her, a blot of darkness leaned and fell through a galaxy of retinal feedback. Shoshone's arm shot out. Claws caught and dug, then furrowed down her forearm as she felt herself being pulled away from the trunk.

An arm wrapped itself around her waist. She slipped slowly to the side. Then the pressure eased. The claws withdrew from her flesh.

"Climb down as far as you can." Benedict's voice was surprisingly close to her ear. "We may have thirty seconds before the shock wave hits."

To her surprise, Shoshone could remember the sequence of limbs and knobs she had used as holds on the way up. But then, the first few meters down were easy, along the parallel limbs that formed the spars of the living sails. Only lower, where the sunlight reached intermittently and the limbs had withered to dry, skeleton branches, often broken off, leaving only knobs behind, did the holds become more irregular and treacherous.

She was moving from a branch ready to snap to a knob that felt to her booted foot slippery as melting ice, when she heard a sound like approaching rocket engines.

"Hold tight!" Benedict yelled.

It was not a sound but a blow that slammed into the trunk, pushing it over so that it was nearly horizontal. The force released, and the trunk seemed to become an enraged animal, trying to throw her off as it whipped back. Branches snapped like firecrackers. They soared through the air in lazy arcs, twirling slowly on their way down. Shoshone flattened herself against the trunk. Giant's fingers tapped her shoulders and brushed down her back.

That was when she realized her sight had returned.

She guided Benedict the rest of the way down. The reef was heaving as if in agony. Wave crests surged through the upper levels of the reef, flashing golden as they broke into the sunlight. Shoshone watched, almost hypnotized, as the reef lifted into foam and surged over her. For an instant she floated, holding her breath. Then the waters fell away, and she was facedown in a tangle of vines. Only meters below her, the sea roared like lions.

A hand clamped around her ankle and drew her effortlessly up. She was deposited, gasping, on a seesawing bracing root.

She looked around for her rescuer and found herself staring at D'Argent. His eyes dropped to her forearm. Her own gaze followed them. For a moment she could not remember why the salts in the water should make it hurt so. Blood oozed to the surface and spread until it was like a liquid layer of skin.

"That was an unforgivable loss of control," D'Argent said.

"I put out my arm so that you could grab it," Shoshone protested. "You would have fallen to your death if you hadn't grabbed it."

"Death should not matter so much," D'Argent said.

"What about Benedict?" Shoshone asked suddenly.

They found him still clinging to the trunk. It was water-darkened nearly two meters above him. "Perhaps," he suggested, attempting a smile, "I erred in telling you to descend."

Thinking of how the tree had nearly thrown them off, Shoshone murmured a negative.

One by one the other Gens made their way from where waves and reef had tossed them. There was one broken leg and a dislocated shoulder. D'Argent insisted that Shoshone have nu-skin sprayed on her wounds before anyone else was treated.

"*Rénard.*" Harriman's voice, hoarse and curiously flat, seemed to be coming from a new direction. "*We must know what other traps have been set for us.*"

Morgenstern's eyes flickered from D'Argent to Benedict and back again.

"I am afraid," Benedict said, his voice shaking slightly, "that I am not immediately up to making that climb again."

"I don't believe you will have to," Shoshone replied.

All around them the reef was still shrugging with the waves, shifting itself into new configurations. Debris hung thickly on the lower branches. Cracks and crashes sounded in the distance.

"My guess is a lot of the intervening foliage has been suddenly cleared." She stepped up the tree to see if she was correct, but the trunk was still water-smooth, and her right arm refused to bear weight.

"Fox," D'Argent said, "clasp your hands together around my neck, like—so." He swung up lightly, as if Benedict were no more than a cloak about his shoulders.

"*Was it Mantei? Did you send her to the armory to sabotage the bomb?*"

Benedict's voice was surprisingly high and thin. Wind whipped the words away.

". . . Mantei could not . . ." Shoshone heard. ". . . was done . . . first smuggled on board . . ."

"Why?"

". . . to be used," Benedict said. ". . . supposed to fail . . . leave only wreckage . . . Both sides would point . . . Hatred . . ."

Benedict fell silent. There was no response from the *Crucible*. After a few minutes D'Argent descended with Benedict. The Gens' leader was taking huge controlled gulps of air. Benedict leaned against the trunk as if gathering his strength.

"Was it true what you said about Harriman?" D'Argent asked. His eyes were wide with something like fear.

Benedict nodded. "It's all in his record. The time as second officer on the battlestar *Invincible*, the ostensible reason for choosing him for this expedition, is real enough. But the real reason had more to do with the time in the internment camps, the charges of mistreatment . . . And the years before the war, when his byline appeared in dozens of the on-line-zines subsidized by the Defenders of Humanity. The topics of his articles ranged from the monsters supposedly created by genetic manipulation to threats to employment posed by the Gens."

"He was chosen because he was a bigot," D'Argent said.

"Assuredly."

"And the rest of us?"

Benedict shrugged. "Look around you. Every one of the Gens on board either distinguished himself in or was greatly hurt by the war. You can work out the odds against that happening naturally."

"And that was why I was chosen?"

"That . . . and because you hate greatly. You could be counted on to set the self-destruct sequence in motion even if Harriman did not."

XXI

Two flurries of panic disrupted the rest of the morning. The first occurred when a roster check disclosed the absence of a Gen named Vangard. Vangard, it so happened, was the repository of the optical switches.

D'Argent organized search parties. In less than an hour Vangard was discovered, stunned and half-drowned, in a layer of reef less than a meter above the wave crests. The optical switches were in a pouch securely fastened about his waist.

It was while searching for him that they realized that the Scout was missing.

Fortunately, it had left an obvious trail: a large vertical hole edged by broken branches. But, Shoshone realized, it would not have been obvious in another watch. Even as they descended, the trees shifted and the branches closed in. In a few hours it would be almost impossible to tell there had ever been a gap.

The network of vines and branches ended two meters above the water. The current sped quickly beneath them. The Scout, Shoshone thought, should be buoyant, but given the amount of time since the explosion of the antimatter bomb, the craft could be kilometers away by now.

The searchers spread carefully across this living ceiling. In the half-light Shoshone found herself reminded of Romanesque arches in old, very old, churches. She stepped cautiously. Nearly everything was dead and brittle this far down. Moreover, the waves caused by the explosion had splintered many of the branches. Each step threatened to extend itself down to the water.

A shout came from one side. Shoshone moved as quickly as she could with Benedict, but they were among the last to converge above either of the two trunks between which the Scout had wedged itself. A wave formed beneath one curved surface as the current tried to push its prize free. The trunks twisted slowly, one way and then the other, trying to accommodate the strain.

Stellato dropped onto the hull and rolled as it bobbed beneath his weight. He spread-eagled to stop himself, then sidled along the upper surface to the open lock. He let himself fall into the lock and disappeared. Less than a minute later Shoshone felt a familiar subsonic hum vibrate her joints. The wave subsided as the Scout lifted itself above the water and away from the trunks. Stellato reappeared at the open hatch.

"I can fly this back-up, but given the present state of the reef, I can't promise that it won't fall through again."

"Don't bother," Benedict suggested. "This is the level which requires our exploration now. Furthermore," he continued as objections began to erupt around him, "it will be that much more difficult for Harriman to attack us here. Scout Five taught us that he can't come at us from below. Although he could smash through the vegetation above us, I think he would have a next to impossible time deploying troops in this sort of growth."

What Benedict meant by exploration at that level did not become obvious until after the midwatch meal. The battle armor that had been stripped from Kim and Nujoma was found to fit Rebekka and Herald. Benedict proposed that it be used for diving gear.

"Uh, are these suits buoyant?" Herald asked.

"The armor makes them too heavy to float," Benedict admitted. "You will find that this makes working underwater much easier. Ask Shoshone: The buoyancy of her pressure suit made her work in the flooded portions of the *Crucible* extremely awkward."

"But if we were to fall off the reef . . . ." Herald said uncertainly.

"You would keep on falling," Benedict agreed. "You will be secured with lines to prevent that."

"We are going after those dots we saw on sonar," Rebekka guessed.

Benedict smiled, pleased. "You will observe and report on all aspects of the submarine reef structure," he corrected gently. "However, if you can descend that far, I will be very interested if you can locate whatever it is that is hard enough to return such a bright echo but still buoyant enough to float when cut loose from the vines holding it. It could be very important."

"Unless it's edible," Gerard muttered, "nothing can be that important."

Shoshone listened to their discussion while lying atop the Scout. It was much easier than the perpetual balancing act in the overhead foliage. The slowly rippling reef ceiling held in much of the heat expelled by the hot water plume and for the first time since leaving the *Crucible*, Shoshone was not cold. Muscle knots she had not known she had relaxed in the moist warmth. Blood had begun to seep from the edges of the nu-skin. Seeing it, Stellato began to fuss about her in a most agreeable way, redoing the dressing and fetching her food and water so she would not have to exert herself.

It was more of a relief than she cared to admit that Stellato had not been selected to make the descent. Anything that dissolved the hull of a Scout could make short work of safety lines.

Benedict and D'Argent were coming to a compromise concerning the assault lasers. Rebekka and Herald would have one between them to cut off samples of the lower reef. The other would stay above in the event Harriman launched another attack.

"Speaking of that possibility," D'Argent said, "I think we should have someone up above to keep watch on the *Crucible* and any Scouts it might send out."

There was a murmur of assent.

"Then I nominate Mantei for first watch. She's not a member of the survey team, so she is easily spared. And in the event she were captured by Harriman, he would be more constrained in his treatment of her than he would be of us."

"Her arm is still bleeding," Stellato protested.

"Pipe down," Shoshone said without rancor. "If Father Benedict can do without me for a few hours, I can make myself useful this way. I can certainly lie in a tree for a few hours without hurting myself."

Benedict, surrounded by Gens, assured her that he would be able to cope. D'Argent gave Shoshone a light radio headset.

"Anything you broadcast will be in the clear and almost certainly monitored by the *Crucible*. So call in only when you have something of immediate interest."

Gerard, piloting the Scout, lifted her up the side of the nearest trunk. "I'm going to match its surge on the next wave," he said through the open hatch. "Wait . . . now!"

Shoshone hopped easily to the trunk, grabbed a limb, and began to climb. Limbs sprouted more thickly as she approached the ceiling, imperceptibly becoming a thicket around her as she continued to ascend. Wind whistled through odd pathways. The sound joined with the rush of water below and the creak of interlocking branches. The murmuring voices below her were lost in it.

She paused every three minutes or so to catch her breath. The breeze was already noticeably colder. Sweat cooled on her forehead and shoulders. During her third stop there was a series of sounds—scarcely heard impacts, snaps—that ceased almost as soon as she was aware of them.

She considered that phenomenon, a mental exercise in perceptional psychology, as she resumed her ascent. In the midst of this natural cacophony, what aural cues caught her attention? Concepts from half-remembered lectures and readings floated across her mind. The eye picks out movement. Eyes and ears both seize on patterns. But so great is the mind's thirst for meaning that it will impose patterns on random sensory data.

The next time she paused, she looked all about her. Foliage swayed to the conflicting rhythms of winds above and waves below. No longer did the mass of moving detail totally bewilder her eye. Creatures no larger than her thumb moved in short columns along the vines, jumping from one to the next when they could. When the distance was too great, their backs seemed to explode in a blue and green metallic blur, and they zipped through the air with quick, erratic movements until they found another place to alight. Sixers hurled themselves frantically from branch to branch, searching for something they never seemed to find. Occasionally the movement of the main trees would open a gap, and a broken limb would be released to crash into the depths, sending sixers and all manner of unnamed creatures scattering out of its way.

But there was nothing Shoshone could relate to the sounds that had caught her attention.

The thicket thinned, and she recognized that she had emerged at the level they had somewhat arbitrarily designated the surface of the reef. The tip of the trunk she had been climbing burst into leaf less than three meters above her, long, living tassels streaming in the wind like kite tails. Shoshone looked around. Almost directly behind her three sail trees towered above the rest of the reef. She scanned the intervening space, constructing in her mind a zigzag path across interlocking bracing limbs that would end at the nearest sail tree.

She trotted the first part of the course, feeling the vibration her stride set up in the branch beneath her feet, conscious of the slow turning that would cause her to slip and fall unless she compensated for it.

In the corner of her eye, below her, she saw a rippling movement of shadow.

She dropped down to the branch that crossed beneath and increased her pace. Another branch, nearly as thick as she was tall, barred her way. She vaulted onto it.

More movement, converging. Closer. Faster. Whatever was pushing those fronds out of the way had to be fairly massive.

It was pretty much a straight run now to the sail tree. Suppose, she wondered, Harriman had decided to try subtlety. Send in troops stealthily, have them pick off the Gens one by one, and subject them to chemical interrogation in order to learn their disposition of forces, their defense plans, the location of the optical switches.

Would it not make sense in that case to pick off the lookouts first of all?

She reached the trunk of the sail tree and pressed her back against it. The huge leaves billowed and snapped above her. Her gaze swept left to right. Fronds bowed and tossed beneath continuous wind waves. Everything seemed natural. Yet the impression of being stalked had been so strong . . .

She switched on her headset. "Shoshone calling. Shoshone calling. I believe I have been tracked ever since emerging from—"

"It does not work."

D'Argent's voice startled her so much that she nearly fell off the bracing limb. He was below her, climbing up the side of the trunk. Hands and feet gouged holds in the spongy surface that took the place of bark in sail trees.

Shoshone let herself go limp with relief. At the same time

she kicked herself for not checking the headset in the first place. D'Argent had had to race all this distance just to make repairs.

He reached the limb on which she was standing, embedded his claws in its side, and swung atop it in one flowing, incredibly strong movement.

"Have you brought a replacement?" she asked, smiling.

"I bring you death."

Silence except for the wind. Shoshone shook her head disbelievingly. "You can't—" She stopped. Obviously he could. "Why? I am not your enemy. *I saved your life!*"

"Yes," D'Argent said heavily. "Through no fault of your own, you are more deadly to us than a hundred Harrimans, than all the Defenders of Humanity put together.

"If you do not resist, I promise you the quick, painless death you deserve. And you cannot resist. I am faster than you, stronger than you, and you are unarmed."

Shoshone watched, almost hypnotized, as he moved slowly closer. Her right hand moved up to her throat protectively. There would have to be three separate movements. She would never live to complete them if he attacked quickly. But if he really regretted having to kill her, if he really believed her defenseless . . .

Her hand dropped inside her robes, grasped the APT clipped to her blouse pocket, and pulled it out, twisting the setting rings to maximum laser setting. D'Argent's hands shot out to strike. But the APT was already sweeping its beam across his eyes.

D'Argent's roar was deafening. His arms pistoned, knocking her aside. She fell off the branch, found the knob of a long broken branch with her hands, and, hanging, miraculously found the nub of another with her toes.

The trunk shuddered with the force of D'Argent's impact. His fists ripped out chunks of spongy bark and tossed them aside. Blind eyes streamed tears as he screamed. Then the screaming stopped, and his head moved jerkily from side to side. Listening. Shoshone opened her mouth wide, trying to breathe without sound.

Something brushed against her fingertips. Looking up, she saw a tree snake, its nearest end tapping the trunk beneath it in perplexity.

D'Argent snuffled, lifting his snout to catch the breeze. Shoshone realized suddenly that she was upwind of him. His arm slashed the air next to her face.

The tree snake, attracted to her warmth, slid slowly over her wrist to her forearm. She tried to relax her arm, to keep it perfectly still.

"You are near," D'Argent muttered. "I can smell you. I can almost hear you. And if you have stayed this close, it must be because you cannot run." He kicked his foot into the bark and stepped off the branch toward her.

The tree snake had completely curled itself about her forearm. Slowly Shoshone lowered the arm until it pointed at D'Argent. The tree snake's serrated grasping surfaces relaxed, not having to fight gravity.

Now, gently . . .

She let her arm fall, then swept it upward, tossing the tree snake. It twisted through the air before falling on D'Argent's face and neck. He grabbed it with his claws and ripped it off. Half his face came with it.

The bleeding tree snake fell away. D'Argent stood for a moment, rocking. His hand extended toward Shoshone, as if for help. Then his knees buckled. Shoshone heard the increasingly distant crash of branches even after he was lost to sight.

When her shaking subsided, she managed to get back on the bracing limb, using the foothold D'Argent had kicked in the bark. She began retracing her path. Halfway across the clearing, she heard shouts. Two figures advanced on her. The nearer was Morgenstern. She sat down to await him.

The last three meters of his approach was almost wary. Shoshone wondered if he was going to attack, then decided she was too weak with reaction to care.

"Are you all right?" Morgenstern asked. "Have you seen Dr. D'Argent?"

"He—" She had to stop and clear her throat. "He just tried to kill me." She saw with relief that Stellato was coming up behind Morgenstern. "I blinded him with my APT, then threw a tree snake at him. He fell."

Morgenstern's face twisted. Stellato pushed past him and knelt at Shoshone's side. His hand brushed her cheek. She flinched away involuntarily. He dropped his hand quickly and picked up her wrist to examine it. She saw, curiously, that it was bleeding from roughly parallel rows of scratches and wondered where they could have come from.

"Is D'Argent dead?" Morgenstern asked urgently.

"I don't know." She gestured behind her. "He fell from that sail tree, the closest one."

Morgenstern reached for his radio, then stopped, looking at Stellato.

Stellato bit his lip. "We can break silence, but just to ask for additional help. Don't say what for. In the meantime, you can search while I get Shoshone back to the Scout."

Morgenstern nodded, then began speaking into the radio. Stellato helped Shoshone to her feet. She protested without much conviction that she did not need his help. On the descent through the reef ceiling she was grateful to have him below her. Just in case.

They had reached the Scout and Shoshone was having her cuts attended to when a stream of bubbles broke the surface of the water. Herald burst from the waves, riding what seemed to be a deep-sea leviathan. Water streamed from its flanks as the current caught it and sent it whirling away.

Watching from the open hatch, Shoshone felt the deck tilt and surge beneath her as the pilot set the Scout on an intercept course. Shoshone saw that the thing Herald was riding seemed to be a huge shell. The Scout came alongside and gently wedged it against a trunk.

Up close, the shell's surface was patterned by raised, swirling ribs. Herald stepped from it onto the Scout, casting off his safety line. He stepped down through the open hatch.

"What do you have?" Stellato asked.

Herald pushed back his helmet, grinning. "I have no idea."

In the distance Rebekka climbed from the water on her own safety line. Already some Gens were making their way to the Scout through the ceiling of branches. Others, impatient or tired of climbing, threw themselves into the water and let the current and the long swell carry them.

Benedict was lowered to the top of the Scout, from which vantage he directed the examination. Despite Stellato's cautions, Shoshone swung herself out so that she could describe the progress to the blind man.

Assault lasers on their lowest settings made precise cuts in the shell wall. Air whistled inward. For all the volume of the shell, the exterior walls were extraordinarily thin. Inside, clean emptiness was divided by curved interior walls. A decaying organic mass outside the largest of the inner chambers had apparently been what had extruded the shell.

Benedict was most interested in what lay at the nether end. Whatever it was, it was heavy enough to hold the rest of the shell upright in the water above it. It was covered with the vines that Herald and Rebekka had burned through to release it. Because the ends of the vines were still oozing the virulent acid that had scoured the hull of Scout Five, work underwater proceeded very cautiously.

In the end, a line was passed through the uppermost chamber of the shell and tied to a winch in the Scout, which pulled it lower and lower until water began to rush into the chamber. The winch wound tighter yet. Without warning, the line went slack as the top chamber became heavier with water than whatever was attached to the base. The shell rotated with solemn gravity until the base, Medusa-headed with severed vines, reached the apex.

Lasers burned away the vines. Beneath them, scoured by acid as well as the lasers, lay a large nodule, midnight-blue but veined, where a shaft of sunlight struck it, with every color of the rainbow.

"The source of the reef's nutrients," Benedict said when Shoshone had described it to him. "You remember Rebekka saying that there were not enough nutrients in the plume to sustain the reef? Her calculations were impeccable. There were other clues. Before I woke you on the reef, you muttered something about rainbow flames. Rebekka confirmed that the fire glowed with myriad hues. This indicated that at least some of the vegetation was absorbing a disproportionate amount of heavier elements.

"Beyond that, everything we had learned about the submarine portions of the reef intrigued me. Echo returns from something hard as metal, yet with a partial halo, as if it were surrounded by something not quite as solid. Then there were the acid vines. Several of you thought they were protection against predators even though we had seen nothing to warrant such protection.

"Lacking facts, I fell back on analogy. I thought of how humans make use of acid."

"In our stomachs," Shoshone said, feeling the beginning of a revelation.

"Just so. So I began to wonder if the vines could be part of an elaborate feeding system. Perhaps they had coiled around Scout Five because of its resemblance to their natural sustenance. Where could that come from? We saw that when released from the vines, it bobbed upward. I drew a line in my mind and looked at its origin."

"The seafloor," Shoshone said. "Hot vents, smokers . . ."

"In whatever peculiar ways they manifest themselves on Thetis," Benedict agreed. "Food on the seafloor. Energy, in the form of sunlight, on the surface. An ecology as lush as the reefs required a stronger link than could be sustained by the solutes and particles carried in suspension by the plume."

He fell silent for a minute. "The tidal tug of war between A.4 and the other satellites on Thetis does more than just heat the ocean and the atmosphere. It also churns the crust through the mantle on a fairly regular basis.

"That nodule should have pretty much every rare earth Lumbongo needs to restore the superconductors of the fusors."

Figures were emerging from the branch ceiling. They moved slowly down the trunk, carefully lowering a large and apparently heavy sack.

"The third thing!" Shoshone said suddenly. "You told D'Argent he had three resources Harriman needed. The first was the Scout, the second, the optical switches. You wouldn't tell him the third. This was it, wasn't it?"

Benedict's face conveyed as much surprise as it could with the eyes masked. "Not at all," he replied. "At the time all I had was an educated guess. I had no way of knowing Harriman would provide us with the lasers and pressure suits we would need to see if I had guessed correctly."

More and more Gens were hurrying through the overhead branches to the descending rescue party. From this distance Shoshone could not tell if the burden was moving on its own.

"I think they have found—"

"All Gens. All Gens. Attention. Attention. Nova lasers are ready to fire on the reef. All will be incinerated unless Benedict presents himself for truce talks within thirty minutes."

The announcement began to repeat. Shoshone looked anxiously at Benedict. "Walking into Harriman's clutches doesn't sound like such a hot idea to me," she ventured.

"It doesn't sound like I have been given a choice," Benedict replied.

XXII

THE TWO GUARDS STARED STRAIGHT AHEAD. NEITHER HAD responded to any of Shoshone's queries. They held their blackly gleaming assault lasers rigidly before them. The fact that they looked worried was not at all reassuring.

Shoshone gnawed her lip nervously. Scarcely three-quarters of an hour before it had seemed almost certain that Benedict would not be allowed to obey the summons. A shaken Morgenstern had feared Benedict would sell them out. Benedict had pointed out that there was nothing he could betray if he wished. He did not know where the optical boards were hidden, and aside from that, he had nothing to betray.

"What about the nodules?" Morgenstern countered.

Benedict shrugged. "You need labor to obtain and expertise to exploit that resource. Harriman has denied himself both by stranding you out here. It will be a bargaining point."

"If he doesn't just throw you back in detention," Stellato objected. "Or have you killed."

"Both are possibilities," Benedict agreed. "The odds are more favorable than burning."

"But what are the odds he can hit us, firing blind?" Shoshone asked. "Can he even generate enough power to fire those lasers?"

"Oh, yes." Benedict nodded. "Lights will flicker, but he should be able to get off a dozen shots in less than a minute without seriously inconveniencing shipboard operations. None of these need hit us. These are nova lasers. The amount of energy in a millisecond pulse will cause the reef to erupt in a ten-kilometer-long fire storm.

"Were I Harriman, I would put a beam to a hundred meters on either side of the Scout. The conflagration would make it

161

impossible for any of us to interfere while his men, in battle armor, secured the Scout and transferred it back to the *Crucible*."

Ten minutes of intensive debate produced little more than a consensus that Harriman might indeed mean his threat. So, with grave misgivings, Shoshone found herself inside an ominously quiet *Crucible*, waiting to see what Harriman wanted with them.

The door to Harriman's quarters opened. A face looked out briefly. Shoshone recognized O'Leary. She had not seen him since the day they had both been discharged from sick bay. His eyes darted about quickly. Seeing only Shoshone, Benedict, and the two guards, he motioned Shoshone to come in. He indicated two chairs flanking a low glass table. Shoshone guided Benedict to one of the chairs and seated herself opposite him. He looked frighteningly frail. Perhaps the ordeal on the reef had weakened him more than anyone had guessed. Or perhaps, despite his brave words, he was feeling the effects of defeat, of having escaped once only to be brought to bay again.

O'Leary caught her eye. He seemed about to say something, when the door at the far end of the room opened. Harriman strode in, an unfamiliar hand weapon holstered at his hip. He almost threw himself into his chair.

"Thank you, Mr. O'Leary. You may leave us."

"Sir, are you sure—"

Harriman unholstered his weapon. It was a smaller version of the assault lasers with which the guards were armed. The barrel was one-fifth as long; the light splashers extended only as far as the wrist instead of all the way up the forearm. He dropped it negligently on the table before him. Shoshone stared at it in horrified fascination.

"If I cannot use this to protect myself from a girl and a blind man, well . . ."

O'Leary nodded, saluted, and stepped out into the corridor. The door sealed itself behind him.

Harriman sat back in his chair, rubbing his eyes and barely stifling a yawn. Shoshone realized that his studied air of nonchalance was only a cover for exhaustion.

"I'm glad you were able to come. There are important matters we need to discuss."

"It seemed preferable to the alternative," Benedict replied.

"The what? Oh, that." Harriman waved a hand. "I had to

threaten something to get the Bestials to release you. That was all that came to mind.

"Look, I think it's obvious that things . . . are not going well just now. Repairs have almost come to standstill. Even with the crew on twelve-hour shifts, between the extra security details and our material shortages, very little can be accomplished. I have tried to have additional crew members revived from cold sleep, but the resuscitation program has revealed short, unexplained power drops. Anything less than a completely controlled revival could bring death by resuscitation shock.

"Three watches ago we broke the access codes to the complate you left in your office."

"That should not have been possible," Benedict said, interrupting in a low voice.

A sudden smile pulled Harriman's lips apart. "I think you underestimate us, Fox. We Norms can be very smart at times. Take O'Leary, who just left us. A less personally impressive individual you will not meet on this starship. Yet he was the one who noted your complate and realized it might be important. He was the one who put in extra time when he was off shift to deencrypt your access codes, who guessed that pride might be your weakness and that 'Sky Marshal' might be the key word that would unlock all.

"He also found, amid the clutter of files for planetological modeling, a file on the *Crucible*. Specifically, a set of equations relating crew positions to the efficient functioning of the starship. You had just begun writing the manpower program for ship repairs when you were kidnapped by the Bestials."

Shoshone blinked, wondering how much reality editing Harriman was doing simply to manipulate them and how much he was making himself believe. She looked quickly at Benedict, but his face disclosed nothing.

"The problem is, we have completed those programs and run them. Only whatever we postulate concerning access to raw materials, whatever permutations we work on crew assignments, there is no solution which ends with the *Crucible* becoming fully operational. Each of them sooner or later ends with a breakdown in hydroponics followed by starvation.

"That's why I—that's why all of us needed you back, why I had to use the most powerful threat at my disposal to get your release. We completed the program as best as we could, but it does us no good. You need to work on it, to show us how to devise a plan that will work.''

''It sounds as if you have completed the programming correctly,'' Benedict said. ''There is nothing I can do to change the relationships embodied in the basic equations. They simply *are*. Your solution lies in providing additional factors for the equations to work with.

''All you need are presently on the reef.''

Harriman shook his head forcefully. ''They are the enemy. I cannot have Jean D'Argent and his cronies fomenting mutiny on this ship.''

''You have no need to worry in that regard,'' Benedict informed him dryly. ''Ms. Mantei disabled D'Argent not two hours ago. It is not certain that he will survive the next twenty-four hours.''

''Did you indeed?'' Harriman's eyes shone as he turned to regard Shoshone. ''I *knew* you were no traitor, no matter what D'Argent said!''

''Then if D'Argent was your concern,'' Benedict suggested, ''you should be able to allow the rest of the Gens back inside.''

''That is out of the question. You must find a solution using our crew of Norms.''

''There is no such solution.''

''You cannot know that without completing the programming yourself.''

''I can know it because I designed it that way.''

Harriman paused long enough to swallow. ''You designed the computer program that way?''

''No,'' Benedict said gently. ''I designed the crew that way. The deck has been stacked since before we left the Periphery. Neither Gens nor Norms have had it in their ability to complete a mission successfully by themselves. The damage to the fusors, the problem with the cold-sleep cubicles—these have only highlighted what has always been the underlying reality.''

Something seemed to break in Harriman's face. He picked up the hand laser and ran his fingers nervously along its shattered-mirror surface.

''I had hoped you were not the enemy,'' he said. He stopped to clear his throat. ''Now you have declared yourself. I will give you one more chance. Perhaps you are not insane. Perhaps you care for your own life, if not for that of anyone else. If so, you will reconsider your decision not to help us.''

He lifted the laser and pointed it at Benedict. "I have this laser at its lowest setting. If I depress the firing stud, it will almost instantaneously burn a hole through you roughly one centimeter in diameter. It will be self-cauterizing, so you will lose hardly any blood. Unless I hit a vital organ, and I can assure you that I will not, you will sustain only minimal damage.

"But you will know pain. I have heard that Multi-Neural Capacitants are especially sensitive to pain. Is that true?"

Benedict nodded, as if not trusting himself to speak.

"That is good. It should speed things up considerably. I may not have to cause you much harm at all. I—"

The muzzle swung around to center on Shoshone. "Sit back, Ms. Mantei. If you attempt to interfere, I will have to react quickly. I cannot be sure of not killing you."

Shoshone forced herself back into the chair. "What is the point?" she demanded. "If you kill him, he won't be able to do anything for you."

"Ms. Mantei, I am doing everything I can not to kill the Rénard. I respect his abilities too much to throw them away. But you just heard him admit that he has been part of a conspiracy which tampered with crew selection. I think that is just the first of his secrets, that his protestations of impotence are just the latest in a series of lies.

"Now, if you will move around to sit beside—"

The door to the corridor hummed open. Harriman turned to bark an order. His voice died in his throat.

"Turn over your weapon to Engineer Mantei, Mr. Harriman."

Harriman's hand moved as if in automatic response to command voice. With a visible effort, he brought the laser back to bear on the figure in the doorway.

"Captain Nickerson." Harriman licked his lips. "Ma'am, there has been a mutiny during your disability. I have isolated the mutineers on the reef and forced them to release Engineer Mantei and Father Benedict."

"I know all about the mutiny," Nickerson said evenly. "I am reassuming command. Hand over your weapon."

She took two slow steps into the room. Looking closely at her, Shoshone could see the signs of resuscitation shock. There was a slight uncontrollable tremor in both stride and voice; bloodshot eyes blinked rapidly, as if against too-bright light.

"Ma'am, I'm afraid you are still unwell. Please return to sick bay."

"I am well enough, Mr. Harriman. The laser."

Harriman's face worked as if he were trying to keep from crying. He straightened his arm, keeping the muzzle centered on Nickerson.

Shoshone looked desperately for anything she could use either as a weapon or at least as a distraction. The table was clear. Like all furniture used in spacecraft, it was bolted to the floor; there was no way she could upend it on Harriman.

His forearm tensed.

"No!" Shoshone shouted.

The muzzle suddenly pointed between her eyes.

Harriman had not really seen the fight between Benedict and Alexandrov. A press of bodies had blocked his view, and when he had been able to see through the gaps, his impression had been of a tangle of limbs, of a blind man grabbed by a Gens in the throes of *testrarch* madness. He had not seen, as Shoshone had, Benedict dodge his opponent's blows at the last moment, had not realized that Benedict was able to hear movement and sense position.

Harriman's head snapped back, blood suddenly smearing the lower half of his face. The laser waved about crazily, as if the arm holding it were suddenly boneless. Shoshone threw herself forward and grabbed the laser from limp fingers as Harriman collapsed onto the table.

Benedict pushed himself upright and massaged his bloody knuckles. He turned in Nickerson's direction.

"Captain, it is a delight to have you back in command."

XXIII

It took their Scout several trips to transfer all of them back to the battlestar. The fusion drives of the other Scouts had been hardwired into the ship's electrical system, and Lumbongo was loath to let any be disconnected just to speed the repatriation process.

Shoshone was with the last load. She helped Benedict down to the deck. Looking around, she was surprised to see the ship's company standing in formation for the first time since they had left the Centauran system. Nickerson and Lumbongo, as senior officers, stood in front of the formation. Facing them, the returning party of Gens was drawn up in two ranks.

Uh oh. Formality time, Shoshone thought.

Following Benedict's murmured instructions, she led him to the front of the Gens's formation, directly across from Nickerson.

"Captain Nickerson," Benedict said. "The Thetan Expeditionary Force is pleased to report."

"Welcome home!" Nickerson said. Her voice echoed off the bulkheads, encompassing them all.

"We have a few things we would like to present," Benedict continued. "Mr. Vangard. Front and center."

Vangard stepped forward, stopping opposite Lumbongo. He unclipped a pouch from his belt, unwrapped its contents, and handed them to the chief engineer. Lumbongo took the optical switches cautiously and lifted them to the light. Rainbow pinpricks scintillated as he rotated the smooth, unblemished surfaces. A slow smile spread across his face. His whole body seemed to relax.

"Thanks for taking such good care of them," he said. He rewrapped the switches and prepared to step back.

"One more thing," Benedict said. "Mr. Stellato!"

Stellato came up with a pouch similar to Vangard's but clearly carrying something much heavier. He opened it and handed laser-cut blue rock to Nickerson. She held it so that Lumbongo could examine it with her.

Bay light caught the swirl of colors on the surface of the cobalt-blue matrix. The cut surface showed a fine layering of brown, maroon, and violet.

"We have not been able to run an analysis," Benedict murmured, "but we have been able to determine that this is the concentrated source of nutrients for the reef. It should have everything you need in the way of repair material."

Lumbongo nodded, hardly able to take his eyes away from the nodule slice.

Nickerson's gaze swept them all. "Your places await you. Fall in."

The two ranks of Gens dispersed as their members sought their positions in the larger formation. Shoshone was the last to get to her place with the engineering contingent, having first had to guide Benedict to his place at the head of the planetological group.

"Welcome home," Nickerson said again. "The *Crucible* is now whole in crew. Soon the ship, as well as its complement, will be fully functional. We have defeated a mutiny which, had it succeeded, could have plunged the entire Periphery into war once again. We are fortunate to have taken so few casualties in doing so. I know that it was not easy for those of you who remained on board, but those marooned on the reef were exposed to double doses of danger and hardship. You will resume your duties in due time. First, though, you will want showers"—Shoshone's eyes flicked left to right, taking in how frayed and downright grungy the Gens looked, how straggly her own hair was, not to mention how ludicrous she must now look in Steward's robes—"and rest. You have earned it.

"Dismissed!"

Right foot back, pivot, one step. The formation dissolved into small groups. Old friends came up to Shoshone, greeting her and slapping her on the back.

Lumbongo looked up as she approached. "Glad to have you back," he said. "I have a lot of work for you if I can pry you loose."

"I'm ready to report," Shoshone said.

Lumbongo permitted himself the hint of a smile. "Nobody as exhausted as you is getting near any of my circuitry."

She waited for Benedict to free himself from a prolonged discussion with Ueda and Timakata, then escorted him to his quarters. By the time she had made her way through the maze of companionways, side corridors, and catwalks to her own door, she realized that she was just as tired as Lumbongo had discerned. But despite the sensuous invitation of her sleeping pallet, there was one thing she had to do first.

She stripped off the borrowed Steward's robes and her own coverall. Undergarments followed. Stepping into the shower, she set the temperature as high as the safeties allowed and had the water jets scour sweat, grime, and the assorted microflora of the reef from hair and flesh. Sonics kneaded her muscles and massaged her joints. She came out feeling flushed and sleepy and as clean as a baby who had just been passed over Benedict's baptismal font.

She fell onto the cool white sheets, wondering what heaven could be more delightful . . .

She woke up fifteen hours later. Swinging out of her pallet, she staggered across the room. For a few seconds she could not understand why she was lurching so unsteadily. Then she began to laugh. For the first time since they had splashed into the ocean of Thetis, she was standing on a completely motionless surface.

That meant that something close to full power must have been restored. Shoshone picked up the clothes she had let fall earlier and dropped them in a now-functioning clothes chute. After dressing, she punched Benedict's identifier into the comm unit.

The locator's artificial voice responded. "Father Benedict is currently in sick bay undergoing surgery. He will be back on net as soon as his doctor considers him sufficiently recovered."

Lumbongo put her to work immediately. The entire nodule was in the main shop, encased beneath an airtight hood. Shoshone was put in charge of the lasers mounted inside the hood. She set them to deliver precisely calibrated packets of energy across the surface of the nodule, the exact amount depending on what Rebekka or Ueda deduced from spectrographic analysis of the surface they were working on. Each layer was to be vaporized, the vapor sucked out of the hood by a fan, then recondensed on chill plates. Thus, slowly, over several watches, Lumbongo was building up the inventory of elements he needed to repair the fusion generators.

Shoshone ended her watch tired but excited with the progress they were making. She met Kryuchov in the mess and asked him how Benedict was doing.

"I don't know," Kryuchov admitted. "I'm just going on watch. However, with Spartacus handling him, you have nothing to worry about. Her specialty is neural regeneration. She just lives for her medical practice. That is why, when Harriman had her put in detention and the rumor was that she might be implicated in poisoning Nickerson, I decided it was time to put an end to all this nonsense."

Shoshone favored him with a slightly skeptical smile. "*You* ended the mutiny?"

Kryuchov seemed unaware that he had said anything extraordinary. "It was just the final straw. First there was this plague, with vague and contradictory symptoms and only one victim, the captain, who should have had the least exposure. Instead of being taken to sick bay for examination, she was whisked through just long enough for me to witness the fact that she was indeed unconscious and then dropped in a cold-sleep cubicle over my protests that that was extremely dangerous for someone with uncertain life signs.

"Then there was the question of what we were to do for the crew quarantined on the reef. Surely keep them supplied with food, at least? Well, eventually, maybe, but not right now. The plague had given them hallucinations, made them violent: a set of symptoms totally unmentioned when the captain was brought in.

"Then the rumors changed. It was not a plague, after all; it was an attempted mutiny by the Gens. The first step had been to poison the captain. Harriman had been able to quash it by tricking the main perpetrators outside. He had spread the story about plague to keep tempers from flaring among the crew."

"You believed that?" Shoshone asked.

Kryuchov shrugged. "It made more sense than the plague story. D'Argent had been testy ever since coming aboard. I could see him leading a mutiny. Father Benedict has what you might call a checkered past. The only unlikely thing was that Harriman would have been smart enough to trap or force him outside.

"Only then he started clamping down on all the Gens who had remained inside. This was popular with some of the Norms at first, but it got old really fast. With all the Gens outside or detained inside, it meant that all the rest of us had to work twelve- or sixteen-hour watches. For a while he even had people watching all the locks and the corridors leading from the flooded sections because of that trick your boyfriend pulled.

"When he had Spartacus arrested, I decided the whole thing had been a fraud from the start. Command gyrations became increasingly frantic. There were murmurings that we had all been set up and that we would never get back to the Periphery. So I violated both direct orders and, arguably, medical ethics by taking a blood sample from our hibernating captain. I didn't find any odd microbes, viruses, or prions, but I did discover enough secobarbital sodium to make me wonder why she hadn't gone into respiratory arrest.

"After that it was just a matter of running her bloodstream through the dialytic filtration system and initiating the resuscitation process."

"Wasn't that terribly dangerous, given the problems with the cold-sleep cubicles?" Shoshone asked.

Kryuchov's face split in a naughty-boy grin. "There was nothing wrong with the cubicles, nor with the resuscitation program. You have to understand how disgruntled everyone, nearly everyone, was becoming with Harriman. The extra hours were the least of it. The rumors that the captain had been drugged, that you had discovered an arms cache, set everyone on edge. The final straw was when the antimatter bomb exploded prematurely. Nobody wants to be vaporized so industrialists can get even richer selling war matériel.

"When I heard about that, I was certain Harriman would give up. Instead, he decided to write off all the Gens and make up a skeleton crew by reviving Norms who had been kept in cold sleep up till then to conserve resources. It was child's play to write in a few lines of program to trigger all the alarms and shut down the entire system as soon as the resuscitation sequence was started. It was even easier to suggest that Benedict had somehow sabotaged the basic hardware. I don't think Harriman found it easy to imagine a Norm working against him. In any event, he was so shorthanded that he couldn't spare anyone to do a detailed analysis of the program. He would have eventually, of course. All I wanted, though, was time enough to revive the captain and get her in contact with those crew members I knew were loyal."

Looking at him, Shoshone found it difficult to imagine anyone who looked less heroic. "That was very well done. You may have saved all our lives."

Kryuchov scowled, as if praise made him uncomfortable. "I had to do it if I was going to get my boss back. Anyway, the captain nearly threw it all away by confronting Harriman. I wanted her to order the guards to blast him, but she wouldn't hear of it.

"Look, I'm late for my watch. Stop by or query us on data net any time you want on Father Benedict's progress."

Later, as she drifted off to sleep, Shoshone felt memories fitting together in her mind, as if they would solve a puzzle that had bothered her for a long time but that she had been too busy to work on.

An unmeasured time later she woke in her completely darkened room, shaking with anger. "*Nothing* has been explained!" she shouted at the ceiling.

It took a long time after that to fall back asleep.

Next watch, the press of work drove everything else from her mind. By the end of her watch Lumbongo had teased apart enough yttrium, barium, and niobium to begin shifting work crews to the job of the actual repairs of the fusors. Shoshone found herself too excited to quit. With the chief engineer's permission, she continued her work vaporizing the reef nodule into its constituents. They were down to the last slice. A second nodule had reportedly been released to the surface and would be flown into the *Crucible* during the following watch.

Four hours into her second watch, cheering erupted from the fusor bay. A ripple seemed to pass across the ceiling. She blinked at the abruptly stronger lighting.

Shoshone shut off all her lasers and fans. She stood up carefully, all her joints and muscles protesting. Slowly, she walked from her workshop to the exit that gave onto the second-floor walkway surrounding the fusor bay. Gens and Norms were clustered in small groups all along the catwalks. On the floor of the bay, small among the line of towers that constituted the quantum drive, lay the cylinders that were the fusors. Scars and burn marks were still visible on the fusor closest to the wall. So were the steady green lights indicating it had been restored to operation.

Someone passing by with a tray pressed a tall, cold tulip glass into Shoshone's hand. The contents had the vaguest fruity smell. Bubbles exploded around her nose and made her sneeze.

"What *is* this?"

"Genuine Centauran champagne," Stellato informed her, appearing out of the crowd holding a similar glass. "Courtesy of Chiang Biosynthetics. Lumbongo ordered it out, with the captain's permission, that we might be properly festive. As I think he is about to tell us."

On the floor, Nickerson made a gesture to Lumbongo. A brilliant smile flashed across the chief engineer's face.

"We have done very well," he said without preamble. An invisible microphone picked up his words and relayed them to the wall speakers. "Although we have a great deal left to do, I am declaring, with Captain Nickerson's permission, a mini-holiday. The next six watches will be on half staff. After that we will work all the harder. I have promised the captain that we will be fully operational in less than a week."

A ragged chorus of cheers erupted from all three levels.

"That sounds like the signal for some serious partying," Stellato said. "Care to join me?"

Shoshone slipped her hand through the offered arm. "Absolutely."

They were still together two watches later, and if anyone saw anything remarkable in that, he kept his thoughts to himself. What the shipboard gossips might indeed have found remarkable was that Shoshone and Stellato had spent the whole time together—well, nearly the whole time—just talking. Now, walking down the corridor toward the duty stations they would have to resume in engineering in less than two hours, Shoshone felt slightly light-headed from lack of sleep yet at the same time utterly relaxed.

They approached a lounge just across from the entrance to sick bay. A Gen sat with his back to her, his head bowed as if in deep conversation with a nearly bald man seated across a small table from him. The Gen's companion raised his head. Ice-blue eyes she had never seen before met hers.

A shock shivered through her. How could I ever have thought this man an overrated academic? Shoshone wondered.

His gaze was filled with measureless intelligence but with something more besides. Grandfather Fox, the Gens called him, yet apt as that was, it was only a two-dimensional slice of the reality she now perceived.

In one of her early school modules she had been in a holo-room programmed to reproduce an old Earth jungle. Sweating from the heat, dazzled by a greater variety of plant and insect life than she had ever imagined possible, she had been startled by a roar that had seemed to come from all directions at once. Turning, she had found herself face to face with a lion. Its image had fixed her with its stare for an instant, then had turned away from her, too well fed to find her interesting.

Benedict might, despite his ascetic leanness, be too well fed to menace her. Or perhaps he had domesticated his inner violence in return for—what? Companionship? Promised salvation? Simple respite from an unending Hobbesian war of all against all? The precise reason did not matter. The thing she must never forget was that however banked it might be, violence always existed just beneath the surface.

All this between one step and the next.

"Shoshone. And Stellato. I am delighted to see both of you." The voice was as cultured and precise as ever. "Please join us."

"I'm sure," Shoshone began unsteadily, "that you're delighted to see anything."

An almost shy smile flashed across his face. "That is true. Especially since I was so blind even before my eyes were damaged."

As she took her seat, it occurred to her that Benedict had been lucky to be blinded. Had Harriman been confronted by an unmaimed Benedict, he would never have treated him so lightly as merely to confine him to quarters.

Or perhaps her vision of the real Benedict was a purely private epiphany. None of those passing in the corridor showed any sign of noticing what lived among them.

Stellato stiffened as he identified Benedict's companion. Coal-black fur flecked with silver. Eyes covered by re-genepaks.

"Dr. D'Argent is here for the first of his retinal treatments," Benedict explained. "Spartacus wanted his bones completely healed before beginning regeneration of the optic nerve. This will be a delicate procedure, since the Gens's immune system counteracts most medicines as soon as they are given.

"In the meantime, we have been discussing the dangers of reason. Jean has been setting out his rationale, step by step, for all of his actions. While it may not be completely satisfactory to a court, it is understandable to a confessor. I have been trying to console him by explaining how my errors nearly cost the lives of everyone on board."

"You, Grandfather?" Stellato asked. "You guided us to a safe landing on Thetis, kept us alive out on the reef, and so discredited Harriman that his mutiny collapsed. What errors are you thinking of?"

"The errors of excessive cleverness," Benedict said, shaking his head. "You have to understand that I first heard of this expedition while in hiding beyond the edge of the Periphery. I performed those tasks for the Order of Stewards which were within my capabilities. In return, I was granted obscurity so total that I was generally believed to be dead.

"The Father General forwarded to me the request for crew member nominations. I had no thought of nominating myself. It would have meant exposing myself to unnecessary danger when there were at least a score of candidates within the Order alone who would be more than qualified for the position of planetary ecologist. Almost as an afterthought, I asked for a list of those already selected, thinking that I might select for complementary personalities.

"As soon as I had the first partial list, I knew something was wrong. The captain was to be a woman with an impeccable string of ratings and honors in staff positions but one who had never held a command position before. Harriman's name I recognized from his association with the Defenders of Humanity before the war and his record in the Loki prisoner-of-war camp. A few others had similar backgrounds. I began to think that someone was pulling strings for the Defenders of Humanity, but then I came across D'Argent's name and that of Morgenstern and half a dozen other Gens.

"Fully seventy percent of the Norms chosen seemed to be individuals especially antagonistic to Gens. The percentage of antagonistic Gens was almost as great. The only conclusion I could reach was that the deck was being stacked for failure. My worst suspicions were not confirmed until Shoshone told me of the antimatter bomb. Mere failure was not enough. It had to be catastrophic, violent failure, something violent enough that it would send shock waves through the Periphery, undermining the Treaty of Chiron and the fragile bonds of trust and cooperation which had been growing slowly since the end of the war. Something which might even restart the war.''

''Why didn't you stop it?'' Shoshone asked.

''You mean, why didn't I convince more than two dozen mutually antagonistic sociopolitical entities that they had been manipulated into selecting crew members who would self-destruct?'' Benedict smiled humorlessly. ''I think that would have been beyond my powers of persuasion. Yet had I succeeded, I would only have forced a pustule below the skin, from whence it would do its poisonous work unnoticed.

''Instead, I tried to restack the deck. There are those throughout the Periphery who owe me favors. A few of them had nominated candidates. I suggested that a few, only a few, of these be withdrawn. Other friends and former clients were on the selection board. I made suggestions. In all, I changed less than twenty-eight percent of the selections, in ways which did not immediately point to me. But as I told Harriman, the result was that neither Gens nor Norms could crew the *Crucible* by themselves. This was the third resource of which I alluded to Jean. Yet Gens chauvinist though he is, he never really believed that his own people were crucial to the mission.

''This was as much as I could do, but I was dissatisfied. And curious. I arranged that I would be a last-minute substitution for the Stewards' candidate.

''Learning from the experience of a former patron, I programmed the cold-sleep system so that it would wake me should any other cubicle resuscitate its occupant out of the officially planned sequence. When the program activated itself, I discovered that an assault team was trying to take over the *Crucible*.''

''Who?'' Shoshone asked.

''Norms,'' D'Argent said quickly.

''Defenders of Humanity,'' Benedict agreed. ''But the only difference between their actions and what you had planned is they struck first.''

D'Argent dropped his eyes and said nothing.

''Finally, when I was brought to bay,'' Benedict said, ''I swelled with self-congratulatory pride for having been intelligent enough to position myself between the leveled assault lasers and the fusors. For no one would be insane enough to fire a beam which might well destroy the ship.''

He sighed. "Prostrating myself before the idol of my own rationality, I forgot that the very thing about my enemies which made them enemies was their fanaticism, their lack of rationality. We have all paid for my error."

Shoshone looked from Benedict to D'Argent, wondering how to politely initiate a conversation with someone who had tried to murder her at their last meeting.

D'Argent saved her the effort. "Shoshone Mantei." His head bobbed left and right like a mole nosing about in the sunlight.

"Over here," she said as she realized that he was trying to fix her position. She shifted closer to Stellato. Even blind, D'Argent was intimidating through mere muscular bulk. Shoshone's calves and thighs tightened as if she expected him to spring.

"Twice my actions have nearly caused your death." D'Argent's voice was low and grave. "Neither attempt was justified or honorable. I . . . am . . . sorry."

"Twice?" Understanding dawned. "You cut my acceleration netting!"

"It was Morgenstern's hand, but I should have controlled it. Soon after we were revived, I noted all the signs of a failed coup. I contacted as many Gens as I could, telling them to be ready for whatever action would be necessary.

"Morgenstern overheard certain remarks you made to Stellato, deduced that you were with the faction which had attempted to take over the *Crucible*, and feared that you would kill Stellato, perhaps making it look like an accident while you were outside. He cut the netting, intending it to part while we were air-braking through the outer reaches of A.4's atmosphere. He miscalculated. It did not let go until we crashed into the world ocean of Thetis."

"What remarks?" Stellato asked.

Shoshone covered her face, hoping to hide the blush that was heating her entire face. Had everyone been listening in on that channel? Nordstrom and Harriman had heard and come to the same conclusions as Morgenstern. For conspirators, it seemed there was no such thing as simple ill temper brought on by exhaustion.

"I'll remind you of them later," she told Stellato. She turned back to D'Argent. "Okay. The first time was a mistake. You gave Morgenstern the idea I was a dangerous enemy, and he took it from there. But the second time was different. You knew I was not part of Harriman's group: I had killed two of his men and alerted you to the antimatter bomb, for God's sake! I had been helping all of you on the reef.''

"A foe like Harriman strengthens us," D'Argent said. "We see him clearly as an enemy and know that to survive we must be smarter and tougher than he is. But a friend like you weakens us. Had Harriman succeeded, an insignificant number of Gens would have died. Yet when I looked in your face, I saw the extinction of all my race."

Shoshone shook her head slowly, without comprehension.

"No, he is not insane," Benedict said gently. "He is not even incorrect. You represent a danger to the Gens greater than all Williams's Defenders of Humanity and the Allied fleet. In his way, Jean made his version of my mistake. He examined the relevant facts, came to the correct conclusion, and did the wrong thing."

"He came to the wrong conclusion," Shoshone protested. "Even during the war I was never a personal enemy of the Gens." She cast a quick look at Stellato, then back at Benedict. "I *like* Gens."

"That is the problem," Benedict murmured. "How unfair it must have seemed to whoever realized it. Not only were you from a frontier colony which had been greatly at risk during the war, you had been raised by exiled Rational Ethicists who named you and your sister Sapi after extinct tribal groupings. Someone read undying bitterness and resentment into those names."

"Which I did not share!"

"True. Despite all that might be expected from your circumstances, you are not the desired repository of fears and bigotry. Underneath all your professional training you are a young woman with a warm heart and perhaps warmer hormones. Please, don't bother to protest! I may have been blind, but I had my ears. Even when the surface emotion is exasperation, the tone of voice between lovers is vastly different from that between strangers."

Seeing her confusion, Stellato asked, "Why is this a problem? Or even anybody's business?"

Benedict sighed. "It is not a problem for me. How can I criticize anyone for obeying the first commandment God gave to all living things? As to the reason it is a problem for Jean . . .''

He turned back to Shoshone. "How many Gens do you think there are, all totaled?"

Shoshone cast around in her mind for a figure. "Well, inhabiting the entire circumference of the Periphery, they have to be at least ten billion—"

Dry laughter interrupted her. "Less than a billion," Stellato said.

"Fifty million would be generous," D'Argent muttered.

"Because of the scattered nature of the Clans," Benedict explained, "there is no exact count. But the range you've been given is representative of the best estimates."

"That can't be!" Shoshone protested. "All during the war—"

"All during the war the Allied populations were fed inflated figures," Benedict said. "First by Defenders of Humanity so paranoid they believed their own propaganda, later by Allied military men attempting to justify their unsuccessful conduct of the war. They saw themselves surrounded by Gens whose territories stretched out into the galaxy. Instead, the Gens were and are thin as the skin of an apple."

"When we were first created, we were 'protected' from the hundred-billion-plus population of Norms by distance and our status as work animals," D'Argent said. "Only perverts lie with beasts."

"The war raised the wall higher between the two populations. Now the war is over. Legal equality has been declared. I looked at you, I saw Stellato's ease and joy in your company, and I realized that I was seeing the beginning of a tidal wave which would wash through the stars and wipe away all trace of my people.

"All of my people who died in the war would have died in vain. I had lost most of my influence with Stellato, and attacking him would have defeated my whole purpose. The only course of action left open seemed to be to remove you."

"I think everyone is taking intentions too much for granted," Shoshone said, choosing her words carefully. "More than that, you are turning me into an idealized mother-of-nations figure. The role doesn't fit."

"If you were a saint, you would not be so dangerous," Benedict replied. "For most purposes, saints are so rare that one need not worry about them. Much more deadly the doom which comes through a young woman of moderate beauty and unheroic goodness, for her army numbers billions.''

"Now you may be taking me for granted,'' Stellato said. ''If this is true, why should I cooperate in the end of my people?'' His voice was even. But Shoshone, who was learning his body language, saw that he was greatly disturbed.

"At our height there were never more than a dozen Multi-Neural Capacitants,'' Benedict said, seeming to ignore Stellato's question. "Now it appears that I am the only one left. All the Gens were created on the premise that if you could breed in special talents while exempting the product from the rights pertaining to humans, profit would result. A costly war demonstrated the error of that premise.''

He shook his head as if clearing his thoughts. "You will do nothing to harm your people. What you will do is marry a woman to whom you are strongly attracted and raise children who are in some ways like both of you. They will be more hirsute than Norms but with less stamina than Gens. And as they grow, you will be more and more convinced that you did the right thing. A combination of genes on both X and Y chromosomes is responsible for *testrarch*, although the genes manifest themselves only in the presence of high testosterone levels. Any boys you have will still go through *testrarch*, but it will be briefer and less violent than Stellato's was. You will look down the generations to come to a time when the characteristics of Gens mean no more than blue eyes or kinky hair today, and people will wonder why there ever was a war.''

Shoshone looked at him askance. "You are overoptimistic. It will never be that easy.''

"Only if you consider the destruction of an entire people easy,'' D'Argent said bleakly.

Thetis had disappeared from the lounge viewscreen. Even A.4 appeared no more than an unusually bright member of the star field. The viewscreen looked out toward the edge of the Milky Way. Among the sparse scattering of stars, Shoshone could locate the spark that was Sirius.

These days the lounge was often packed. Over frosted flagons of ale or steaming mugs of tea, survey crews would exchange their latest discoveries: worlds baked down to cores of heavy metals, covered by thin silicate crusts near the caldrons of the A and B stars; outer subjovians that had been stripped from their natal orbits and now looped from one star to the other in century-long figure eights. Volcanoes percolating bizarre mineral combinations with promising properties unknown within the Periphery.

Metals and ices. Extremes of heat and cold. Only Thetis had breathable air, but the entire dual system was rich with all the resources needed to make a strong interplanetary economy. In the table conversations Shoshone heard the excitement of sudden discovery: how Gens's experience in working in hostile environments combined with Norm technology might convert a curious and unreachable crustal formation into a major asset.

At the moment, however, the lounge was nearly deserted. Nearly all the survey crews were out on their last missions before the *Crucible* gathered them in for the long jump back to Cygni and Alpha Centauri.

Shoshone became aware of a presence at her back. She put her hand up behind her. Lightly furred fingers, their tips hard with retracted claws, slid into her palm. The silence lengthened, a gentle insistence awaiting an explanation.

"The problem is not with you," she began, not sure that she could explain her feelings even to herself. "I just don't like people making my choices for me. My parents tried to choose my friends when I was a girl. Harriman assumed I was part of his Defenders faction just because I was a Norm from Aquaflamme and thus would have no objection to becoming his spy. Benedict seems to think he can map out my religion, my mate, and my descendants down to the third and fourth generations, at least. He's more subtle than most, but whenever I feel someone pushing, I instinctively want to push back."

Stellato came around and sat next to her. "Then perhaps what I ought to do is push you away and play hard to get." Thoughtful brown eyes regarded her over a grave smile. She remembered how, oppressed with the dry intellectualism of the Rational Ethicists, she had always preferred the wolf to Red Riding Hood. She had been taught that it was bad to prefer feral emotion to reason. Yet for how long, despite the tables of safety factors and breaking strains that her pragmatic engineering training had thrown up as protective ramparts all around her—for how long had she wanted to be bad!

"Now *you* are trying to manipulate me," she said, licking her lips nervously.

"Of course." The smile split into a bright, wolfish grin. "I think our race has been doing that since just after we learned to walk upright.''

The smile vanished. ''But I also know that even if I wanted to take away your freedom entirely, I could not. My father once told me that the greatest horror of a parent is that no matter how well you train and educate your children, they remain free to do the wrong thing. But that's what freedom is, after all.

''So,'' he said wistfully, ''if I can't rely on having engendered a grand passion—''

Shoshone looked away, trembling, afraid that one word, one look, might unravel her entirely.

''—perhaps I can use a more businesslike approach. My mother used to say that true love was a mate who kept the recycling vats clean and made sure that air-lock doors never opened out of sequence.''

Shoshone laughed. That was so exactly like something she had heard from her grandmother.

Suddenly she felt herself relax. They had first come to know each other hurtling through emptiness, working frantically to save the almost dead shell that was the *Crucible*. In the anonymity of a pressure suit, Stellato had been neither an attractively available male nor a menacing Bestial but instead a coolly competent colleague, able to ignore exhaustion, discomfort, and a downward-ticking clock to do what had to be done to save their lives. Later, on the reef, he had been willing to set himself against his own people in her defense.

Dependability, loyalty . . . Stellato had quietly demonstrated all those stodgy, unglamorous virtues that had somehow become twisted in Harriman. And if, alloyed with that solidity and competence, there was an attraction that might give rise to a ''grand passion,'' why, she would be a fool to fight it just because others thought it a good match for their own reasons.

''All right, then,'' she said. ''The hell with all of them. The Fox knows many things. Too many for me to keep track of. I know only one, but it's a big one.''

As he leaned closer, she told him what it was.

ABOUT THE AUTHOR

Born in Massachusetts in 1948, Robert Chase was educated at Phillips Exeter Academy, Dartmouth College, and the Duke School of Law. He currently lives in Maryland, working as an attorney for the U.S. Army, with his wife, three children, dog, and cat.